The Shop

i Siôn
gan ddiolch am sylfaen y siop

The Shop

Emyr Humphreys

seren

Seren is the book imprint of
Poetry Wales Press Ltd
57 Nolton Street, Bridgend, CF31 3AE, Wales
www.seren-books.com

ISBN 1-85411-390-9

A CIP record for this title is available from
the British Library.

The publisher works with the financial assistance
of the Welsh Books Council.

Cover photograph: Helen Sweeting

Printed in Plantin by Gwasg Gomer, Llandysul

One

FREDDY HELMUT is in genial mood. I sat up half the night translating and, he admits, improving his paper on a knotty problem of seed and food distribution in Ethiopia. It is one of those days when he likes to treat me as his particular chum. On his desk there is a neat pile of application forms passed down to him for useful comment from the higher-ups. He has years of experience in the United Nations Food and Agricultural Organisation and he likes to think that his experience, in the office and in the field, is valued. 'They like to know what I think,' he says, showing modest satisfaction. He has the reputation of being an easy-going unambitious sort of colleague, with a taste for gossip and office politics. I have to admit he has been my benevolent guide, philosopher and friend. More than that, he has a chalet in his vineyard near Lago di Bracciano that is more or less at my disposal.

'Surname, given name, date of birth, education, career to date…'

He grunts contentedly as he drops another application form into his out-tray.

'Eddie, old fruit…'

He leans back in his chair and points at me. This means he is about to indulge in one of his pseudo-philosophical discussions. I am ready to join in. To humour him as much as anything else. It's an interesting relationship. I exercise my independence while tacitly acknowledging his patronage. After all he is my immediate senior and he signs my progress reports.

'These come in from all points of the compass…'

He fingers another application form. I'm not sure whether it is a gesture of indifference or ephemeral power.

'How do we define who we are? Or more precisely, how does one define who one is?'

I don't really have an answer and this troubles me. At this moment it is much easier for me to define who Freddy is than who I am, and that seems totally inadequate. He is a north German with excellent English and he likes to decorate it with phrases that he considers characteristic and idiomatic. He pursues his philosophical hares as a form of entertainment, which is fair enough, because he takes our international relief work just as seriously as I do. All the same, the questions he raises as a matter of interest are always liable to trouble me at a deeper level: and it is little comfort to me that I know the reason why. My elusive self is to be found in the care of a certain Bethan Mair Nichols and wherever she happens to be at any given moment. I want that girl on a more permanent basis and I would say that these days that is more than sufficient to define me.

'It's a funny business.' Freddy loves to display his colloquial English. 'People may not know exactly who they are, amid the confusions of the modern world, etcetera: but they bloody well know what they want. And furthermore, Eddie, old fruit, they are liable to turn very nasty when they don't get it.'

A conclusion to alarm me. He must know I am not the type to turn nasty. The fact is he knows more than I would wish about me. Since the day I came to work with him, he has derived a generous measure of amusement, even *schadenfreude*, from what he pleases to call my amorous entanglements. 'What's the latest?' he used to say. Inside information about my love life was more exciting than the Italian football results. I suppose with a degree of resentment I used to accept his chuckles, and an inclination to slap my back, as the rent that's due to love.

In my own old fashioned way I am quietly appalled that Freddy Helmut delights in an independent existence in Rome and rarely sees his children in Flensburg and Bremen from one year's end to the other. Two ex-wives and two lots of children, and yet happy to footle around the eternal city in search of more exciting relationships. My search was always for a soul mate, not an expression of delayed adolescence. And indeed, beyond that, having discovered her, you could define me by my preoccupation with a desire for marriage, progeny and domesticity. I owe it to Freddy that Bethan and I have enjoyed a series of reunions in that discreet and delightful chalet between the vines and the almond orchard. I'm not certain that 'enjoy' is the last word on that subject either. Bethan pulls my nose and calls me a displaced Puritan. I say marry me, marry me! I need a family in an endless variety of formulae and she always replies with, 'It would be nice of course.' *Sed noli modo*, not yet, not yet.

Strange to admit the first time we met I barely noticed her. Strange and yet not so strange. It embarrasses me deeply to recall that my mind at that time was aching from the loss, or more precisely the flight of Rosie Lorenz. She had been transferred from Rome to Lisbon and I had directed much energy and ingenuity in obtaining an assignment that would enable me to follow her. I was in thrall to her drifting ethereal charm. It haunted me like a tune I couldn't put out of my head. For several weeks, night and day as the song goes, I concentrated on Portuguese because my affable boss, Freddy Helmut, wanted, more for my benefit, he joked, than his, an in-depth report on the state of the cork forests and allied industries in the Alentejo. Freddy has ensured that my superiors in the department appreciate my knack for presenting facts and figures in clear and unambiguous prose in a range of languages. This is a gift I owe to my Swiss mother and her devotion to my education.

However, when I arrived in Lisbon, as breathless as a greyhound as Freddy Helmut likes to put it, I discovered that Rosie had taken up with a dashing naval attaché at the

American embassy. She was caught up in a whirl of social engagements. She sighed, if only to show some appreciation of my devotion and then got rid of me with a finesse that at this distance has to be admired. Heartbroken I must have been for at least a fortnight. There seemed to be roses in bloom all over Estoril and I could hardly bear the perfume: and yet, at this distance in time, I recall the nature of my dismissal better than the features of her face. What also lingers is the residue of truth in my father's more penetrating comments on my behaviour patterns.

Dear boy, you will turn yourself into an academic zombie condemned to rummage through life in search of a female to whom he can offer his brain on a plate. He loves to deliver his lines. O God, what a father. Hubert Cynddylan Vaughan-Lloyd, better known, if known at all in this day and age, as the ex-matinee idol and booming Shakespearean actor, Orlando Lloyd. It could be my father's fault that there is such a tight bundle of 'me's inside me pushing and shoving to get away from each other. Are there so many 'me's?' In the event they always merge into a persistent yearning for a missing loved one. We define ourselves by our repetitions. How many times do we use the expression 'never again'. You'd never make a leading man, dear boy, if you insist on being led. Who in his right mind would want to take up such a footling role if the end product is sitting in the shade among the pines of Juan-les-Pins listening to the monotonous applause of the cicadas? Of course theatre life still has a touch of the brothel about it. It's not a place where you learn to idealise women. You need to be disillusioned, Eddie, my boy. It's more elegant. When I register another failure I always hear his voice booming in my head with would be mellifluous reproach.

The work remained to be done. The comfort of statistics and the study of the cork industry of the Alentejo. Heartbreak mends faster in a warm climate. At Evora I met this ebullient Franciscan; a weekend conference on The Environment. No subject, according to Freddy, apart from the lady-friend gap, closer to my heart. We sat next to each other and in no time at all we were chatting like old friends. We took the same line in urging discrimination and restraint in the use of chemical deterrents. We recited chapter and verse on global warming with the unanimity of a Greek chorus. That made us smile at each other. He had charm, he was a philosopher, capable of challenging remarks. He was a man of the world in the widest sense: much travelled, talkative, interested in everybody and everything and only lightly constricted by the Rules of his Order. It seemed he had been given a licence to roam the continents in order to demonstrate the power of his religion to make people cheerful. He may have sensed I needed cheering up. He had a fast car and he insisted I should see the prehistoric stone circle at Almendras, so off we went. The roads were narrow and he drove like a maniac and reassured me by saying that dashing around the world was some compensation for being celibate. We bumped and stumped our way through olive groves.

Dogs barked furiously and a range of poultry scattered in all directions. The ridged and deeply rutted track through the shadowed woodland slowed him down. Then suddenly on one bounce we were faced with the stone circle exposed in the bright spring sunlight. There must have been as many as a hundred tubby smooth standing stones, eight feet high, fixed for ever in their inexplicable ceremonial positions and in the middle, interlopers from our day and age, a film crew apparently enjoying a picnic break.

In no time at all, Father Afonso was in their midst demonstrating his habitual good will. He wore traditional black, but his smile and his good humour were resolutely up to date. The man we took to be the director was tall and willowy and I judged deep in a restrained dispute with a slight female figure in outsized dungarees and a vast straw hat. The tall man looked defensive, flinching even, under a cool but measured attack. The cockney cameraman gladly turned his attention to the clerical visitor and gave his name as Billy. Afonso brought his own brand of oil on troubled waters by expatiating in his rough and ready English on the merits of a range of Alentejo wines. His evident good nature was difficult to resist. The young woman, I thought, resented the interruption and slunk off to sulk among the stones. The filming wasn't going too well I gathered because either Billy the cameraman or the director had neglected to hire a piece of equipment called a 'cherry picker' which would have allowed a far fuller artistic choice of high angle shots of the stones. There was magic to be revealed by the photographic process. The young woman's attitude was enough to make her frustration apparent. Both the director and the cameraman were guilty of not taking their profession seriously. There could be further outbursts. At the first opportunity, I tugged at Afonso's black sleeve and we left the crew to their devices. It seemed to me that in the whole area there were numinous qualities that no camera yet invented could hope to capture.

My fateful encounter with Bethan Mair Nichols occurred the following evening. I was mooning about among the prolific display of geraniums on the hotel terrace in Evora, when the willowy film director spotted me. I must have been harbouring nostalgic thoughts about Rosie Lorenz and he must have been looking for company. I felt obliged to ask how things were going. He was in the mood to unburden himself. I found his amiability a striking contrast to Father Afonso's, although in my morose condition I was grateful for both. I suppose the Franciscan asked for nothing except for you to accept his goodwill. The film director was looking for sympathy. Of course so was I. What else keeps us going?

Over our drinks he told me his name was Barry. Barry Parrott with two 'r's and two 't's. He wondered whether I had noticed he was having a bit of difficulty on the set.

'I mean the stones of course.'

He had a very winning smile and a trick of brushing back his long fair hair from his forehead.

'She's an extremely talented girl. No doubt about that. But very intense. Bethan Mair Nichols. Welsh. Very keyed up sometimes. Very touchy. Something to do with her background I suspect. You can take these things too seriously in my view. It's only a documentary after all. And those stones have been there two or three thousand years. And they will still be there long long after we are gone and forgotten. Helps us to put things in perspective, wouldn't you say?'

I heard nothing to disagree with. The kind of elegiac attitude that suited my mood. We had a second drink. He imagined it was possible our paths had crossed before. I don't know what it is about me. An anxiety to please perhaps. People seem to regard me as a useful mirror in which they can catch an agreeable and reassuring glimpse of themselves. He had a further need to unburden himself.

'I was an actor you see. I always felt acting was my true vocation. But the fact is, it's a tough world out there. It really is. And it's getting tougher. I don't think she quite grasps that, you know. Loaded with degrees and Film School and all that sort of thing. All these aesthetic principles. In my time we were only too glad to get the work.'

'My father is an actor. Or was.'

It just slipped out. This odd sense of obligation to respond with a matching degree of friendly frankness. As soon as I had spoken I knew I could be making a tactical error. This abiding naive streak my mother used to worry about. 'Hold back a little,' she used to say. 'Consider the shape of the situation before you open your mouth, my love.' How right she was. As far as my father was concerned there was always more to conceal than reveal.

He knew about Orlando Lloyd. He stepped back demonstrating amazement and repeating 'Really? Really?' My response could have been interpreted as diffidence: in fact it was lingering regret at having made the revelation. Barry Parrott collected old theatre programmes reaching back decades, 'Quite a valuable collection really'. A show of modest pride. And then I was required to step into a better light so that he could check on the resemblance. 'No wonder I had the feeling we had met before.' Not a point to please my father. I am an inferior copy of his distinguished self, almost two inches shorter with red hair and big feet, 'with a nose directly traceable to your great-grandfather, the Geneva Jew.'

By now Barry Parrott was ready to embrace me as a kindred spirit. He was dining with Simon and Vanessa Potts, the travel guide writers, a delightful couple, who were passing through, and wouldn't I please join them?

'Always a good move,' he added roguishly. 'Guarantees the best of the cuisine.'

So there I was, a more or less willing victim, caught at a table of travellers' chat. Would I have been any better off dining alone and brooding over the loss of Rosie Lorenz, wondering what exactly it was she found lacking in me? An excess of passivity perhaps? A lack of sparkle. An absence of presence. Simon and Vanessa would have us know they dined here in the line of duty. They were staying with their dear friends, the Count and Countess of Something-or-other, at the Quinta das Torres and they had to be as objective and judicial as possible but this part of Portugal had a very special place in their hearts. After all, Portugal, our oldest ally and all that. In no time at all they were at it, as travel connoisseurs placing the principal holiday countries of Europe in what they called an order of merit. The man and wife team were arguing about fish and vegetables when Bethan Mair Nichols appeared on the open staircase. A singular moment. Could that have been the moment that Rosie Lorenz flew out of my mind for ever?

I sensed Barry Parrott's nervous hesitation. Was it his intention to ask her to join us? I must have fixed an eager smile on my face in anticipation of a pleasant diversion. She looked so elegant in her dark blue, it was only her boyish determined step that related to the girl in the vast straw hat I last saw skulking among the standing stones.

She was a model of calm and stillness as she took her

place between myself and a Barry Parrott anxious to please. There is a confidence and ease that goes with so much restrained beauty. Her mere proximity was pleasantly disturbing. Barry resolved to be ostentatiously cheerful. He introduced his colleague as very gifted and strictly Welsh. He wondered whether Simon and Vanessa had contemplated a Travellers' Guide to Wales. That sort of thing. He was smiling like a genial host putting up a topic for conversation. The Pottses declared that they absolutely loved Wales, rain or no rain. They had once thought of an Arthur's kingdom sort of thing, joining up Wales and the West of England. Oh, they had tried more than once. Their last attempt came to a full stop at Bala as it happened. 'We like to follow our inspiration don't we, Van?' Simon Potts said. 'With the better kind of guide book you need a thread, or you'll just end up with a telephone directory.' A voyage of discovery was the basis of their technique. And the more obscure the place the greater pleasure it gave them to extol its uniqueness. 'And the friendliness and hospitality and all that.'

'Alas, I'm afraid that in Bala we met our Waterloo.'

'Oh dear,' Barry Parrott said. 'What happened?'

'A charming pub, wasn't it, Van? Can't remember the name. Can you?'

Vanessa shook her head ready to listen intently as Simon spoke on their behalf.

'So rude, we felt. These people kept on talking Welsh. It put us right off. We knew they could speak English. Of course they could. And we were there to help. It put us right off. Most unfair perhaps. But there we are. Our guides have the personal touch and are based on our personal reactions. We like to praise without being fulsome. A full and fair appraisal. We like to think that's what makes our guides unique.'

'So much for Wales,' Barry said cheerfully. 'The Land of Song and all that. Land of my Fathers and my fathers can keep it!'

The laughter subsided. They were looking at Bethan

waiting for her to respond. She took her time. I can remember distinctly my eagerness to hear her voice again. It was slow and almost childlike and I judged the accent to be more north rather than south.

'What did you want them to do then? Those people in Bala?'

I thought she was making an effort to deepen her accent, roughen her naturally dulcet tones.

'Offer you Welsh-cakes or commit hara-kiri?'

While we were still wondering whether or not she was making a joke, she made a further solemn observation.

'I don't know whether it is inherent in the language or in the psyche, but I find it a very odd way of looking at the world.'

Now she was being positively gnomic. I ventured to ask: 'What do you mean exactly?'

'To assume the planet exists to provide holiday destinations for well-to-do English-speaking tourists.'

She had made herself only too clear. A frost descended. I tried to fill in another uncomfortable silence by speaking up.

'I'm Welsh,' I said. 'Or at least half Welsh. My mother was Swiss.'

Bethan was amused by my effort.

'Is that a fact?' she said. 'I shall have to see you get a medal.'

She was kind enough to smile at me and even laugh. I was captivated. In fact her attention must have inspired me. She may have been paying me more attention in order to further punish Barry Parrott. Briefly I had the impression of being either a prize or a bone of contention. He even went so far as to hold my arm and repeat his complaint that Bethan Mair Nichols could be very punchy. If it was meant as a warning it was one I was very ready to ignore.

On the pretext of admiring the ruin of the so-called Temple of Diana in the moonlight, I found myself walking alongside Bethan and listening intently to her quiet voice.

Everything she said seemed to be given an added significance by the starlit sky above us. There was enchantment in the air and yet her utterance was resolutely down to earth. To me it was an intoxicating combination.

'It's quite comic really,' she was saying. 'I had Welsh and Welshness shoved down my throat ever since I can remember. I took this job to get away from it all. And what do I find as soon as I get here? Having to stand up for my blessed heritage. Just one more time.'

'Good for you,' I said.

I was too eager with my approval.

'Good for nothing,' she said. 'It's like a family curse. My mother spent one or two spells in prison after making language protests. The sins of the mothers shall be visited on the daughters. Until the third and fourth generation.'

If she found it comic I found it comic too. I was so imbued with sympathetic understanding. We could muse and meditate together, merge into a new element, acquire in the moonlight modes of communication never known before.

'Ideologies are meant for the upbringing of children.' she said. 'The citizens of tomorrow and all that sort of thing. When you become an adult and creative, what you need above all is to breathe free. That's what I think, anyway.'

They were not propositions that had occurred to me before. Now that Bethan had put them into words they seemed important and profound and I was nodding in vigorous agreement.

'If you are a woman, of course, being free means not being crippled by worrying about what other people think about you. Shaking off the long trail of shackles from the patriarchal past.'

She was giggling with pleasure at the sound of her own inventions and perhaps the impression they were making on me. We were completely comfortable with each other. I suppose there is no better source of inspiration than an attentive admiring listener. I took it as a compliment that she wanted me to understand her attitude to the work they had in hand and how it differed from Barry Parrott's.

'Those stones mean something. You have to look at them long and hard to find out what the message is. To me photography is a language. It's a language you can use to make everybody understand. Make everything clear. You can escape from the language you were born with into a bigger yet parallel universe… Oh my goodness. Listen to me. I'm getting on my own nerves. But you know what I mean, don't you?'

Of course I knew. As we moved in step around the square with the ruined temple raised at its centre, it seemed the whole earth was paved with secrets we were destined to discover together. This entailed a degree of frankness between us that made me shiver with delight. She had a tangle of emotional commitments she needed my help to unravel: not just family. The state of the world. We moved through shadows. She drew a thin shawl over her head and I peered anxiously at her delicate features as though to reassure myself of the vital connection between them and the soft voice that held me in thrall. She is a person who lives on a practical plane where activity because it is creative is a sufficient definition in itself. She has no difficulty in making up her mind. Just to be close to her would make me less indecisive. More than that, she would be a source of animating magic.

'I don't want to be unfair to Barry,' she was saying. 'He has been good to me. If there's one thing I detest, it's women who flutter their eyelashes in order to get on. There are career moves and career motives. It's the kind of world we live in. I wanted to get into directing. He is good-looking and he has a lot of superficial English public school charm. But he is a lightweight.'

Lightweight. The word was a verdict in itself. A condemnation. It cast Barry Parrott into the intellectual outer darkness. I almost felt sorry for him.

'I don't want to sound like a bad-tempered harpy

16

trying to justify her own behaviour. Which I admit was not very good by the Sunday School standards I was brought up with. It's just that there is a whole world of meaning that Barry hasn't the faintest inkling about. He seems designed to be superficial. And there isn't that much difference between superficial and slipshod.'

Even in my state of moonlit exaltation I realised that the standard this beautiful young woman set was extraordinarily high. I hardly measured up to it. I am a born amateur, very curious about the world of course, but curiously lacking in ambition. That could be my father's fault: a distinct unwillingness to strut on any stage. I listened even more intently in an attempt to fathom the extent of this girl's aspirations. Nothing in the world now seemed more important than understanding Bethan Mair Nichols. It seemed that effective photography could be an aid to tutoring the masses. It was an instrument that could be used to counteract the manipulative power of big business and politicians. If that power went unchecked those monsters could always work up the irrational anger of one lot of masses or other to reach genocidal boiling point. If I understood her reasoning correctly, slipshod workmanship was the equivalent of indifference among the well-intentioned. Things had gone too far already. There was evidence everywhere. What the stones were saying to her was that the planet was a Garden of Eden we were threatening to turn into a blighted desert. As much as I could keep up with, I said 'amen' to. My neck muscles told me I was nodding repeatedly.

'We seem to understand each other,' she said. 'It's quite strange really. I feel quite silly saying it. We only really met this evening. But I feel as if I've known you all my life.'

Two

THAT NIGHT my room in the hotel was flooded with moonlight and I was too excited by my encounter with this amazing girl to sleep.

When we parted in the foyer she abruptly reached up to kiss me on the cheek. It was like a benediction. She murmured something about my gift of listening and thanked me. It was like a seal on a new friendship. I struggled to recall whether I had said anything to demonstrate that I was more than a simpering soft-headed romantic, on the rebound, sinking from one condition of infatuation to another. I made one point I think she listened to. That photography is a language like any other language, a tool of expression: but didn't everything depend on what you had to say? She agreed with that. So the delicious flow of our warm communication continued without further obstruction.

This was different from all my previous romantic encounters. Barry Parrott said she was punchy. It was clear to me she was punchy with a purpose. She was beautiful enough. She had no need to pose as a delicate fragrant flower or be what my father would call a 'pretty little thing'. Even in this brief space of time I could believe our relationship had a solid intellectual base, and that in itself was an exciting prospect. It was possible my destiny had arrived and was standing wordless at the open door ready to take over. Rather like my good friend Father Afonso. He decided to help my research. I was completing my report on the cork economy in record time. He led me to statistical resources that would have taken me days to discover on my own. He also made time for more sight-seeing and to my delight Bethan was willing to join us. The documentary at Almendras, such as it was – a poor thing, I was given to understand – was finished, and she was glad to shake off her part in it. Afonso took her under his wing just as he had taken me. The film crew had left and Barry Parrott had mysterious business of his own to attend to.

Within easy reach of Evora there were five more neolithic sites Afonso was keen for us to examine. For my part I was happy to go anywhere in Bethan's company. She appeared to like the Franciscan as much as she liked me. Bumpy journeys in his open tourer she didn't mind a bit. They made her laugh and sitting in the cramped rear seat I did my best to be cheerful too. There was a stone sanctuary about twenty miles south east of Evora that seemed to rekindle her professional displeasure with Barry Parrott.

'The things we have missed! It's unbelievable.'

I followed her attentively among the standing stones and passage graves. Afonso had stopped to chat with two old women feeding their chickens in the yard of the white-washed red-roofed smallholding.

'Honestly. He is so superficial it amounts to incompetence. I mean it's a programme commissioned for a series on prehistory. Low budget admittedly. So what does he do?'

I am eager to be taken further into her confidence. Together we examine more closely a motif carved on the surface of a menhir. What did the wavy lines and zigzags mean?

'He's just a fixer who loves to fix. Only one degree above a con man. Very smooth and delighted with his own smoothness. What Mr Parrott was trying to do on the side was a series of shorts he could sell to the Tourist Board and the airlines. That's where he's disappeared to. Will he pull it off? That remains to be seen. Meanwhile he makes a shoddy superficial job of the original commission. I blame myself. I let myself into it. How was I to know he was so superficial? I dread to think what his acting was like.'

That was a joke to end her condemnation on a lighter note, more in keeping perhaps with the blue sky and the enticing shade of the cork trees around us. I had still to reveal my father was an actor. For a moment I heard his voice like a rattle in a cupboard. These days my priority was to hold on to her confidence, her respect and friendship. Each day I hoped to get closer to her. However the Franciscan was in charge. It was his fast car and we were his grateful guests. Bethan even went as far as to make cheerful jokes about 'The Three Musketeers'. No doubt they added to the gaiety of the occasion. They also had a distinct neutering effect. We were so to speak, all boys together, classmates on an outing. We were indeed three persons of like mind and goodwill, and as we drove around or ate together in quiet establishments, where more often than not Afonso was a welcome visitor, we had discussions of surprising depth on a surprising range of subjects, but all strictly impersonal, on the condition of the world or the meaning of this or that, nothing really calculated to bring the girl and myself emotionally closer. Afonso was as much a chaperon as a guide.

Bethan was at least four or even five years my junior, but these animated discussions were enough to show that she had a joined-up view of the world far more positive and comprehensive than my own. And for one so young she had a forceful way of expressing herself. It seems that the world is an astonishing place that has to be explored with humility and reverence. Father Afonso was in enthusiastic agreement. I nodded of course, harmoniously, although their combined fervour made me feel a hedonistic academic with an ingrained habit of muttering 'on the one hand' and 'on the other'. If I was to keep up with this girl I needed to take myself in hand and subject myself to an altogether new and perhaps sterner discipline.

I was stretched out on the warm ramparts of Marvão, listening to Afonso explaining the significance of the place on the frontier between Spain and Portugal, when Bethan made one of her sharp remarks about politicians.

It seemed they ranked even lower than actors in her estimation. They should be as useful but as short-lived as disposable nappies. I'm not sure whether that was her own pleasantry or something she had heard. However when they discussed the Iberian Peninsula as part of the European Union she began to soar to speculative heights that made me feel quite nervous.

'True leadership should rest with disinterested thinkers,' she said. 'You know, like those Shia Ayatollahs. Issue edicts on the public good. And private passions of course. How to reconcile them. I mean it is remarkable how they do it, isn't it? Those mullahs. There's always got to be some way of transforming the volatile masses into disciplined citizens.'

I was not encouraged by such oracular discourse. I listened intently because I wanted to get to know her better. It was clear to me she was looking for a Career she could combine with a Cause, or the other way around. In my own case I cherished the hope that my search was over. I had found her, and she was what I had been looking for. Edicts on the public good, if I understood her correctly, would be a serious threat to the individual freedom which I cherished greatly. As she did hers surely, judging by the evidence of her life-style. Or at least as much as I had seen of it. The cleric was again filled with enthusiastic agreement. I thought to myself, well, he would be, wouldn't he? Priests were the nearest thing we could provide to mullahs. Broad-minded and free-spirited as he liked to think himself, he was an ordained officer of a church always ready for a re-run of the mediaeval struggle for power between the ecclesiastic and the secular.

I kept my reservations to myself. My confidence as a suitor had been dented by the defection of Rosie Lorenz. It was up to me, as that ancient but resourceful woman-iser Freddy Helmut puts it, to create the opportunities where the short-hand of friendship could be converted into the long-hand of love. In spite of the marvellous weather and the stimulating intellectual callisthenics, it came as an enormous relief when we discovered it would be possible for Bethan and me to become fellow travellers on the long train journey from Lisbon to Paris. Vistas opened up full of exciting opportunities to establish closer understanding.

I never liked Afonso more than when we bade him a fond farewell on Lisbon central station. He was still full of enthusiasm for the prehistoric. There should be a next time, he insisted, when he would drive us both north to the Côa Valley to see the rock art of the Palaeolithic period. There were wondrous representations of ibex, strange fish, and even such modern things as horses. Bethan responded with near rapture at the prospect and as usual I nodded. I owed him so much, and I should have been stricken with inward grief and shame at being so pleased to leave him. The fact was the girl and I were setting out on an adventure that was designed for only two. He stayed on to wave us goodbye, as he said, in a good old-fashioned way on a good old-fashioned journey. When he raised his arm, it began with a wave and ended as a silent benediction.

So what else could we do but sit back and murmur our admiration for our remarkable friend? He was unique we agreed. A special person. A pearl of great price. Bethan seemed to think more deeply about him as she stared at the shifting landscape. He had to be lonely she surmised. And yet his faith gave him strength. And that was something to be envied. Of course it was, I agreed. It was something she lacked, she confessed. Something she was searching for. It had to account for her restlessness. It was all very well to talk about voyages of discovery and ambitious projects, but in the end, what could be more important, more vital than an inner stillness, an inner strength? We agreed that it was more than likely that Father Afonso had it, whatever it was, and it had given him the power to do us a power of good. We were smiling happily at each other, prepared for the journey and for listening to each other with increasingly rapt attention.

What did we know about each other, except an eagerness to know more? For the time being nothing could be more important. The business of living could be on hold while this vital journey was in progress. She knew my father was an actor after all. A famous actor. 'I don't know about famous,' I said. She was interested. It was gratifying to know she had gone to the trouble of extracting the information out of Barry Parrott. Unless of course he had told her for some obscure reason of his own? I needed to make an effort to control the emotional turmoil this unique occasion was already stirring inside me. Did falling in love have to mean losing your foothold? Talking about my father would be enough to remind me of his so often repeated verdict about Eddie being too susceptible. Only a fortnight ago I believed I was in love with Rosie Lorenz. And now she has faded into a pink and fluffy memory. What am I confronting here if not my destiny? This was the girl to talk to. There was sympathy as well as strength in her steady gaze.

Frankness was all. I had to admit my father was a burden. He had been married three times, and he was well into his forties when I was born. Dancing with the devil of old age on the Riviera and shuffling about in a surprising variety of stratagems to restore or at least relive the dubious glories of his heyday. She was interested. She leaned forward and her violet eyes seemed even bigger as she paid close attention to everything I had to say. Once the floodgate was open of course reminiscence came pouring out and in no time I was paddling in a confessional pool. I told her about my mother and how devoted she had been and how much she had suffered. I was distressed at the degree of emotion I was stirring up inside myself. It was what my father would describe as 'unmanly', one more attribute that marked Edward Lloyd, – red-haired and disfigured with a flattened nose broken in a childhood accident – susceptible and softhearted, 'a walking target' as he would say for predatory females on the look-out for easy prey. As my eyes cleared

I felt Bethan touch my hand to comfort me. There never could be a less predatory or more delicate girl. Her face wore the dedicated expression of a young nurse attending a wounded patient. I told her about the Trust Fund and the numbered accounts in Geneva, but by then she was embarked on a reciprocal study of her own relationship with her mother.

It wasn't a case of not being able to get on. She had been most tenderly brought up and there was plenty of loving attention around. It was a case of divergent aims. You could get stifled by being too well brought up. Her mother had been in league with enthusiastic teachers at the Welsh school who were too eager to tell her what to do and what to believe and what to like. 'So that's why I cling to my camera, I suppose,' she said. 'It helps me to accumulate evidence. Work out things for myself. Do you know what I mean?'

Of course I knew what she meant. Nothing could ever be quite the same again. Our consciousness seemed to be expanding by the minute. This journey would bring about transformations of seismic proportions. Our mode of communication had become so close we became blissfully unaware of other passengers. The train and its amenities existed to serve and sustain our dreamlike condition. On the way to the dining car, when there was no one about, I took her in my arms. It seemed so right that our true companionship should be sealed with a close embrace. We were there to take comfort from each other. Our bodies had the right to know each other. Over our meal, which seemed curiously insubstantial compared to our private communing, she explained that her birth mother had died within a matter of weeks after her birth. Lowri, the mother with whom she was in perpetual loving contention, was her father's second wife. There may have been some genetic defect which Bethan may have inherited. A possible heart murmur? The defect took on an immediate romantic overtone. She was something precious and delicate that needed my protection. It

24

was all 'may' and 'perhaps' and she had always preferred not to inquire further. On the other hand her origins could account for this curious sense she had always had of an individual mission. There was some purpose, some goal, she was meant to achieve. This accounted for her restlessness which I might well have noticed. We started to laugh together and this smiling and light-hearted determination became characteristic of our relationship: the mere joy of being together.

This was temporarily shattered, at least as far as I was concerned, when we returned to the compartment to discover that we would be sharing it for the night with an elderly American couple who were doing Europe, they told us, for the last time. They bustled about in a studiously unobtrusive way, making themselves comfortable. In fact they were more than elderly. The wife said they had been married fifty-four years and that there was nothing they enjoyed more than travelling in each other's company. If you had to be worn out, she said, this was a good way to do it, except that sight-seeing killed her feet and would we mind if they settled down early since they had discovered years ago that horizontal was the best way to travel.

During the night, as the train rumbled on, wide awake and daring, Bethan crept into my bunk. She whispered into my ear that we were vagrants with no fixed abode and therefore it was better that we clung together – this was the perfect transport – and let our bodies do the talking. She straddled me and I listened hard to soft endearments in Welsh that I vowed to understand. She swayed gently like a boat at anchor shifted by a rising tide. We had created a world within a world, distilled, without dismal mundane concerns, serving each other with unceasing rapt attention.

Until the elderly American switched on the blue light above his head and blundered his way to the toilet. We heard his wife in a quavering voice asking him if he was alright. We heard the short grunt of his reply and the compartment door opening and shutting. Bethan clamped her little hand over my mouth and allowed herself to shake with giggles. Every detail seemed unique and delightful and never to be forgotten. All lovers assume there is magic in their mutual attraction. The impulse I needed to restrain was growing too possessive. I felt I had discovered something rare and beyond price: a treasure to hoard to keep to myself alone, and it was with some effort that I reined myself in.

By the time we reached Paris, Bethan had allowed me to take charge. I have this rather childlike pride in knowing my way around great cities and I suppose I made an extra effort to impress my girl with my unerring sense of direction and easy command of the language. I think she found this naive pleasure in the accomplishment rather endearing. She was inclined to give me spontaneous kisses and say she found me so sympathetic and unthreatening. She would emphasise that my honesty and sincerity were the qualities that appealed so much to her and we both laughed together at my hesitation to accept her verdict as a compliment.

We laughed a great deal. We shared a room and a bed with an ease that seemed natural and inevitable. We agreed that we had become more than we thought we were. A combined force. We emerged from our lair after mid-day to conquer Paris and make it an annex to our private paradise. There were new exhibitions that Bethan had decided it was vital for her to view and ponder. I was obliged to confess that I had, so to speak, only come for the ride, and the way I said it amused us both greatly. In between serious study we were innocents abroad, standing on bridges peering down at the swirling river, ourselves ready to float in and out of churches. In one we sat down to listen to the organist practising Bach and we held hands and declared ourselves moved and uplifted. For three unforgettable days we saw everything and we saw nothing except each other in a fresh and glorious light.

It was all brought to an abrupt end by Bethan's mobile phone ringing in the depth of her handbag. We were on the moving staircase on the outside of the Pompidou Centre, and debating whether to take in the Brancusi studio or take an early lunch. She turned her back on me to engage in a desperate argument with what appeared to be a malevolent invisible spirit. I was filled with instant foreboding.

'It's Barry,' she said. 'Let's go and eat and I'll tell you about it.'

As things stood it appeared that Barry Parrott exercised what amounted to a stranglehold on her career. They were due within two days to start filming at Tustrup.

'Where on earth is that?'

She smiled sympathetically at my agonised cry.

It was in Jutland. Yet another complex of standing stones and burial chambers and so-called stone age temples. It appeared that one of the burgeoning themes of this project was the primordial unity of Europe. Hence the extra cash from Brussels. I listened to her expositions making an effort to hold back the misery welling up inside me. It had all been too good to last. It would all vanish like a dream. As she was speaking and explaining, stratagems, plots and ploys to hold on to her were flashing through my brain. No career change would be out of the question if it kept us together. She had to understand my desperation and how committed I was.

Such was my anxiety to hold on to what we had won or at least what I had won, as we discussed the problem I felt my understanding of her character begin to wobble. I had already observed she read newspapers and magazines with an avidity I found hard to understand. She was much concerned with trends or the cutting edge as she inclined to call it: where was it? Berlin? New York? London? San Francisco? Who was wielding it all and that sort of thing. I dismissed the unworthy and Orlando-like suspicion that this was a variant of the eternal feminine search for fashion. Bethan dealt in ideas and concepts even more than I did. She did not appear to suffer from my need to establish emotional stability. All I needed was a secure platform from which I could conduct in comfort my own variety of spiritual researches. Like a born researcher I was happy to travel hopefully and never be over-anxious to arrive.

Suppressing disappointment and dismay, I listened patiently to Bethan expounding the extent to which her intentions and ambitions were intertwined with short-comings in the character of Barry Parrott. He may not have been a creator or even a competent technician, but he certainly was a fixer with a wide range of connections. I had to appreciate the stark nature of her dilemma: sticking with Barry's setup, trying to make the best of it, even with all the compromise and shilly-shallying it entailed; or bending to the will of a loving but overbearing mother; living at home and teaching or at the very best trying to squeeze into the Welsh language television channel.

While I was silent in my misery she became vehement.

'I want to achieve something! My own effort and nobody else's. What we are here for is more important than where we came from. I'm not here to fulfil another woman's frustrated Cymric dreams. What is wrong with a touch of ambition, Eddie? You have to measure your own success or failure. By the time you reach forty what have you done? I'm twenty-seven already. My time is running out.'

I would like to have made a joke there, but I didn't dare to. Her birth mother had died so young. I imagined it brought too much pressure on her. For my own part I was in sight of the middle of the thirties road and it didn't worry me unduly: except – and I couldn't say it in the face of her tumultuous and unconventional ambition – I would like to be married and even starting a family. I saw now that I would have to keep such unseemly longings secret and on hold. I did consider suggesting we could make a brilliant success of living together. I have a small but steady private income she would be welcome to use to pursue her artistic endeavour. If I mentioned this at this point would she see it as yet another trap: an inhibiting commitment?

'I don't want to be safe, imitative and unoriginal. The whole point is make something new or find something new. That is the point surely? I take that to be a duty. You can call it a way of life if you like.'

As we strolled along the embankment of the Seine I was struck dumb with a sense of being inadequate. It was a direct challenge to which I should respond. Trembling and apprehensive with the fear of some inseparable loss, how could I? Bethan sensed my misery and laid a comforting hand on my arm.

'I am a self-absorbed bitch,' she said. 'I really am. It's the history of my life really. I don't know how you put up with me.'

This was a release in itself and I hugged her. We seemed to have spent the rest of the day making fun of ourselves, making absurd confessions, particularly the bits and pieces of our failed affairs of the past. At Cambridge she had a crush on a certain Tim, and was so enamoured she took up acting which she hated. There was a Raymond who studied Old Norse and so on and was now making a fortune in an investment bank. These names stuck in my memory like burrs on the back of a coat. They were there to remind me that this remarkable phenomenon at my side was human. But not as fallible as myself when I told her about Paola whose father was something secular in the Vatican, and whose mother was a social climber with crampons who found me completely wanting. I even mentioned in passing the defection of Rosie Lorenz, and Bethan was soothingly sympathetic.

I told her more about the sufferings of my mother and the embarrassing infidelities of my father and how he could flaunt them even more than his pedigree. Bethan seemed interested in both. We took some pleasure in exploring what she came to call my Cymric Connection. She said it was about as substantial as the bad breath of a mythological beast! She teased me about my lack of knowledge of Welsh topography. If my father claimed to be a grandson of the third baron of Carreg Wen, how could that possibly matter if he didn't know where Carreg Wen was? She laughed when I told her of our quarterly trips to Geneva to draw on his allowance from my mother's money and how I had to countersign everything. She said that was the best place for a parent: under lock and key, a fly stuck to the fly paper. She would be interested to meet him, but couldn't be pinned down to a definite arrangement at the moment.

Our brief season in Paradise had come to an untidy end. I was too eager for assurances. She said our bond was cemented and there would never be a wall between us. We would always tell each other everything either one of us might wish to know. The sinister mixture between the past and the subjunctive made it too clear that a brief season of bliss was about to vanish for ever. I had a premonition of a life-time to be spent striving to recover this dissolving dream. There would be mobile phoning and e-mailing and even long letters if there was time. I wanted to nail it all down, there and then, construct a calendar of movements and meetings. She promised to do her best but I could see that precision in these matters was not to her taste.

The following morning on the way to Charles de Gaulle she returned to the litany of the shortcomings of Barry Parrott. For my part I would have wished she had not. It gave rise to uncomfortable spasms of intense jealousy. If he was all that weak and useless, where did he find the power to attract her to his side away from mine? Professional ambitions were all very well but there had to be some other quality as well. He was good-looking. I had heard her murmur she rated him physically attractive. I hung on to her in that last embrace, hungry for warmth and reassurance. I watched her walk towards the escalator without turning around. A small determined figure that could be heroic and pathetic according to the way you were inclined to view the human condition.

As far as my own condition was concerned my world within a world had vanished or at least had shrunk to a damp despairing orb. I had shameful tears to shed. Quite disgraceful for a man of my age, and I could only shed them in the privacy of a cubicle of the public toilets. Paris the annex to Paradise had lost all its savour. The great capital where I knew my way around, the sights and sounds and smells that had held us together from Les Halles to the Bois, from the Tuileries to Saint Sulpice, threatened to asphyxiate me with loneliness.

Three

AND THAT WAS IT. My life would never be the same again. A terrible beauty had been born. I had stepped into a new world. When I caught myself tramping the streets muttering such apocalyptic phrases, so that heads turned to look at me, I made a staunch effort to take myself in hand. I bought a newspaper, sat at an outdoor table, ordered a coffee, watched the world go by and wondered whether I was suffering from a delayed adolescence. Bethan Mair wasn't there to talk to and I had an urge to try and record every word she had spoken before she had left me. Then again there were all the questions I had neglected to ask, all the arguments I had failed to deploy. All my questions shrink into a whine: 'when do I see you again?' And an even more pathetic: 'shall I write or ring?' And the unforgettable coolness of the answer. 'Both of course. But not just yet, dear Eddie. Not for the next few days. I shall have a lot to concentrate on. I'll call you. But you'll be in my heart, day and night. I promise you.'

I learned them by rote, the guidelines laid down by those soft lips and the delicate pressure of those fingers, all in less than one afternoon. I've heard it said by know-ledgable people, Freddy Helmut prominent among them, that relationships are more often than not fatally weakened by prolonged separation. With Bethan and me I would argue exactly the opposite is the case. As far as I am concerned certainly her life has taken over mine and the longer the gaps the more absorbed I become in trying to fathom the mystery. Of course there are routines that never seem to change. I am grateful to them. They are handrails that help me to cross the abyss of absence. For weeks on end I immerse myself in the knottier problems of Food Data and the Under-utilised Commodities. And there are problems of translation and statistics that positively entertain me. Also to get closer to her, I begin to study Welsh.

This amuses Freddy Helmut no end. It allows him to make elaborate jokes about Penelope doing the wandering and Eddie Odysseus staying at home keeping the Welsh hearth warm. At weekends I bring my lexicons and grammars with me to the chalet between the vineyards and the almond trees, and the sound of Welsh words on my tape recorder is some compensation for Bethan's absence. 'My God! Not another tome!' Freddy's patience is liable to give out. He snatches the grammar out of my hands and urges me to race after him down the slope and plunge into the lake. Well into his forties he still fancies his athletic prowess. I believe he is quite envious of my linguistic skills. His French was never up to much and in the office he always brings me any memos or correspondence in that language to be corrected. He says I have my uses which I think is meant as a compliment. I admit I have always been an addict of lexicons. Just as Freddy is a lifelong sybarite disguised as a dedicated international civil servant. We all have our little failings.

Except Bethan Mair of course, especially in her absence. Not only does my heart grow fonder. It grows ever more concerned with her heroic struggles towards freedom and fulfilment. She has much to contend with and my role is to provide her with unstinting comfort and encouragement. That series on neolithic stones was a success, thanks to her steady input. With some effort she kept Barry Parrott on the rails. As I was given to understand, he was liable to chase off after will-o'-the-wisp get-rich-quick schemes such as an American series called 'Ancestry Videos', cooking up fancy genealogical trees to reassure rich Americans about their pedigrees and their roots and all about where they came from. Bethan was very amused when I said 'everyone comes from somewhere. So what?' It was Barry Parrott that had the bright idea of making a video film of my father. 'Whatever comes of it,' he is reported to have said. 'We can always sell it to Archives.' I suppose my initial indignation melted into amusement, particularly when I saw that Bethan was enjoying the unlikely venture.

I have to say they get on rather better than I would like. Orlando switches on what he considers his deadly charm and Bethan responds with what I can only describe as delighted amusement. She seems oblivious to his patent insincerity. 'He is an actor, Eddie,' she says. 'Therefore he acts.' She exercises such a degree of tolerance I can't go on repeating that the man drove my poor mother to distraction with his petty philandering. I can't go on repeating that when she died, I was distraught, inconsolable. I have to accept it was the cancer and not his serial infidelities that killed her. In her lifetime she never stood up to him but in her last will and testament she took her quiet revenge. I was her son and only heir. To her husband, Henrietta, his third wife, left a quarterly allowance for his lifetime, and the withdrawal at the Geneva bank had to be countersigned by his son. I have to confess that this is the only exercise of power that has ever given me a frisson of pleasure, and that didn't last. The journey could be inconvenient and my father's frequent shortage of cash a source of persistent nagging. 'If you could just let me have such and such a sum, dear boy, to tide me over.' And the trips lasting two or even three days could be nerve-wracking beyond words. 'Let's pop over to Ferney, dear boy, and take a butchers at dear old Voltaire's establishment.' He had this ridiculous habit of claiming an affinity with the great man, even to me, so well aware that the posturing buffoon had never read a word of his works, or even used his French language, except to the shops or the *femme de chambre*, if he could possibly avoid it. The aim was to pull off the confidence trick of acting the part. Nothing else mattered: except the money to feed his appetite for further impersonations. It's an awful thing when a father brings out the worst in his son. All I have ever asked of life is to be left alone to indulge in my harmless pursuits and I suppose my dear mother left me my modest private income for that express purpose and, as she used to say in her sweet but tired voice, 'do a little bit of good in the world.'

Bethan is not put off by him. Finds him 'interesting'. This does make me wonder, makes me jealous even. It seems inconsistent with her view that family is an institution a creative artist such as herself is obliged to escape from, or at least keep at a long arm's length. She claims to enjoy staying in our rather claustrophobic apartment in Juan-les-Pins and is even willing to make supper for us on occasions just for the pleasure she says, of seeing the great Orlando rubbing his hands and demonstrating relish in anticipation. 'All his gestures are so delightfully theatrical' she says. And yet she quite firmly puts me off any visit to Cardiff and her nice family home in Cyncoed with a damning 'Oh they're very nice but too Welsh bourgeois for words'. I would quite like to understand what she means by the phrase. She is never willing to elaborate and I am not eager to waste our precious minutes together indulging in arguments or recriminations.

The Barry Parrott video film project of Orlando Lloyd was an absolute non-starter. There was no money in it and the mere mention of the word archives, my father said, gave him the smell of the mortuary. What he did enjoy was showing Bethan a selection of his massive scrapbooks bound in uniform mock leather of a green and gold hue that I found particularly sickening. I had to admire the patient attention she paid him as he went into detail about his faded triumphs. He even gave her sample renditions of the more prestigious roles. His early and I may add his only Romeo – 'O! she doth teach the torches to burn bright. It seems she hangs upon the cheek of night, Like a rich jewel in an Ethiop's ear'… Bethan was my rich jewel. I study the fresh contours of her beauty as she listens to my father prattle and I give myself a congratulatory hug that I should be the one to possess her. I move to the window to study the view of the palm trees and the sea that is the chief consolation of the perched apartment, and quietly restrain myself from crowing. She is mine and I am hers and on that private axis the whole world turns.

Orlando Lloyd was happy to linger over his triumphs in the fifties when he was, I have to admit, a much photographed matinee idol, famous for his good looks and languid upper-class English manner – 'before the toughs took over', as he put it, and 'those bloody angry young men.'

He was much more cautious in Bethan's presence, parading his pedigree. This I found intriguing. He was like an actor in a read-through who couldn't understand the lines and was still uncertain how to play the part. Bethan was liable to know more about the whole business than he did. He was christened Hubert Cynddylan Vaughan-Lloyd and could claim to be descended from Elystan Glodrydd. Since he couldn't even pronounce the name properly he had to be vaguer than usual invoking shadowy claims of yesteryear to vast estates in mid-Wales and the Marches. 'The eldest son in the family must have 'Cynddylan' among his names. I suppose that goes back to the Dark Ages. Curious really'.

He pronounces the name 'Kin-dilan'. Bethan corrects him gently. Then she points at me.

'So you must be Cynddylan too? Eddie Cynddylan. I like that.'

'There's a castle somewhere,' says the great Orlando. 'I'm afraid I have no idea where exactly.'

Bethan listens with wonderfully polite patience and even related possible ancestral figures of ours to the literary renaissance of the twelfth century. This excited me but caused my father's eyes to glaze over, even as he nodded his practised signals of appreciative understanding.

I was puzzled by Bethan's response to our Welsh connection. On the one hand she seemed to take it lightly and was ready to tease us about aristocratic fantasies. On the other, when it came to our ancestors patronising the poetic art, it became a more substantial matter. She suggested an excursion into the territory so that we could make a thorough exploration of the subject. Orlando showed superficial enthusiasm but was plainly relieved when no dates were set for such an excursion. He was never one to allow his comfortable routines to be disturbed. Myself I was disappointed. Any arrangement that allowed me to look forward to being with Bethan was always more than welcome: and language study had to take root somewhere to be effective. Orlando was always a man who lived for the pleasure of the moment. Such as clutching at Bethan's waist as she made her way past him in the narrowest passage of our apartment and holding on to her breasts when she was in danger of losing her balance. It made me realise how potent a force sexual jealousy had to be in history, when sons could be driven to kill their fathers even at the risk of destroying a dynasty. In the kitchen, as she bent over the stove I caught him stroking her hair with both hands. He even had the nerve to wink at me when he saw I had caught him at it. It meant that he was demonstrating innocent fatherly affection. All he was doing, for my sake, was making her feel welcome.

For the first time ever I experienced relief when the time came for Bethan to leave. And even at the last moment he scored a miniature triumph as he declined to be photographed. 'Ah, my dear. Not even for you! I've had too many taken. I can't be doing with any more. Age has withered me. Unless of course you want to film me jumping off the jetty at Port Galice. Positively last performance!' He was the host, genial to the last, bidding the parting guest a fond farewell. No sooner had she gone, he continued to add insult to injury.

'She rather overdoes this Welsh business, don't you think? And don't you think you should do something about getting her accent ironed out?' He gets my answer from between my teeth. I know it amuses him to rile me. 'You are Welsh yourself, for God's sake. You never tire about boasting your pedigree. If that's what you can call it.' Orlando has perfected a superior sniff. 'Ah well. That's something quite different.' 'Is it? Is it?' He thinks of his pedigree as membership of a small but exclusive club under long standing royal patronage. I am caught in the time-wasting exercise of trying to make him show where the difference lay. It is quite extraordinary how his banal pronouncements manage to reverberate in my brain. I might stop thinking about him and our impossible relationship for days and even weeks on end, when for no reason at all I hear his mellifluous baritone boom nagging away in my brain.

'Eddie lad…beware of developing a history of being dependent on some delightful female or other…You need to watch out for it. You really do. It could be your mother's fault of course. She gave you a gilt-edged education I have to admit but I'm afraid she spoilt you rotten, as the saying goes. The thing is, with the ladies, dear boy, you always need to locate a weak spot or two and bear them in mind until they come in handy. As they most surely will. The only things to put on pedestals are statues. And embracing statues is a waste of time, dear boy.'

Why should I ever want to scratch around for weak spots in the smooth perfection of the girl I love? There are no more blemishes in her character than in the body I idolise. She is all the more beautiful because she disregards her beauty as much as she disregards convention and what she calls 'things that don't matter' such as money. On that subject she has interesting views of her own. She distinguishes between dull money, dirty money and clean money. 'Clean money' is what she earns by the sweat of her own brow. 'Dull money' is my modest private income. 'Dirty money' includes excessive millions grabbed by banks and arms manufacturers and earth despoilers. I suspect she has invented the category of dull money out of regard for my feelings. 'I am happy for you Eddie. I really am. At least it gives you a little room for manoeuvre.' I find these casual remarks of hers profound.

We spend so much time apart they seem to grow in my mind and proliferate in unexpected directions.

I literally rack my brains for possible interesting projects we could embark on together. They tend to bear an unnerving resemblance to the labours of Hercules, but at least thinking about them keeps at bay the pains of jealousy that lurk on the edge of these prolonged periods of being apart. I am too aware that on the fringes of the film industry there are under employed lascivious males ready to pounce and thrust their attentions on any unattended attractive female. Bethan regularly sets my mind at rest by saying these were sources of minor irritation she could easily cope with. It was professional imbroglios, the unreliability of colleagues, that always caused her most distress. About these I was often called upon to soothe her with long-distance sympathetic sounds.

There came a moment when by dint of much thought and manoeuvring I created, with the help of Freddy Helmut who said he was a middle-aged cupid, what is known these days as a window of opportunity. There was a need of a report on food shortages in the Southern Sudan and a subsidy available for a video film. I acquired the authority to steer this commission in the Barry Parrott/Bethan Mair Nichols direction. I was quite beside myself with the possibilities... My hopes were dashed. Bethan had transferred from the good ship Parrott to a more stable vessel. In Denmark she had met this exciting experimental director Jens Strangerup and had joined his crew as first assistant for a film to be made of the plight of the native coffee growers in Nicaragua. She was so sorry about what she called 'the clash' but I had to appreciate the value of the experience. She would be acting as stills photographer as well. In my disappointment I was tempted to draw her attention to a pattern in her career that was beginning to emerge. She was liable to get involved with wonderful people about to initiate nothing less than an artistic revolution in the industry. No doubt these paragons would be charmed by her intelligence and enthusiasm and good looks. Within weeks obstacles like icebergs would emerge from the idealistic mists to threaten their endeavours. Things would come to a sorry end not so much in tears as resentment and acrimony.

And indeed so it happened. While I was in Lucichokio a sad message arrived from Houston airport. The money had run out and they were stranded. Could she borrow her fare home? Jens retired to the converted schoolhouse in Jutland to lick his wounds and Bethan was driven to seek refuge at home in Cyncoed, Cardiff, in the bosom of her bourgeois family. In my words of comfort I ventured to tell her she was too much of an uncompromising perfectionist. She replied she would never want to be anything else.

Four

THE GREAT ORLANDO is a very important person, and for my sins I am his only son. Above the door of his fourth-floor apartment there is a closed circuit camera and the lock has been changed. I ring and he takes ages to come to the door. It is not all that late but he is wearing a blue silk dressing gown. He puts his finger to his lips and sends me down the narrow passage to my cramped quarters where at least I have my own bathroom. There are whispered explanations that I barely catch. There has been a burglary in the building. And he has a guest who will be gone in the morning. He gives me one of his naughty-boy giggles and closes the door. How can I be anything but mortally embarrassed. This is one of his habitual 'harmless flirtations'. It doesn't stop as he gets older. Her husband away, some idle 'middle-aged-or-older-for-god's-sake' woman, has fallen for his faded charm. All the result of a lifetime of cultivated selfishness.

Not that my father and mother quarrelled or even bickered much. She was too much in awe of him. Henrietta Lloyd (née Reiss) was a quiet dignified woman, a classical scholar and dedicated teacher who gave it all up to marry a posturing actor who had made taking advantage of his charm and good looks a way of life. What a ghastly mistake. But that makes me a ghastly mistake too. 'My one chick Hen' he called her when he was in a good mood. I doubt whether her English was ever perfect enough to detect the nuance of contempt he sometimes put into the silly phrase.

I could have done with a brother or sister. I said so in many ways to my mother on many occasions. I received different answers I took as excuses. My father had to concentrate on his career. There was a world tour coming up and she had to look after him. The world was too dangerous to bring more children into it. She wanted to concentrate on the best for my father and me. My father always came first. She adored him and he accepted her adoration as due and proper tribute. She adored me too in a quieter way and took my education in hand so that I could move with ease and familiarity through all the languages and cultures that touched upon her native Switzerland. French in her view had priority as the natural heir of Latin as a *lingua franca* and the source of the most rational discourse. This was ironic because her own life had been distorted forever by one irrational impulse.

And come to think of it, rational discourse does not appear to be my strong point either. I am driven by emotional weather fronts. Such intellectual resources as I possess at the moment are directed at getting my father out of this apartment for a reasonable length of time and getting Bethan in. A reasonable time would be as long as it takes to gain a grip and a foothold so to speak in the process of properly understanding her. Sporadic reunions with a laughing loving girl, so much in charge of her own life inside her menstrual cycle, repeated, over time, could degenerate to the banal level of a holiday romance. It is imperative we come to perceive each other in greater depth; and how better than in some bearable equivalent to a humdrum domestic existence? Bethan will escape from family tensions in a damp climate and together here we will pursue the task of educating each other towards a closer understanding, like dedicated scientists working under laboratory conditions and taking occasional time off, walking alongside the blue sea or sitting in the shade of the palm trees in the public gardens.

At breakfast the great man is no longer in a cheerful mood. The *femme de chambre* had forgotten to bring him his usual mixture of yoghurt and muesli, and in the newspaper there was a glowing obituary to an English politician who had been in school with him. The fact is he should have gone into politics. All successful politicians were actors of one sort or another. Ham actors mostly trying to peddle goodwill and sincerity. All that 'trust me' stuff. And what have they ever done when it comes to the push except give the Empire away like damaged goods in a closing down sale. There hadn't been one decent politician since Winnie died. Not one. That woman paraded around squawking like a battery hen Boadicea, hadn't a clue how to keep the lid on the pressure cooker and lining up with Krauts and the Froggies and the Wops, a bundle of Dagos and Dutchmen, forever squabbling over the shrunken cake. It was all very difficult for a man like him to swallow, coming from a family of empire builders. Spreading civilised language and cricket to the four corners of the earth. The Vaughan-Lloyds had done more than their bit, and precious little they had to show for it. It was all a bitter pill to swallow. A bitter pill.

This is the usual way he goes on. A Eurosceptic lying in the sun and dreaming of Agincourt. How am I to bear it? Grit my teeth and wait for Bethan. There was a photograph of a strange woman on the bureau. She had white hair and she was smiling. 'Who's that?' I ask. If there were to be photographs in this room they should be of my mother. There was one I particularly liked of me, aged three I should think, nestling against her. Orlando swept up the picture and put it in the drawer. Another trophy. Probably the woman who was here last night. Fooling her to believe she was the only girl in the world, and similar doses of romantic slush she would have been only too ready to swallow. And the old dog was nearly eighty, pickling away in the Mediterranean sun.

'You know Eddie, I've been thinking about you.'

Am I supposed to welcome his attention? Quite comic really. All these years he has taken my range of accomplishments for granted: they were the result of the educational attention his wife, and my mother, had lavished on me. And of course they were of an inferior work-a-day order, rather sterile and uncreative and not to be compared with triumphs on the stage, or even on the screen.

'Put it this way. Why hide your bright light under a bushel? Don't you think all this Food and Agricultural business is a bit of a bureaucratic dead end? I mean what does it amount to except being a glorified translator or a frustrated do-gooder? I still know what's going on in the world you know. I advise you very strongly to consider going into politics. I took a look at *The Telegraph* down at The Galaxy yesterday. There's been a bit of a reshuffle and Pongo Ethington's boy – what's his name, Alastair is it? – has been made a minister in the Home Office. Good God, I said to myself, he can't be all that much older than Eddie. Now you give that some thought. You've got a lot to offer and a most honourable name. I still have a few connections.'

Fond illusions. He wears identities like costumes. He played Disraeli once on an Australian tour; Prime Ministerial roles he slips easily into. If he ever deigned to define himself, all he would discover would be a wardrobe full of costumes. The stuff I have to listen to. The great Orlando tucked away in Juan-les-Pins, wrapped in his prejudices, cultivating his eccentricities, indulging his bad habits, spicing up his days with adulterous duplicities, squandering my inheritance.

'Look, I'm off to Biarritz tomorrow. So you and your little maid of the mountains can have the place to yourselves until I get back. And keep a look-out for the Mafiosi. That's what the cameras are for you know. They say they're Russians. I don't know what the world is coming to.'

The indestructible hedonist. When he does get back he'll be itching to get me to Geneva so that we can sign papers and he can replenish the old kitty as he likes to put it. The cool nerve of the man swanning around the Riviera like a moulting peacock. He feeds on illusions and will go on doing it to the very end. Is that the sum total of the human condition?

'Bye the bye,' my father says as he checks on his ridiculous crimson cravat in the mirror before leaving on his latest adventure. 'There's a phone bill to pay. Would you settle it, dear boy, before those creepy phone chaps cut us off. And you can tell them that beastly answerphone isn't working properly. These gadgets can be a damn nuisance can't they? For all I know your pretty little sphinx may have left a message on it.'

And he was gone. An exit carefully calculated to leave me on an empty stage in a state of quiet panic. He would never lose the ability to undermine my confidence. Had she left a message? Had she turned against the idea of being holed up here with me, and was she rummaging around for excuses? No need to think of obligations and duties when a relationship is on an open voluntary basis. Am I being selfish in my pursuit of greater certainty? A message. I need a message. Without it my world is wrapped in ominous silence. The phone was out of order. I charged down to pay off the bill. Service would not be restored for forty-eight hours. All I could do was march the streets within close range of the Résidence des Oranges, in case she turned up, and keep my mobile in my pocket. Why should my life hang on such flimsy arrangements? I sat in a small public garden between a wall of bougainvillea and a hedge of blue plumbago and wondered about creation and my own part in it. At Evora I conducted a smart exchange with Father Afonso who had taken me to task for making fun of the pepper-pot turrets on the cathedral. He accused me of being a visionless humanist as I remember. I had a smart reply ready, rather like a worn visiting card printed during my undergraduate days. 'If you say God is the Creator, he must be a captive of his Creation just as much as we are.' He had an even smarter answer too. If only I could remember it. Something about all captives needed rescuing. Certainly true in my case, trapped in this climate of flowers with a view between the palm trees of the sunlight glittering on the sea; or more correctly, trapped in my own neurosis. The flower garden and the view would get along even better if I wasn't here.

The ring of the mobile sets my heart racing.

'Eddie! Listen. Change of plan. Would you mind terribly coming here, instead of me coming there?'

Would I mind…Where's 'here?' The apartment lies in wait for her. Here is here, not there. And this damned little instrument next to my ear has too much control over my life. I must find somewhere to sit down. I am a seething mass of perturbation and disappointment.

'Eddie! Can you hear me? I need you. I'm in trouble basically. Nothing all that serious you could say but trouble all the same. Family trouble. I don't expect you to come running every time I whistle, but if you could manage it dear Eddie I need you to hold my hand.'

The dust settles with amazing speed. The way ahead becomes clear. I am needed, therefore I am. That is all one needs to know really. All the rest is the operation. Having gained my breathy assent she goes on in a more cheerful mode calculated to cheer me on and lift my heart. I feel as committed as a well trained sheepdog.

'Eddie, I've worked it out. We can kill at least two birds with one stone. Your bird of ancestry and my beastly burden. Could you make it to Shrewsbury by next Friday? Could you? Do you know where it is you cosmopolitan gadfly? I'll be waiting for you at the Lion, with my trusty rusty Land Rover.' I said, 'The Lion… No problem'. 'Eddie you are a marvel! I love you. Can't wait to kiss you. Must fly now. A bit of editing to finish. Clear the decks and so on.'

No problem is quite a problem. All the way. And quite a bit of expense. But as chaff in the wind at the prospect of our passionate reunion. Only in Bethan's embrace it seems my unstable universe settles into place, sustained by the smell of her skin. This is a pattern in our life-style, mine at least, that resembles the random peaks on the monitor of a life-support machine. With her I am where I should be, even though I don't really know where I am. Border country is never marked on the map. Her trusty Land Rover comes to an abrupt stop. She is lost in admiration when I manage to restore the ancient model to life. It is all part of a great adventure. Off we go, Bethan says, in search of castles in Wales instead of castles in Spain or Languedoc.

She has vital appointments and mysterious crises looming, but my presence she assures me has already diminished their threatening proportions. Meanwhile the weekend is ours to devote to the search for my ancestral Cynddylan. I am at a loss as to how precisely to distinguish between her seriousness and her amusement. Is it all funny or is it important? She says her game plan is to chase up or turn up Castell Cynddylan and see whether Eddie C and his onomastic origins match up to each other. We go up hill and down dale through sunshine and showers. Bethan says I am a rootless wanderer being presented with an ancestral home and there should be a distinct musical tone poem to go with it. When the sun comes out there's plenty of birdsong. When you stop to listen warbles and musical signals break out all over the place. This is a country birds certainly like, overwhelmingly green and wet and wonderful. A far cry from the dusty palm trees of Juan-les-Pins.

A new spring has to be a new beginning. I need to linger to familiarise myself with the unfamiliar. This is a country which may be mine, but of which I have no recollection. Once as an undergraduate I went on a walking tour on the coast of Pembrokeshire, but that was in my life before Bethan, a period that has reversed at speed into the mists of unrecorded time. At every turn we take, there seem to be sheep with lambs, and as we climb higher up, mountain ponies with foals that Bethan stops to photograph. She is ready to photograph anything: in close up, primroses nestling around the base of a blackthorn or the protracted glitter of the sunlight on a winding stream. We have our luggage and her equipment piled up in fine disorder at the back of the Land Rover. The sun strikes on a great patch of gorse and sends its heavy scent exploding towards our nostrils. I have this intense desire to be one with nature and with Bethan. We should be part of all this verdant renewal and growth, but even as she lies under me I sense Bethan is restless to press on and make some fresh discovery. It is as though the green world and the given moment are not enough for her. The idea of me and my forebears takes precedence over my physical self. It undermines my confidence as a lover to suppose I have dwindled to a plaything, an object of amusement. She strokes my cheeks and kisses me to restore my spirits.

Bethan has an old chum at the Centre for Advanced Celtic Studies, and she has made notes of the stuff he has ferreted out about my funny family. It amuses her as we bowl and bump along the twisted country roads to dole out bits of information mostly calculated to astonish and disturb me and allow her to laugh at the bewildered expression on the face of the person she has taken to calling 'dear Eddie C'. The Cynddylan bit, she says flows directly from cattle thieves and raiders passing themselves off as princes with pedigrees going back to the Romans and the Fall of Troy. They play fast and loose with royal authority and hook themselves up to the Marcher Lords to give themselves tenure and respectability. My particular branch have turned out to be the weaker brethren who have clung ever more fervently to the Cynddylan mark as they slid down the social scale to get submerged in a genealogical swamp of small-town lawyers and impecunious parsons, stiffened with pretensions like my great grandfather who was an archdeacon in the West of England.

I have joined in this enterprise with evident gusto although I suspect it all interests her more than it does me. She delights in a heady mixture of maps and theories while I try to look happy instead of dazed. She says genealogy is a Welsh weakness that she tries to take lightly. Yet she cannot resist the fascinations of digging around our origins. 'You never know what dark and dreadful secrets we might uncover! Mind you,' she says, 'it can all descend very quickly into a meaningless mythological morass. An absolute mess in fact. It's what we are in ourselves surely that really matters, otherwise we might be forever taking the word as a substitute for doing something'... I make a light-hearted plea for my ancestral birthright.

'What about my link with Wales?' I say. 'I was counting on it.'

She shakes my arm.

'I'm your link with Wales,' she says.

That makes me feel authentically cheerful. She is the real reason why I am here.

'A peasant girl with a camera. Instead of a basket on her head.'

After much climbing and clambering we reach a summit mound with ruined walls which she declares is 'either Carreg Wen or Castell Cynddylan, or quite possibly both.' To the east at the far end of a wide valley there is a glimpse of what I take to be the Shropshire plain. Bethan sits me down on the highest point of the ruined wall to photograph me. The sun plays hide and seek with the high cloud and the light fluctuates in a way that makes her quite impatient. She is cross with herself for leaving her tripod behind in the Land Rover and I am obliged to sit still in the chilly breeze while she reads her light meter and makes adjustments.

When she is satisfied with her shooting she launches herself into comments that are too excited to be taken all that lightly even though she is laughing and I am so delighted to be looking at her, so vital and poised and relaxed on this draughty hillside.

'That's it then! Cynddylan in his original 'Ystafell'. No ceiling of course. No roof even. Only the cloudy sky. Let me take one more long shot to be sure. You can move if you're getting cold. Jump around. But stay in shot!'

Ever since she extracted the Cynddylan business out of my father she likes to quote the famous lines. As far as I can follow she sees something of what she calls 'The Welsh Condition' in the lines of that celebrated ninth century poem: 'Ystafell Cynddylan ys tywyll heno... Cynddylan's hall is so dark tonight, no warmth, no bed, I shall weep a while and then be silent'… His sister mourns his killing, the destruction of his court, the devastation of his land. 'Ystafell' can mean a room or a building. Anything with walls and a roof. A habitation where a human can feel at least as safe as an animal in his lair. As far as I am concerned, it's Cynddylan's room in my gloomy flat in Rome. There's nothing worse than the silence in that room after she has left it. Up here in the draughty acres I am admitted to Cynddylan's Hall like a visitor to an airy tomb. My father's palace littered with sheep droppings and fallen stones. I am the liege lord of regiments of clouds on the run.

Bethan, my beloved poet of the camera, develops her theories from day to day and I listen with rapt if not desperate attention in my effort to understand her. The gathering darkness in Cynddylan's Hall is symptomatic she says of a crisis in the Western World, the clash between the local and the global. I have to admit that I have never seen things quite in that way before. But then I had never met Bethan in the days when I saw myself as a burgeoning international bureaucrat. There is something about her touch, in the spirit as well as in the flesh that makes me tingle with a new awareness. You can't define yourself it seems until you discover for what purpose you occupy your allotted space.

The mission had been completed to her satisfaction if not entirely to mine. It seems as though we had been chasing ghosts or at least trying to lay them to rest, and that all we had was the photographic print of a solitary figure sitting on a hilltop ruin. All halls and rooms are empty in the end. It could be anyone anywhere and I was displeased with my inability to attach any symbolic significance to the event or the record of it. All I could do was attach myself even more closely to Bethan's cheerful vitality. Her intimate knowledge of all this undulating topography is at least substantial, unlike those vast mythological Marcher estates that exist only in my father's melodramatic mind.

Below the hill at the farm where we had left the Land

Rover we sat down in a conservatory extension to enjoy what they called an old fashioned Welsh farmhouse tea: freshly made scones, barabrith, homemade jam and cake. I showed a professional interest in the process of diversification. At F.A.O. we have an entire section codifying this global problem, from the poppy growers of the golden triangle to the coffee growers of Columbia and Kenya. Quite a key word. Diversification. Brynbach claims to be a sixteenth century farmhouse at the heart of two hundred acres; a working mixed farm that derives a substantial part of its income from tourism and the holiday trade. Its claim to fame: being two miles away from Offa's Dyke. So much for Cynddylan and a thousand years of progress, from cattle raiding and border battles to parlourised tea in a surprisingly clean working farm. In the orchard among the primroses and the bluebells there were little children playing and in the kitchen in the depths of the old house there was a woman singing. The idea of rural domestic felicity moved me far more than the ruin on the top of the hill. It seemed so much more like what I was looking for.

There must be a melancholy expression on my face. Bethan touches my arm to comfort me.

'Dear Eddie, you are really so sweet and patient. If I am pushing you too much, you must really tell me.'

I cannot decide whether it can be me or herself that Bethan is putting to the test. She does seem to be in a state of alert of a higher awareness than when we are together in the warm south. Could this just be the difference in climate? We have never been together in Wales before. All these hills and rivers and woods speak a green language that seems much more alarming and various and volatile than when studied in black print on a pale neutral page. I feel obliged to demonstrate a visitor's politeness and say something complimentary about the old farmhouse and the successful diversification and the excellence of the tea and the charm of the children's voices in the orchard.

'A little bit more sun,' I say. 'And it all becomes a relaxed version of the Garden of Eden.'

Her response is enigmatic.

'After the Fall,' she says.

I fail to understand.

'If you listen you'll hear the children are playing in English. The parents have failed in their duty. That's the way I was brought up to look at it. The Welsh manifestation of original sin. I am sitting here feeling guilty on behalf of Mister and Missus Farmhouse Teas. I can't shake it off. It's been drummed into me and of course I believe it just like a little Catholic brought up by Jesuits. It's my mother-stroke-stepmother Lowri, really. Unbending is our Lowri. She believes the language is the fountain of youth for a given people. Like that Cranach picture of ancient bodies entering the pool and coming out all bright and youthful on the other side. The language does this because of the elixir of poetry preserved in it. If the language dies the fountain dries up. So there you have it. The gospel according to Lowri.

I follow the argument as sympathetically as I can.

'She sounds a very interesting person!' I say. 'I would like to meet her.'

'Well you are not going to,' Bethan says. 'Not this time anyway. I have two families, Eddie Cynddylan. And I don't really like either of them. They both make me feel guilty. We've dealt with your family. Now we'll set off further north to deal with one of mine. I want to photograph the memorial stone to Griffith Ezra Bowen in the churchyard of Llanfair–iscoed.'

'Who?'

Since it seems her intention to persist in surprising me, I respond in kind.

'My great-great-grandfather. I think I've got that right. There may be another great to put in. In any case nothing as far back as Cynddylan. Peasants don't bother to go far back. A century or two and they're back at the wooden plough breaking their backs. So off we go, dear Eddie. To the north.'

Five

I AM AWARE of the unwisdom of becoming too absorbed in the give and take in a relationship. In an ideal world it should move with the effortless and invisible collaboration between practised eye and hand. I tend to dwell on it in spite of myself and the excuse I make is that Bethan and I spend too much time apart. Every reunion may provide a fresh injection of ecstasy, but it also involves processes of invisible mending, and the shoring up of bulwarks that have in some way been unaccountably weakened. After all, in our separate ways, we are travelling a world that only too easily can become hostile and the element of trust, of faith, of confidence is an essential component that we need to share with equal dedication. Bethan has gone to such trouble to winkle out rumours of my remote ancestry the least I can do is take an active interest in her search for her more recent and more substantial progenitors.

I am anxious to be helpful. I don't know quite where we have arrived. It seems a hollow in the hills over-whelmed by its own green strength. It certainly overwhelms me. I look around as though I was wondering for the first time where the myriad towering assemblies of leaves have come from: there must be a giant green strength of renewal far below in secret caves and caverns. I am ready for some amusing mythological speculations: however Bethan is already seriously engaged. She has her tripod out and is concentrating on a photographic record of this village which she tells me is called Pentregwyn.

I am dispatched to seek out grave-stones with specific names carved on them. To aid my memory I have scribbled them down on the back of an envelope.

The churchyard is large and circular and the parish church squats in the middle with the weight of its rough hewn slate roof appearing to push it down into the soft earth. It's a 'Llan' of course and I have learnt enough to understand the importance of the prefix in the Cymric celtic context. But who exactly the saint in the dedication may be I have no idea. Neither does Bethan even though her mother's people are buried here. In fact she knows very little about them either. All she says is that what she knows does not make her jump for joy. There was an estrangement when her father re-married. I found that intriguing and long to know more. Bethan finds it all irritating and a bit of a nuisance. No part of our exciting life together: no more than ghosts glowing beyond the margin like the lights of a town one has no desire to visit. We have more than once agreed in a light-hearted holiday sort of spirit that families are institutions to escape from. And yet here we are crawling around a sleepy settlement in mid-Wales in search of people, mostly dead, that she might claim to be related to.

Somewhere behind the church there is the sturdy rhythmic sound of a scythe being sharpened. An attack on the long grass between the graves has already begun. The shorn section made all the rest look even more overgrown and overcrowded. In the west corner the wall was crumbling and the graveyard invaded by sycamore saplings and brambles. I am tempted to go around and seek help from the man with a scythe. Would he direct me to the whereabouts of any deceased Bowens. So far I had not seen one. Only endless Joneses or Williamses or Davieses or Hugheses. I hesitate to approach a stranger because Bethan attaches great importance to discretion.

We have moved into strange territory that could easily turn hostile. What is called for is reconnaissance on tiptoe. I move as unobtrusively as I can, which is somewhat absurd since I am the only upright figure in sight capable of moving, and more often than not I have to kneel to examine faint inscriptions.

'Looking for relatives, are you?'

The stocky man in heavy duty working clothes is standing above me, the long scythe over his shoulder. He is holding up his ancient whetstone as if it were some kind of torch. He is there to help me and I understood his Welsh.

'Yes and no,' I say.

His smile grows broader and even more benevolent.

'You are a learner,' he says. 'That is very good. My brother Ifan will be very pleased.'

He shifted his stance enough for me to discern a man engaged intently in restoring a collapsed section of the churchyard wall. He is weighing a stone in his hand and looking up at the great beech tree whose thrusting roots had been responsible for the damage. Preoccupied as I am with my search for the name Bowen, what I see registers as a quiet symbol of the ancient struggle between man and the force of nature. The brothers seem decided to appear ancient themselves. They move slowly to make themselves more acceptable to the forces around them, inventing their sarabande as they go along.

'Ifan is a poet. A hedge poet I call him. He doesn't mind. We are twins you see. Simon Davies and Ifan Davies. Although I'm taller than he is. I don't know why either.'

He smiles quite charmingly. His teeth are in excellent condition and his pink and white cheeks are surprisingly smooth and feminine.

'The name Bowen,' I say. 'That's what I'm looking for.'

He nods understandingly. Life is the better for its little mysteries and finding that name in this churchyard should not be difficult. We should speak to his brother. He has deep knowledge in these matters. Their mother used to say that Simon had the inches and Ifan had the brains. Ifan must have been aware of our approach but as we get nearer he seems to concentrate more deeply on the choice of stones around his feet. He strokes his chin as if there were much to wonder about. He seems less open than his brother, more rigorous, more demanding of reasons.

'Belonging I suppose?'

He stares at me through narrowed eyes wondering still what a stranger wanted and to whom or to what he could possibly be related in an acceptable pattern.

'No,' I say. 'Not really.'

'Research?'

Our conversation is balanced on single significant epithets and Simon's unstinting goodwill. When I show agreement Ifan's face lights up with interest.

'A scholar,' he says. 'Which college shall I say?'

His mouth is still open like a hungry chicken and it would be churlish not to feed him a morsel.

'Cambridge,' I say. 'A long time ago.'

This gives him some cud to chew on. His lips move as he ponders the name Bowen and extracts all the nourishment to be gained from it. He lifts an arm and points at a monument half hidden by branches. It is also tilted by the force of tree roots.

'Griffith Ezra Bowen,' he says. 'Something should be done about it before it falls over. Important man, he was, in his time. But there you have it. Time stays. It is men that pass.'

I consult my scrap of envelope. The monument is to Bethan's great-great-great-grandfather. I enjoy an absurdly warm flush of triumph. The inscription is hard to read but there is 'J.P.' after his name. He was born in 1820 and died in 1895. A man of great solid Victorian muscle. I clutch the information like treasure trove.

'This is a big Bowen for you,' Ifan says.

The brothers are happy to share the great discovery.

'A friend of Mr Gee,' Ifan says. 'They used to travel the country to meetings. Big speakers. I remember my grandfather saying this Bowen had been to London to meet Mr Gladstone.'

Simon's head was nodding with admiration at the depth and width of his brother's knowledge. There is more to come but the words are frozen in his tobacco stained lips as out of the clouds a pair of fighter bombers take a practice run at their target, which has to be this undistinguished village hidden between the green hills. I don't know how much they can see as they scream through: the river perhaps, the churchyard, the war memorial, the village hall, the chapel and the general stores. A stick of bombs from that sleek monster and Pentregwyn would be obliterated. The noise is overwhelming. The earth shakes. Simon clutches his ears and Ifan shakes his fist at the sky. And then the nightmare is over as swiftly as it started. In the quivering quiet both their heads are trembling with protest.

'Devils from Hell,' says Simon. He nods towards the high clouds as though he knew the exact location. He smiles as he repeats the phrase. It must be one of his favourites. His brother spits tobacco juice into the long grass and makes a pronouncement.

'I wrote a piece about it,' he says. 'In free verse if you please. For the Barri Eisteddfod. 'Ban any Bomb' I called it. I was right too. It didn't win though.'

'It got a mention.'

His brother records the fact as a spring board for a bit of teasing.

'Not bad for a hedge poet,' he says.

The brothers look contented. They get on well. It mitigates the impression of a subdued aboriginal species allowed to survive in a lowly habitat thinly protected by an undergrowth of language. It's likely the green leaves offer them food as well as protection. It's not as if anything they say could ever count for anything, any more than birdsong. Especially against fighter bombers. But you can attach excitement to their discovery like a botanist locating a rare plant. Not to mention this leaning memorial where the black marble urn on top of the polished plinth has only to tilt a degree or so more to empty its imagined contents. As if to oblige me before I ask, Simon has brought out a sickle and is clearing away the brambles to afford me a better view. Perhaps when Bethan photographs the monument she might find room for the ancient twins in the shot? Perhaps not. At this juncture nothing is for me to decide. She leads, tense with her own mystery. I follow, proffering obedience.

The presence of a female film maker and her companion seems to have driven indoors such population as exists in this quiescent village. Do I detect the twitch of a lace curtain as Bethan marches boldly about the place wearing her black oilcloth cap and coat and carrying her aluminium tripod on her shoulder. She looks so business-like and in such a hurry, engaged in perpetual combat with the capricious Welsh light. It is true it may rain any minute but I am at a loss to understand quite why there is no time to lose. I marvel at how so small a figure exerts so much authority over this place where nothing seems to happen. There is more going on in the churchyard than in the mean square in front of the village shop. Pentregwyn seems unevenly divided between old people's homes and holiday homes. It does nothing to live up to the beauty of its surroundings.

'Eddie…'

Bethan whispers my name without taking her eye off her view finder. My shadow is falling across her shot. I am of course her shadow because I have elected to be. I reject my self-accusation of being a born parasite. Bethan's concentration on her work is a demonstration of enviable strength. She has a capacity for sustaining silence and very little patience with small-talk. She could have received my discovery of the Griffith Ezra Bowen monument with more approval and even enthusiasm, but I need to bear in mind how little I really know of the depth of emotional or even cultural baggage she brings with her to construct a pictorial record of this apathetic place in such a hurry.

'Could you shift the Land Rover out of my shot?'

I don't understand the need to whisper but I hurry to obey. I even skip in an attempt to make her smile. It's not that she lacks a sense of humour. This even more than usual seems to be a mission. I move the vehicle and crouch behind the wheel so that I can study the girl through the clean arc of a dirty windscreen. Could it be a love-hate relationship for our origins that we had in common? I don't know enough about psychiatry to know whether neuroses are transferable or infectious. I realise I have to rein in my appetite for reassurances or renewed terms of endearment. We are too well disposed towards each other, too well balanced, to engage in those emotional power struggles that can so easily wreck relationships. I'm not sure whether it's the tradition of *amour courtois* or my inferiority complex, but I must take for granted that I need her far more than she needs me. It seems to fit in best with the steps of the courtship dance. It may be that we sleep together. My goal however distant, remains marriage. I comfort myself that she called for me urgently and I came at once. There is no one in the world she trusts more, she says, and that is a very high priority. It has to warm me as much as any fervid declaration of love. About the precise quantity of love secreted in the other, there is no mode of measuring. That's why love is linked so closely to faith and hope. The last spontaneous gesture of unrestrained love and affection that sticks in my mind was when I restored the recalcitrant Land Rover to rumbling life. She jumped for joy and threw her arms about my neck. She hugged me and kissed me.

She is waving. She needs me.

In that moment the whole place seems to cringe as some fresh faced trainee pilot brings his howling machine down so close that I imagine I can see his cheeks twitching as he threatens to tip Pentregwyn over the edge into annihilation. Bethan claps her hands over her ears. I howl out loud knowing that no one hears me. What are these machines intended for except to batter natives into submission and flatten their dwelling places. I have a Jeremiad to get off my chest. The power of silence and stillness returns. If I spoke there would be no one to hear me. Bethan is waving again. She needs me. Her mind is back on the work in hand. Not a time to air my fruitless speculations.

'Eddie. Stand in front of the shop, won't you?'

I am promoted to foreground object. There are witty remarks I could make but Bethan wants to get on with it. She looks as determined as a clenched fist.

'Turn your back to the camera. Put your right hand on the latch as if you are about to open the door.'

A portrait of Pentregwyn General Stores. Not exactly the Taj Mahal. I am the ghost of a customer. Over to my right there is a raven perched on the top of a dead tree. All is silence and the purple blinds of the shop are lowered in mourning. I feel a quotation coming on.

'Bethan! What were those lines about shame on my beard if I don't open this door to see if what they said about it is true…?'

'Shush. Face the door and keep still.'

What for heaven's sake is so significant about this depressing building? I have to put the blunt question.

'Well, among other things, it's mine. And I still don't know what to do with it.'

Six

'BEHOLD, a monarch am I... Lord of all I survey...'

Bethan peers through the grimy plate-glass where the mournful blinds have failed to meet. I consider putting a protective hand on her shoulder but decide against it. She is cheerful and resolved and in command of the situation: encouraged if anything by my puzzlement and confusion.

'Of this place anyway and all that goes with it. And a handful of cottages and maybe a couple of smallholdings. Well now then Socrates-Cynddylan. What should I do with it all?'

She asks the question and it vexes me a little that it can't matter all that much to her what I think. If she really wanted to know she would have put me in the picture at the very start of our journey. Plainly she was more intent on astonishing me. So where does that leave me? Where I began. Her devoted admirer feeding off his devotion like a pelican off its own blood.

'You're not vexed that I've sprung all this on you?'

'No, of course not.'

I smile and tap the window with my finger. In this involvement I am partially sighted and the only guide stick I hold on to is whether it will bring me closer to my very own cherished goal of marriage. I could say she is a frustrated film director doing all she can to dramatise her situation, but I won't. For the moment I have the debilitating sensations of being marooned in a forgotten world that is shaping up to make demands on me that I would prefer to avoid. Bethan draws me closer and our heads are touching as we peer again into the crepuscular interior.

'Isn't that just something?'

I am prepared to be surprised. Gathering clouds part, and a convenient shaft of sunlight pierces the gloom of the interior. I find it distasteful, a place of dispiriting shapes and shadows. I make an effort to accept it as now part of her world. The shaft of light picks out a galvanized zinc bucket dangling forlornly from the dim ceiling.

'Just look at that.'

Bethan smiles as she points at the bucket. At the same time I feel her shiver.

'That could be an awful warning, Eddie C. My great-grandfather hanged himself somewhere in there.'

I want to sympathise but she doesn't sound in need of sympathy. The idea of suicide alarms me more than it does her. It seems a design flaw in the human condition hostile to my cherished expectations of marriage and progeny. Life is not a gift to be so brutally rejected. Her objective attitude adds to my confusion. Is it that a professional photographer looks on the distortions of living always happening to someone else? To suppress disloyal thoughts about a streak of coldness and even calculation in her character I enlarge on my discovery of Griffith Ezra's monument.

'So the one I found in the churchyard must be your great-great-grandfather. Or even great-great-great! Think of that, Hedda!'

At least she smiles at my Ibsenish joke.

'There you are you see. My mother warned me of this place. Forbidden fruit. Poisoned Chalice. All that sort of thing. It doesn't look so bad though. My unexpected inheritance.'

With arms outstretched she twirls around on the pavement outside the shop. She stands still to take in the surrounding scene without being confined by the viewfinder of her camera.

'My mother brought me here when I was less than four years old. All I can remember is a brown hen with yellow chickens crossing the road. That's all. It's all just as new to me as it is to you, Eddie Cynddylan. If new is the right word. More substantial than the lost acres of the Cynddylan Vaughan-Lloyd's though?'

She was pleased and excited and yet apprehensive.

'We happened to be passing, is the story. From some eisteddfod or other. But then you have to remember my mother hardly ever just happens to do anything. She is governed by her purposes. Purpose-driven. My goodness there's a thought! Could it be possible I'm rather like her? Oh my god...'

Comic despair and laughter. I restrain myself from saying how important it is for me to meet this central force in her upbringing: or from complaining that she has taken my father in her stride while it doesn't seem I'm ever going to meet hers.

'The one and only Lowri. My father's devoted second wife. She happened to be passing. Right here. With my father's little daughter in her hand. And that Sulwen Bowen creature did not even ask her to sit down or offer her a cup of tea or both. There you are Eddie my love. On such pivotal events whole buckets full of family lore and legend hang.'

It is more becoming to treat the whole business light-heartedly. Our relationship is always at its best when we are laughing together. We pride ourselves on having the ability of not taking ourselves too seriously. Even when film enterprises or projects go wrong, we reserve the right to take it lightly in the end. Bethan is shaking the handle of the locked door.

'It's ridiculous,' she says. 'This place is mine and I can't get in.'

She presses her nose against the glass of the shop window.

'He went bankrupt when rationing came to an end. That took some doing surely. Some women burnt their ration books in front of his eyes. And he had lost his only son in the war. People turned away because he was a pacifist. What a tale of woe. I don't have to inherit all that as well, do I? Ancient history. Nothing to do with me, is it?'

'Of course not,' I say.

And yet her visible attachment to this dismal complex of granite buildings suggests that it might. The one-time heart and soul of the village, Pentregwyn General Stores served the living, just as the churchyard down the road serves the dead. Bethan takes me by the hand and we move to the rear of the outbuildings. It occurs to me that in this romantic encounter it is the man who is being swept off his feet. She confronts the blistered green paint on a massive wooden double door. We push at one half until it creaks open, and Bethan marches in determined to exercise her proprietorial rights. She stands at the centre of the paved yard surrounded by gloomy two and three storey buildings, rubbing her hands with the pleasure of contemplating the potential of the premises.

'Illuminations and Revelations! What do you think?'

I don't know what to think until she tells me. All I can manage is a complaisant smile.

'Transformation. What else. Jens has the right idea. Good old Jens.'

Jens Stangerup. I don't know what it is about that name. The way she uses it gives me an instant jab of jealousy. She seems to admire him and all his works and counts it a privilege to know him let alone work with him. So what exactly is my size and value in her eyes? My languages? My international relief work? Even my minor expertises including playing the piano and the internal combustion engine? What am I worth to her apart from my devotion? A painful condition this devotion. When she chooses to be glamorous, in so many variations, such as in film star mode stepping down a stage lit staircase, I shrink among the line of suitors at her feet. At least here, in her outsize working clothes, I have her to myself.

'He's transformed this deserted school in the middle of Jutland into what amounts to a studio complex: cutting rooms, rehearsal rooms, green rooms and so on. Really impressive. The question is, Eddie Cynddylan, could it be done here? Of course it could. Why not for heaven's sake?'

I am nodding because on the whole I have higher hopes of this desirable creature in her native habitat than when she wanders abroad on exotic schemes and dubious ventures. Easier to set traps, poachers say, in territory where you can find your way at night. Of course this isn't my territory, but at least it's hers and as my aged friend in the churchyard said, I am an approved learning *Dysgwr*.

'Hang on a minute…What's going on down here?'

Bethan stands in front of another locked door. It looks like an outside kitchen opposite a back door of the shop. There is a window to peep through, cleaner than the rest. Inside are signs of untidy habitation: dirty cup and plate on the bare table, the fireplace of the old fashioned kitchen range choked and overflowing with ash and cinders, a yellow jersey flung over the back of a battered armchair.

'Lowri did warn me. In this place there is always more than meets the eye. There's somebody living here. Not a tramp we assume. He has the key to the door. It must be a man. Look how untidy it is.'

I wonder whether we should make enquiries. Outside the forces of curiosity are gathering. Down at the lychgate Simon has appeared nursing his sickle. From the terraced cottages two plump women have joined to give each other support before advancing. There are faces in the windows of the Victorian hotel that has been converted into a Residential Home. In the school yard a yellow minibus with 'Nottingham Schools Outdoor Centre' blazoned in large letters on its side was filling up with children. Pentregwyn, which had lain so dormant and undemanding to be photographed, was now threatening to buzz with life.

'Let's get out of here! I don't want to start answering questions about who I am and what are my intentions. Especially when I don't know myself.'

We roar off in some confusion, Bethan at the wheel. She thinks we might be late for the all important appointment with the lawyer where she has to sign papers, collect keys and, I assume, come to some conclusion, even if it is only temporary. She assures me everything is under control. She will take short cuts and minor roads and with any luck we shall arrive in time or at least not unforgivably late. It seems that photographing the place before taking possession was a necessary process of evaluation. It was the best way to get the feel of the location: a photographic reccy. Always sniff around first. And how else would we have discovered that clandestine occupation of the outside kitchen?

'Lowri did say they were a shifty lot, my birth mother's family. They make all the right righteous noises, she says, and they are as twisted as a pig's tail. That's Lowri for you. Ever forthright, ever blunt. How she can judge, when she has had so little to do with them… I suspect a catalogue of slights and imagined wrongs. Was there a battle for possession of little me? I think there must have been. What do you think?'

What can I think when I've never set eyes on the woman? I imagine some stiff, determined, muscular, middle-aged, childless woman overprotective of the winsome child she has, so to speak, inherited. Probably still baffled by the transformation of a docile picture book little girl into a turbulent, headstrong young woman who at this moment is driving me to distraction by driving at a reckless speed without being at all sure of the way. We find ourselves in a road that is nothing more than a lane with flowering cow-parsley growing out of the hedge banks so high that they form a white wedding arch. Above them the white flowers of the blackthorn lie like snow drifts or confetti waiting to be thrown. How much more worthwhile this journey would be if it led to an altar instead of, as I fear, leading us ever further from it.

We arrive at a junction where the road signs are hidden by overgrown hedges. Bethan leans on the wheel uncertain whether to turn left or right. She is cross with herself and unexpectedly vulnerable.

'I don't care any more,' she says. 'I'm exhausted.'

I know it's the moment to clasp her in a warm embrace. I am rewarded.

'You are with me anyway. You are a patient darling. My

best friend in all the world.'

She detaches herself from my fond stroking and loving kisses. My attentions have given her fresh strength.

'You drive,' she says. 'We'll just have to say we got lost. Pilgrims in a foreign land.'

I enjoy the transitory sensation of being in charge. Once we are back on the proper route the air of magic is restored to the countryside in early May. A remnant of mist lingers around the broken tower of the castle that overlooks the market town. We find the solicitor's office next to a dentist's in a side street; Davies Hughes and Caradog-Jones, what else? Clearly related to those names on the gravestones I studied in the churchyard. I find this interesting to ponder on; like the fact that both dentists and solicitors use clinically polished reception areas to keep anxious patients waiting. We have missed our appointment. We are appallingly late. We are in a chilly sin bin looking at an anaemic panoramic view of Barmouth.

Bethan does not believe in being contrite. Not for any length of time. And any meaningful private exchanges become impossible when an assiduous solicitor's clerk flits in and out. Bethan quietly fumes and studies her watch at regular intervals. I comfort myself with the knowledge that at least I am sitting at her side and not suffering one or other variety of isolation and solitude several hundred miles away from her. I even take time to congratulate myself on my chivalrous response to her appeal for support. I am resolved that my attitude will be to accept whatever happens as a challenge.

When, at last, the solicitor, the regal Mrs Olwen Caradog-Jones rises from behind her expanse of mahogany to greet us, Bethan makes little effort to respond to the warmth of the welcome. From such a large majestic figure the voice that emerges barely rises above a whisper but it is vibrant with sincerity.

'My dear, I have so looked forward to meeting you. And I am not disappointed. You are the very image of your dear mother. I can't tell you how I feel. In our youth, in our childhood, we were so close Ffion and I. We were best friends you see. And to see you in the flesh, you see, so like her, it's like a dream come true.'

Bethan looks embarrassed. So fulsome a greeting smothers her impatience and any residue of indignation. Olwen Caradog-Jones' smile remains fixed. To relieve any tension she is looking at me. It becomes obvious she is waiting to be introduced.

'This is my best friend, Edward Lloyd,' Bethan says. 'He is learning Cymraeg.'

Mrs Caradog-Jones' smile renews itself. Her sculptured hand is extended in my direction. I am welcomed. She would like to learn more about me, but Bethan is bent on being brisk and businesslike.

'He drove me here in the Land Rover. Very sorry we're late. We had a bit of a job finding the place. They said next to the dentist's.'

'Ah yes. The old streets. One way and so on.'

She settles behind her desk still studying us both as though we offer the promise of a romantic picture. She even sighs and raises both hands in what could have been a gesture of muted benediction.

'Forgive me for saying so,' she says. 'You both look so delightfully young. A breath of fresh air in this dowdy old office. All your life before you. How wonderful.'

Myself I am inclined to feel grateful for her unstinted admiration. As to the room I would call it austere rather than dowdy. It is lined with solemn looking tomes that serve to reinforce her air of benign authority. There is a single oil painting of a bearded man who most likely represents the founder of the firm and possibly this well preserved and well-dressed lady solicitor's grandfather? On a mantle-shelf there is a bust of Beethoven to suggest that music provides her with relief from conveyancing, contested wills and protracted legislation. The surface of her desk is clear and the way her hands rest on it suggest calmness and control. I am further flattered by the fact that she considers me youthful. Does a readiness to please reduce the weight of years? Can there be some pleasant equation whereby the lover and the loved one appear to be the same age? I sit there smiling.

Bethan however can't wait to set pleasantries aside. She wants to get down to business and in the first place she wants to know who exactly is squatting in the outside kitchen of Pentregwyn Stores. A sobering cloud descends and Mrs Olwen Caradog-Jones' smile dissolves.

'So you have already been there,' she said. 'What a pity.'

'Why a pity?'

My heart sinks. Bethan is ready for combat. Just as I go through life being diplomatic to the point of being evasive, she voyages forth resolved never to be put upon.

'My co-executor, dear old Doctor Seth, was so looking forward to showing you around.'

'Who is it then? In there?'

The more impetuous Bethan sounds the more measured the Caradog-Jones response. Her pale hands remain at rest on the desk, clasped in unruffled calm.

'Your tenant, shall we call him?'

Bethan's mouth turns down in instant distaste. A tenant is the last thing she would want.

'A strange, sad, yet quite touching story. It's Curig Puw poor lamb. Curig Llwyd as I call him. Because he's so pale. He had a little yellow beard. Children used to call 'Iesu Grist bach' after him. He had no idea how to keep order. That's where he makes what little home he's got. He was a theological student you see. A young man of enormous promise. First class honours and so on. Offered a pastorate of six churches. It was too much for him. Then he rushed into marriage hoping to share the load I suspect. It didn't help. Then he began to harbour doubts about his calling. About his sexuality. About everything. In any case he suffered a breakdown. Not so much an outcast. These days our Welsh society has become indifferent rather than censorious. You could say he cast himself out. Sulwen discovered him in a coma or whatever on the back seat of his old car, which had broken down outside the shop. Five o'clock in the morning. What did she do? Your dear old aunt, or great-aunt I should say, took him in. At least allowed him shelter in those two rooms in the outside kitchen, and there he stayed. To save his pride he paid her a pound a week rent although she said she didn't need it. He still lives there and works on neighbouring farms. Even more of a hermit now that dear old Sulwen has passed away. We decided it was as well to leave things as they stood.'

There is a silence that I at least find uncomfortable. Mrs Caradog-Jones seems quite used to it: an occupational hazard maybe, uncomfortable silences. She is looking at me, a third party at hand to ease the awkward moment.

'And what did you think of our little Pentregwyn, Mr Lloyd? It seems to have been old-fashioned since the world began. Whenever I go there I feel as if the past were lurking around every corner. Waiting to be rediscovered perhaps. Brought back to life. Such a delightful village in the old days. I was sent away to school you see, like my mother before me. Not so much a question of education. To improve my English and acquire a better accent. Those petty snobberies of long ago. They governed our lives you see in those days. To get to Pentregwyn for the holidays was like returning to the earthly paradise.

This is so solemn an occasion I feel obliged to be direct.

'A lot depends on the weather,' I say.

'Yes of course!'

It is a topic to discuss while Bethan confronts the problem of her unwanted tenant.

'Even Juan-les-Pins can look pretty miserable in the rain!'

The lady solicitor considers the question of rainfall in greater depth than I anticipated. Her pondering took the edge off the silence. She is poised for a serious discussion.

'What worries me, Mr Lloyd, is global warming. When wars break out over water, we may come to bless the rain. We are defined by our worries and concerns I feel...'

'A clean slate!'

Bethan had given the tenant problem full consideration and has come to a conclusion.

'I should want to start with a clean slate. Perhaps the best plan would be to give this man a month to find somewhere else.'

She smiles to indicate that she is being fair and generous. She is also taking charge of the situation.

'Yes. I see.'

What Mrs Caradog-Jones sees in the middle distance is a range of obstacles still invisible to the client.

'I have a feeling, you see, that it was Sulwen's wish that Curig bach, as she used to call him, – hardly bach really, he's six foot and as thin as a rake – should be allowed to stay in the outside kitchen. In any event as you know there is the other executor, Doctor Seth ap Tomos. He was here to keep our appointment. He couldn't wait any longer. It is one of the conditions of your great aunt's will that you should read and as she said 'inwardly digest' her letter, her farewell letter to the world she called it, before we make the formal provisions of handing the property over to you.'

'Is that legal?'

A slight flush is rising in Bethan's porcelain complexion which I find becoming. Her determination never does anything to impair her delightful appearance.

'That is a good question. Sulwen was different. We loved her for her sterling character you see. In our separate capacities Doctor Seth and I were devoted to her. And she trusted us. We were very close.'

'Well I suppose I'd better read it then.'

Mrs Caradog-Jones' right hand moved on the surface of the desk and it seemed to me as if she were playing a trump card.

'There lies the problem,' she said. 'Doctor Seth has the letter and Doctor Seth has gone home. Either we arrange a new appointment or better still you could go and visit him today. He should be home by four o'clock. I can telephone to leave a message. It's such a pity you were so late for the appointment. Having come such a long way.'

Seven

YOU CAN BECOME frustrated and impatient with a language which you claim to understand, when you find you cannot express in it reservations let alone nuances. I need more time to digest the significance of the exchanges between the statuesque lady lawyer and my Bethan Mair. Even their difference in size becomes an element in what is developing into a clash of wills. I need to be better informed of course although gobbets of information, however revealing, are no substitute for a session of quiet thought. This is a situation with long term as well as short term implications. We can't allow a few days frantic action to determine our fate, surely? We have this nice tourist brochure about places to stay – out-of-the-way inns, traditional farm houses. Places where you are encouraged to relax and think. Nothing is going to vanish in the meantime.

Bethan is in no mood to put things off. We are being driven by the gale of her impatience instead of taking time to think. We scribble directions on the backs of envelopes and off we go, retracing out steps in the sense of getting back close to Pentregwyn although by shorter safer routes and all in order to confront the impatient Doctor Seth ap Tomos in his lair. Why say 'impatient'? Why 'lair'? Because this is what Mrs Olwen Caradog-Jones wants us to perceive as opposed to her liberal, benign, Olympian impartiality. He is the great obstacle, the difficult hoop we need to jump through. The Task. The Test.

She says he is easy to recognise because he is thin, wiry, restless and he crops his red hair close. His mansion, Coed y Glyn, where we are heading, he lets to a group of

American anglers together with fishing rights. He lives alone in a cottage behind the house. As we wind our way back through more green countryside and flowering hedgerows, Bethan gives vent to her indignation.

'Did you ever see such an absolutely nauseating pretentious female? Queening it! Exercising her little bit of power and importance and expecting me to grovel with gratitude. I never asked to be left that stupid shop. And what do I care about any sacred bonds that bound the three of them together. If there's one thing I can't stand it's this business of trying to impose emotional commitments on other people. How can that place mean anything more to me than what I can get for it? My dear old Dad is absolutely right. When you get involved with one lawyer you always need another one to stand up to him! Or her in this case.'

"Dear old Dad" indeed. This is a case in point. Why don't we stop and consider? What for example do her parents know about this legacy, if that, in fact, is what it is. Can an inheritance depend on just reading a letter? Does she really want it or is she just fuming about her dear old dad not to mention her formidable mother. What do they know and what do they think? Are they as much in the dark as I am? I try to be cool and objective.

'Bethan. You never tell me anything. Your father. What is he like?'

It has to be the moment to press the question, before I am overwhelmed with fresh revelations. Over the year or so of our relationship we have developed our own forms of tender communication. Even text messages under these conditions of frequent separation can develop into embryonic lyric poems. Maybe ancient family trees are shackles to escape from. On this expedition we seem to be getting entangled in another kind of family trap.

'My father. Very sweet and charming, Alwyn Nichols. He belongs to that spineless fraternity you could call the honourable invisible society of Cardiff Civil Servants, waiting in line for their O.B.E. If you need his address, he lives under my mother's thumb.'

A peculiar business altogether having two mothers. Along with Ffion the birth mother comes an entire tribe and among them this great aunt Sulwen who leaves her this outlandish inheritance with an entail that involves reading a letter. A deserted shop hedged about with obscurantist provisions and obstructions. So I need to be ready to share any degree of frustration or indignation Bethan could be feeling. It's what I'm here for.

'He's too nice for anything, Alwyn Nichols. So he lives in an emotional deep shelter. Miles underground beneath his smile. Wouldn't want to be disturbed by anything more violent than the wind in the willows. And there's a reason for that, Eddie Cynddylan.'

I lean further over the steering wheel to indicate an eagerness to learn more. Bethan constantly amazes me. Inside that pretty head there is some kind of pressure cooker at work. This is of course a crucial moment. Does she look upon this strange legacy as a birthright or a burden, a blessing or a curse?

'Squashed in his youth by his father, the great judge David Wyn Nichols for not coming up to expectations. Mind you, relative failure has its compensations.'

She is smiling sweetly at my evident incomprehension. If relative failure is a category, does she consider I belong to it? This girl can be so disturbing. To follow her you can say goodbye to a quiet life.

'Very attractive to women, that large-eyed hangdog look. He was so good looking, I imagine, in his younger days before he lost his hair.'

After all it is springtime of a sort and the weather is improving. All the greenness that surrounds us becomes uplifting when you get used to it. Maybe it helps to give an aura of innocence to the natives. Bethan is cheering up, amused by the inconsequential haphazardness of her own ruminations. And as her devoted admirer I am amused too. Perhaps the trick is to treat this whole adventure as a bit of a joke. Such as pretending to get lost searching for the long drive that leads up to Coed y Glyn.

The drive sweeps up through the trees to the commodious early Victorian mansion, and the lawns spread southwards to give a pleasing view of the river winding below and the high hills on the horizon. The trees on the northern slope grow close to the house, their leaves present a burgeoning chromatic scale of green. We see a thin man, spectacles perched on his close cropped red hair, crossing the yard beyond the house, with a length of wood under his arm making his way to a makeshift carpenter's workshop in the middle of a range of outhouses.

None other, we think, than our great executor, the Doctor Seth ap Tomos. A thin, wiry, foxy-looking fellow who is making a display of having things to do, a man, like time and tide, not prepared to hang around, using a show of indifference to denote displeasure; all the same unable to refrain from taking a sly sideways glance that proves to me his curiosity is roused. We abandon the Land Rover and follow him at a respectful distance to his workshop. In the open garage we see a pair of vintage cars that appear to be in the process of being restored. He is a man of leisure with many interests. We introduce ourselves. For some reason, while keeping an eye on Bethan he chooses to address me.

'Lloyd is it? This place used to belong to a Colonel Lloyd. Long ago, before I was born in fact. Still there could be a connection. Wouldn't it be a fairy tale if he had left this place to you?'

That was a joke. His face is cracked with a frosty smile. He wants us to understand he has a dry sense of humour.

'In any case, Mr Lloyd, what is your interest?'

He hurries on, embarrassed by his own frankness.

'A man should have interests. In my case to ease the pressures of my profession. This sort of thing. Did Olwen Caradog tell you I also write poetry in the strict metres? We are not shy about it. We have a society called Carpenters of Song. Poetic song, disciplined inside established staves, you see. A notation really. A way of saying and a way of looking at the world.'

He gives up on his credentials, folds his arms and leans back on the workbench to study Bethan.

'The living image of her mother,' he says. 'You understand this can be quite upsetting for me. I don't know how much you know.'

'Nothing.'

Bethan speaks for the first time. She sounds determinedly impartial.

'I adored her. There's no harm in admitting it after all these years. You could say I loved and lost. Not that it made me a better poet. A better doctor maybe. I can offer you some tea in the cottage. Not in the house. I let the house to a group of Americans. They call themselves the New York Newts. They don't catch all that much fish and they don't come here all that often. So what could be better?'

He seems to find relief from staring at Bethan by prattling away. It seems to me the nervous prattle of a man who would prefer to think of himself as taciturn.

'We are predators you see. As a species. Predators who have learned to co-operate and diversify more effectively than the rest of the animal kingdom. Hence your social contract, you see. As I keep telling Olwen Caradog, unspoken but more vital than a legal system. That's what the Great Republic has forgotten since it became a superpower. What is it driven by? That's the question to ask. Not manifest destiny as much as messianic greed. I give it to them straight. They like an argument. And so do I sometimes. They're a cheerful lot.'

We are ushered into the cottage.

'We invite you to step back into the nineteenth century.'

I need to lower my head in the doorway. It is deliberately a story book interior. Thin blue curtains on a deep window give the room a pleasant tint. There is a grandfather's clock ticking purposefully in a dark passage.

'I do a lot of thinking in here,' the doctor says. 'Gives me a sense of perspective.'

There is a brass paraffin lamp with a glass globe in a

deep alcove and alongside a button-back easy chair where I imagine he indulges in solitary meditation. Two low country chairs are set on either side of an old-fashioned kitchen range with an oven on one side and a metal cupboard on the other. A round top tripod table with tea things already set out stands in the middle of the room. A mahogany bookcase is stuffed with leather-backed volumes that seem more for show than for use. The doctor is fussing about inside a Victorian schoolteacher's desk, holding the lid high with one hand. We assume he is looking for the vital letter that his ally the lady solicitor declares has to be read before the Will can be proven. Bethan is silent. Still deeply suspicious of the whole proceedings.

'We all live in the past in one way or another,' he says. 'In my case I chose the past which I like to live in. Poverty with the sting taken out. Paraffin lamps and draughts to taste. Now then. Here it is.'

He extracts a battered tin and rummages inside for a photograph he wishes to show us.

'I've been meaning for years and years to put these in an album with a few intelligent notes to match. They don't fade so much as take a pinky tinge. As if you were looking at them through rose-tinted spectacles which of course you are. For my own part I prefer good old black and white. Here we are! A primary document! Three months for contempt of court. That's what they got. A group of us welcoming your mother and three other young ladies. Outside Pucklechurch Prison. '71 or '72 was it? Long hair and short skirts. There she is for you.'

He hands the curling photograph to Bethan. I can see her hand is trembling.

'Which mother?'

I can barely hear her. Doctor Seth is behaving like an amateur conjurer who has just pulled off a trick. Very pleased with himself.

'Right in the middle. Ffion Locksley. Prettiest one of the lot. The beautiful rebel! Not a good picture. You've got to forgive a bit of prejudice. Ffion was even prettier than you are. Your stepmother is there somewhere too. In the background. Lowri Philips. One of the stalwarts. Not to be left out.'

'I don't call her stepmother.'

Bethan seems to have shrunk. For a moment all the power and the protest seems to have gone out of her.

'Quite interesting really. It was your grandfather who sent the lot down. For demanding to speak Welsh in his court. Each one jumping up in turn and the policemen dragging them out. Those were the days. 'Bliss was it in that dawn to be alive, but to be young was very heaven.' That's the time when you think you're the centre of the universe. You spend the rest of your life finding out you're not!'

Bethan sits down with her elbow on the round table and her head lowered. Doctor Seth seems to realise for the first time that she might be upset. I restrain myself from telling him he is a stupid insensitive clown.

'How about some tea now? Indian or China?'

I begin to suspect the whole business is a bit of a comedy to him. Something to enliven the boredom of his existence. What does he do all day except read news-papers, fulminate on the state of the world and fiddle with his carpentry and vintage cars. Why doesn't he practise if he's a doctor? Isn't there a shortage? He can't be all that old. A very healthy and active sixty perhaps?

'We can nip down to take a look inside the shop before you read the letter. Once we've had our cup of tea. You might like to try my home-made blackcurrant jam.'

He wants to make us tea. He wants to make this a chatty social occasion. He wants to be friendly.

'I don't see why that man should be left to occupy the outside kitchen.'

Bethan has pushed the photograph away. She is not going to bend or buckle.

'Curig Puw? Saint Curig. Oh he's quite harmless.'

'That's hardly the point.'

He has fresh scones under a cloth and his blackcurrant

jam is very good. I am pliable enough to enjoy his afternoon tea and remark how comfortable he has made his cottage. My normal mechanism slides into action. If he is ready to make a good impression, then so am I. I will make an effort to be understanding. He was probably as much in love with her mother as I am with her daughter. There is a sense in which we are fellow sufferers. I balance a small spoonful of blackcurrant jam on one of his fresh scones. He has difficulty in not staring at Bethan. He needs to unburden himself.

'I went on protests just to be near her. I was in heaven when she tried to stop a policeman dragging me off to the police van. I danced attendance on her all the way to the Old Bailey. But she came back with my old mate Alwyn Nichols. Meant nothing to the world in general. Meant everything to me.'

Bethan picks up a scone just to do something to fill in an uncomfortable pause.

'The past never goes away,' he says. 'It's a bit of a mystery really. What are we doing, all the time, except building more of it. And yet the present pretends to be so different. There we are, thirty years and more ago, bound together like a band of brothers and sisters. All in the struggle together. To save the language nothing less than a revolution would do. So we had one every day! Not exactly Chile or Vietnam. But quite a little rumpus. In and out of prison. Loyalties and betrayals. All the usual stuff. Ancient history to you. To us, it turns out, the most vital part of our lives.'

We eat in silence and he assumes he has gained a sympathetic hearing.

'A lot to be said for a country practice. I've never regretted coming here. Then again my feeling is if you want to live close to nature, you have to more or less stay in one place. I've done well enough and I've had many consolations. We have our little choirs, you see, and our carpenters of song and our talking shops. All is not lost. The language holds us together in a web of silk you could say, comforting shackles, easy to wear like carpet slippers. And dear old Sulwen kept house for a small cloud of witnesses in Pentregwyn General Stores. Our local talking shop. And there was the chapel too for the likes of holy Joe. Curig the Born Believer. I'm a born sceptic myself. I came to the conclusion long ago that some brains are wired for belief and whatever hocus-pocus goes with it, and others are not. It's as simple as that really. Mind you we all get on very well. Thanks to the Cymric cult of being agreeable.'

Bethan removes a crumb from her lap and drops it in the fireplace. She is on her feet.

'Look. I'm a total stranger here. This whole network of relationships means nothing to me, quite frankly. You can't expect me to understand it all. I don't really want to? Why should I?'

Doctor Seth listens and nods wisely.

'Of course. Of course. I agree with what you say. And it does remind me of one of dear old Curig's little theorems. Little theorems he calls them. The old preachers used to call them Illustrations. About two strangers on a train. The seat had been double-booked so they scowl at each other. Quite hostile in fact. But as the journey goes on they exchange reading material to while away the time. And even a sandwich. And step by step as the long journey goes on, travelling companions become neighbours. That's Curig, you see. No church but never far from a pulpit. I don't believe a word of it myself.'

His lips tighten with frankness and honesty. He enjoys being listened to.

'There are mysteries of course. Beyond reckoning and calendars. There's more to the music of time than the creak of an escalator carrying off one generation after the other in neat battalions. Take Curig and your great aunt for example. Separated by scores of years and yet soul mates. Talk about an odd couple!'

He would like us to join him in a chuckle. Bethan remains firm.

'Where's this letter I'm supposed to read?' she says.

Eight

My very dear Bethan Mair:

For the first three and a half years of your life you were altogether mine and this old shop was your playground, your very own little kingdom. There never was a more radiant or contented little child. You seem to have had enough inner resources to light the whole place up. There was one old lady, Mrs Roberts, Y Felin, who would come in to buy one egg just for the pleasure of seeing you. And old Lewis Jones, whom I hope you will meet again, built you a little wheelbarrow so that you could trundle it around the place: and your little scales is still here too, in which you could measure anything from a pound of sand to a pound of sugar. I mustn't go rambling on about the past. Your grandmother, my clever sister Megan, had a favourite theory that humans are programmed to idealise the Past because it represents the peaceful bliss of nine months in the womb! And the idea of the Fall reflects the shock of birth. She would trot out the same argument to explain our inclination to idealise a monoglot Welsh nonconformist Garden of Eden. She was full of theories. I wonder if you have inherited the urge? I miss her to this day. At the stage I have reached, Bethan, my dearest, you feel the future is already pushing you into the past and you shouldn't fight against it: just behave as though you are already gone.

The wonderful thing about this world is that it will still be here after we have left it, and I can't tell you how happy I am to think that this place and all that goes with it will become yours. I do so much hope so. In a sense you took possession long ago when you played at my feet and it seems no less than poetic justice that you should take it over. You must forgive my old-fashioned flowery language. When I was young I had literary pretensions, I even learned the strict metres but as you can see only too clearly from this letter it came to nothing. Not entirely my fault perhaps. Due to my lack of push and ambition that seems essential for achieving anything; and due to circumstances which at the time I felt were closing about me like a vice.

What the whole story amounts to in the case of Sulwen Bowen is that my life was this shop, Pentregwyn General Stores, and this shop was my life. 'The whole story,' Doctor Seth says is a logical and physical impossibility, since it would involve the entire history of the world! I promise you I won't start that far back. He also says that trotting out the entire panoply of facts and figures won't bring us a step nearer to understanding why it all came about and it's always the why and not the how that makes the real difference. (I hope you will be patient with the doctor, my dear. He can be contrary, and downright grumpy, but he has kept me alive for longer than I deserve and there is a heart of gold behind that sceptical, clinical, long face of his. And of course, like me he loved your mother. I understand that doesn't give either of us an automatic right to interfere in your life. That I think would be a privilege we have to earn.)

Let me get back to my short history of my world. They used to say in those far off days when I was young, that old maids are always obsessed with their family histories. I have tried more than once to exorcise the nagging demon by writing the history of the parish of Pentregwyn. Now there we have a misnomer to begin with. Pentregwyn is a small village in the rather rambling parish of Llanfair Iscoed. I never succeeded in putting it all together but I have accumulated a pile of notes and jottings and cuttings. If ever you were interested, you will find them in the dresser in my bedroom above the shop. I don't claim they are an essential part of the inheritance. Every generation has to make a fresh start, I understand that, and it can manage the manoeuvre better without the leaden weight of the past on its back. All the same we all have this built-in faculty of curiosity, and in my own experience it has grown stronger as I have grown older.

You can see how I am indulging myself in the pleasure, and relief, of talking to you freely. Not face to face it is true. I have been denied that fulfilment. However, it could reach in the end a deeper level. These are my words directed entirely to you: my first and last words you could say. And they come with all my love, along the close link that leads from me to you and you to me. Your mother for as long as she lived was the light of my life; just as you were for as long as I had you. Your mother was the daughter of my only sister and I loved her too. So there you have a complete circle in which my whole life has revolved. My sister Megan and your mother Ffion are dead, and yet for me they are alive still. They live in my mind. These are not just morbid reflections. They are a part of the staple diet of my living. You may think this is because I am an old maid, all her life spent in struggling to keep a shop open, and you may well be right.

My Father, Henry Bowen

I have to tell you first about my father because I fear that his suicide may be all you know about him. He was the kindest and most gentle man you could imagine. So why should he kill himself? I wish I could explain it to you. The foundations of our way of life had already been well and truly shaken by two world wars and now this hideous event threatened to bring the whole edifice crashing down. That was the way I saw it. And still see it. Even writing this down makes me go cold inside and wish I was already dead. Not just the horror. The desperate attempts to cover it all up. I can still hear myself lying to inquisitive customers. His foot caught in a length of rope. He was carrying a two hundred weight sack of flour on his back. He tripped and fell through the open trap-door and broke his neck.

Sometimes history can look like a sequence of nightmares. I think now that was at least part of what overcame him. He had an older brother, Owen Glyn, O.G. they called him, whom he idolised. They were brought up under a regime of what people today might call iron discipline. And the reason for that was their grandfather had been something of a public figure. They were supposed to take great pride in him. They could see his monument in the churchyard: Griffith Ezra Bowen 1820-1895. He was a man in the vanguard of a range of good causes. 'The Cause' was a favourite phrase. It could mean building a new chapel, battling against the Establishment, Temperance, Law Reform, the Secret Ballot. Their grandfather, Griffith Ezra Bowen was there alongside Mr Gee of Denbigh, addressing meetings, travelling far and wide on horseback and on trains and even on ships. He clashed regularly with Archibald Lloyd, the squire of Coed y Glyn, and it still seems comic to me now that that house is the property of Doctor Seth ap Tomos. Ancient history of course – (very ancient to you I am sure) and battles long long ago. I can only say that I still live in the shadow of it all.

Griffith Ezra overstretched himself. Archibald Lloyd had called him a 'jumped up shopkeeper'. That was enough to make him buy land to give himself status. He got caught up in enterprises that went wrong. He had half a share in a merchant ship that went down off the coast of Ireland. That sort of thing. The fact is Pentregwyn General Store might have gone down like that ship except for the industry and iron discipline of my grandparents and it was within the constrictions of that discipline that my father and his older brother O.G. were brought up. I think their lives were governed by rules and regulations, in the chapel and in the shop and everywhere else really,

partly to make up for the extravagancies of that flamboy-
ant headstrong creature Griffith Ezra. It is one thing to
take a tribal pride in the doughty deeds of the head of the
clan, quite another to suffer from his risky ventures.

My grandmother used to say my father Henry had
one skin less than other men. His brother Owen Glyn was
quite different. He was Griffith Ezra all over again: he
didn't give a damn. Then along came the Great War.
That's what we always used to call it. Owen Glyn seized
the chance to escape. He could have been put in charge
of our two farms but he wouldn't hear of it. My father
Henry went because his brother Owen Glyn went. Owen
Glyn was killed and Henry survived thanks chiefly to his
bad eyesight. It kept him away from the front line.

I don't know how that period of insane slaughter in the
trenches appears to your generation. It haunted mine. I
believe the loss of the brother he looked up to, was the
beginning of the guilt that was to ruin my father's life.
This was the time they say when people began to turn
against organised religion. We did the opposite or rather
my father did. Why not try the pious simplicities of the
New Testament? What better could the chapel offer?
Sweep away the old dogmatic debates of the denomina-
tions and love thy neighbour as thyself. Dogmas were not
so easily swept away. My grandmother used to rumble
away about politics and business being a bad mix. She
said my father spoilt his wife and children. My mother
certainly was a pretty woman who used to murmur she
didn't enjoy the best of health. She used to worry about
having a red nose and she drank camomile tea like an
addict. We three had a wonderful childhood. Owain, so
ominously named after the uncle who was killed, Megan
and me, Sulwen. We knew next to nothing of the troubles
of the big world. Pentregwyn, Coed y Barcud, Y Garn,
our great playground. I think we had a sense then of being
privileged. The days were longer and our games seemed
to last for ever. Owain organised and we followed. Megan
and I, along with all the village children. People talked

about the gathering clouds and my father attended pacifist rallies, but our young lives were tranquil enough until Owain was called up and put into the R.A.M.C. then of course the gathering clouds descended and all was blackout, distant air-raids, mess and miserable muddle.

I try to think of it all as it must have appeared to my father. Somebody local painted Conchie Shop on our gates early in the war. That was one reason why my brother Owain joined up. My mother went to pieces. She would sit at a table and stare at a heap of ration coupons and then stir them with her finger, shake her head, blow her nose and do nothing about them. It's the dullness and the monotony of those days I remember, to my shame perhaps, not the suffering. Always shortages to share out and nobody satisfied. People nice to the shopkeeper in hope of small favours and hating his guts behind his back. One of the casualties of that war-time was the withering away of the old neighbourliness, like the emptying of the pews in chapel. The end of the vigorous community spirit of the old Pentregwyn. Of course it was an idealised version of bygone days I heard from my grandmother, and it got even more rosy as she grew older, and she lived to be ninety, so I must safeguard against the same process as I write to you. All the same there had been a rooted community and my generation has lived to see the roots withering away.

My brother Owain was killed on a Normandy beach in 1944. You could say my father lost the two lives he loved most, his brother and his son, to the thing he hated most, war. Perhaps he expected too much from life in the world in which he found himself. And the power of war grew worse. I remember him muttering to himself at the time the Americans dropped those atom bombs on Japan, 'Not once but twice.' He thought it could be the beginning of the end for humanity. I can see his head shaking as if he were struggling to escape from a trance. As soon as rationing relaxed, customers drifted away. Petrol came off ration and people began the habit of shopping in town.

Sometimes I used to think the only genuine commodity we had to sell in the shop was sadness.

The only bright spot in our lives was your grandmother's brilliance. Nothing in those colourless anxious days could do anything to dim Megan's achievements, and the pride I took in my sister. My mother wasted away and I stayed home to help Tada. I thought he would recover. It was the same with the chapel and the life of the village. There appeared to be a resurgence of a kind. A determination to restore things to how they used to be. Restarting the local Eisteddfod and the sheepdog trials, and the Urdd youth club, the choir and the chapel societies. The good old days and so on. At this distance it appears like the final, gasping, twitching of a dying society. What I remember more clearly is yet another war in Korea and that hydrogen bomb melting an island in the Pacific and my father's head forever sunk on his chest. He must have been beset by nightmares, and I suppose the last resort when you are fighting against an advancing swarm of demons is to kill yourself? He couldn't learn to live with what he must have seen as a new world of horrors. That's the way it appears to me and yet I must tell you that not a year passes without my turning again to face the whole enigma like a glacier shifting yet another inch closer to my nose.

From the day Owain was killed you could say that my mother and my father had lost the war: certainly they lost control of their lives. To keep things going, step by step, Megan and I took over: or to be more accurate, I did. I seemed to find satisfaction and contentment of a kind, running a business. Something to keep me busy. Megan approved of everything I did. She said it was a law of nature for children to take over where their parents had failed. There was an exhilarating sense of urgency. The only way to save the family from going under was to make decisions and stick by them and work from early morning to late at night. There was a sense of release too. My father's generation believed that daughters should follow their mothers and submit to docile domesticity. We imagined he had planned to have us working in the shop, keeping the house going: looking after our ailing mother so that he could give his time to his impractical brand of politics. His uncompromising pacifism had alienated half the members of our chapel as well as our customers.

Once we were in charge we set big changes in motion. They seemed big to us anyway. We sold one of the farms, and I expanded the bakery side. I bought two vans and we established a mobile service that more than doubled our turnover in less than two years. I honestly enjoyed the challenge. More than that I enjoyed my sister's brilliance.

My sister Megan

I may have been the eldest, fancying myself in charge, but Megan was cleverer as well as being prettier. Her academic success was my chief comfort in life. She took a first class honours in philosophy and her doctorate was in educational psychology. I remember I used to dream about her becoming a professor in Bangor and living in a nice house overlooking the Menai Straits. I could share the enlightenment education brought her by a slow process of osmosis. In fact she became a research fellow in London University and it was there that she met Chris Locksley a radio producer in the B.B.C who became, dear Bethan, the grandfather you never met.

Old age is such a comic condition. I can't imagine Chris as a grandfather. The great thing he did, of course, in the first instance, was to cheer us up. And that was certainly something we needed. He was handsome and charming as well as cheerful: all qualities my sister Megan found irresistible. She adored him. This was understandable. It is possible that I was jealous; jealous of their bubbling happiness, jealous that he was taking my sister away from me. He laughed a great deal and was inclined to find everything a bit of a joke, especially anything to do with our shop. 'The Selfridges of Pentregwyn', he called it. He had none of our traditional hesitations about hurting other people's feelings. He liked to say what he thought and he placed frankness very highly among the virtues. He certainly practised it. 'Look,' he would say. 'Look here girls! My old man was shot to bits in the Great War and he died of it all when I was six. But my mother and my row of giddy aunts didn't go on about it. He gave his life for his country and when my turn came I did my bit and came through it. And the fact is, if the worst came to the worst, we would do it all over again. In the mean time, children, life is there to be lived. So let's get on with it.'

He took a critical view of what he called 'the natives'. They caused him no end of amusement. He made fun of the way customers always made enquiries about our health before placing their orders. 'You are like a bunch of Orientals' he would say. 'Always bowing and scraping before getting down to business.' And he was never short of advice either. Since there was no pub in the village we should either open one or apply for an off-licence, or both. When I told him it was my grandfather who had been responsible for closing the Bodafon Arms, the last public house in the village, he shook his head in disbelief. There were so many aspects of our way of life that left him at a loss for words. 'So weird', he would say, when he discovered we never bought Sunday newspapers and that our late father had never been inside a cinema.

Between them, Megan and Chris tried to manoeuvre me into a marriage. He had a school friend and boon companion called Courtney Waters whom he called 'Bouncer'. By now, in my mind's eye, I can barely distinguish between the two. Bouncer was a rougher, less elegant version of Chris and he had gained his nick-name they told me by some special tactic he deployed on the rugby field. They were both appalled, by the way, to learn there was no rugby played in our county at that time let alone our parish. One more reason in their view to rescue Sulwen Bowen from the clutches of the dark ages and the darkness of the Welsh middle earth. My recollection now is that I quite liked him and certainly liked the noise the two men made as they trampled about the premises determined to awaken the whole place from its cobwebbed slumbers. They were very amused when they learned that Pentregwyn could mean 'blessed village' as well as 'white village'. No end of jokes they made about it. Bouncer had a VW Beetle he was extremely fond of and I can remember excursions to the mountains and the sea. Megan kept a watchful eye on the whole proceedings. I imagine now she was uneasy herself about the nature of her own commitment. There was a powerful physical attraction between them; anyone could see that. But culturally shall we say for want of a more accurate term, the Bowen sisters and Messers Locksley and Waters, were as different as chalk and cheese.

I would have liked to have been married. A longing for romance was just as much a part of our growing up as with any other girls. Because of our background no doubt and a certain rigidity of upbringing, it tended to be allied to subterfuge and innocent deceptions. Boys were a species of delicious forbidden fruit. Through her brilliance and educational achievements, Megan broke loose and she wanted me to share the pleasures of a new freedom, just as we had shared everything when we were children. She was clever and I was always very willing to learn.

I was faced with a choice. I had no real difficulty in making it. Courtney was a housemaster in a school in Suffolk and he had a professional need of a wife. We had music in common. He had a surprisingly refined tenor voice and played the cello I remember. He would go into ecstasies about the vastness of the Suffolk sky and the muted splendour of sunsets seen from the edge of a great field of ripening corn. Here at Pentregwyn he said he missed the expanse of sky and felt hemmed in by the hills. I don't remember my choice of words when I declined the offer. I must have made an effort to spare his feelings, but I could see he was quite hurt. Masculine pride is something I have never learnt to handle. I treasured my independence. I made that clear. I had acquired a collection of local obligations; several of which, including playing the organ in chapel on alternate Sundays, caused Chris to snort with an open amusement tinged with contempt. It all opened a rift between me and my beloved sister. When there is an emotional tug-of-war the two parties become hypersensitive about each other's shortcomings, suspicious of each other's motives. Megan was quite cross with me. She had an alternative lifestyle mapped out for us which I suspected would relieve the strains and stresses of her own marriage. Chris had been a foot-loose bachelor, settled in his habits and his hobbies and the restraints of married life could make him irritable. For some months you could say Megan and I were estranged.

Ffion Locksley, your mother

Until Megan became pregnant! She needed me just as I would have needed her. Our differences were swept aside. We were beside ourselves with excitement in a way that Chris found difficult to understand. He was pleased, of course, he said, when he got used to the idea. For Megan and myself this was the promise of a new beginning, as though the world was about to be born again. We needed to hold each other's hands as we had done when we lost our father and our mother and had to face a bleak future together. I wondered perhaps whether Chris had lived so long in an exclusively masculine world he did not realise that giving birth could be the most dangerous moment in the life of mother and child.

It all went well. Queen Charlotte's was wonderful and I must admit Chris Locksley was bursting with pride and joy. At least until it came to choosing a name. Megan had settled on Ffion because she had always doted on the name. It had taken her fancy when she was in school because it was the name of the head prefect whom she greatly admired. For my part I thought it was simple and distinctive. The argument arose over the double 'f'. Chris didn't see the need for it. In any case why not call 'the kid' Fiona? The impasse lasted at least five weeks. Chris called the baby 'x'. It was an edgy game that I felt was always in danger of turning sour. I was told Megan settled the problem in her own dry humorous fashion. Chris came back from a day in the studios and she announced she had registered the baby as Marilyn Monroe Locksley. She kept a straight face long enough for him to accept the name Ffion with both the 'f's' when she finally smiled. He was inclined to call the baby 'Phee-phee' to get his own back.

'What's in a name?' A great deal as it turned out. All to do with such weighty matters as identity, solidarity and allegiance. Cooped up in a flat in what they called the wrong end of Chelsea, Megan decided she would want her Ffion to enjoy fresh air and a Welsh education. Chris dared to wonder whether such a thing existed. It was a dispute that developed slowly and lasted longer than it took Ffion to learn to speak Welsh to her mother and English to her father. It reached its climax in a clash of careers. Chris had been moved to television and he was highly thought of by his Head of Department as a dashing adventurous character full of bright ideas; just the kind of right-hand man he had been looking for. Megan had resumed her educational connections and was offered a lectureship in a new educational institute in Wrexham. 'Look here, old boy,' the Head of Department was reported to have said. 'I can't have my right hand man living over two hundred miles away, can I?' There was a period of strain and tension that ended in a reasonably amicable separation that became less amicable as time went on.

Your grandmother and your mother made their home with me and Megan travelled the thirty odd miles to work three or four times a week. Chris came down to see his daughter as often as he could. He took great delight in her as indeed he should. I understood from Megan that he was becoming equally eager to have a son and heir. I stood well apart from such discussions. There were times though when he would turn to me for help and explanation. I was the one, for example, that had to try and convince him that our language was not a barrier designed to keep him out. He claimed to have tried to pick it up in their early days but had fallen off at the first hurdle and really didn't see the need to try and get back on such an awkward mount again. He had no gift for languages anyway, and this seemed to him, quite honestly, more of a stubborn medieval mule than a decent twentieth century hunter. He travelled the globe in the course of his job, and everywhere he went there were always enough people who spoke English. So who would need anything more?

Your grandfather Chris was a fine man, widely respected. He was honest and generous and open-hearted and cheerful, and that in my experience is as much as you can expect from any man. He was sensitive too and in spite of his devotion to plain speaking, easily hurt. There may have been a sense in which he felt his private life was being taken over by a new breed of woman. There was a look of bewilderment bordering on pain that would pass over his frank and open features from time to time that suggested as much. Perhaps in his childhood and youth, having lost his father so early in life, he had been spoilt by that row of giddy aunts he spoke about. They were all either widows or spinsters and I think he had been the masculine apple of a line of admiring eyes. That would mean that 'having his own way' would have been deeply ingrained in his character. He made an effort to compromise and that was greatly to his credit, but he found it very difficult.

My rather half-baked theory is that he tended to take out his frustration in a growing antipathy to our language. It always seemed to be the main obstacle to him gaining his own way. He even called it an obstacle to civilisation and advancement. I tried to explain to him that with us it meant a sense of warm affiliation. It accommodated centuries as well as a breadth of understanding. It inculcated a sense of responsibility to others as well as to the traditions that preserved it, along with the landscape and the weather. If there were to be any renewal, any improved form of society in this corner of the world, the language would provide the essential cement as well as a sense of direction. Perhaps I was trying too hard to keep up with the intellectual skills of my clever sister. When I paused for breath, rather pleased with my exposition, he looked at me as though I had been talking gibberish and walked away.

I am going into too much detail. What I write sounds too critical of your maternal grandfather. What I needed to say was that he was a fine man who found it difficult to adjust to what he must have considered the constraints and restrictions of life at Pentregwyn. In the simplest terms you could say he was just never cut out to be a countryman. I have no means of knowing how much you were ever told about him, if anything at all. I want to confirm that he was a splendid character whose brilliant career was cut short by a tragic air accident. The advanced aeroplane he was travelling in on its test flight disintegrated over the Indian Ocean. There was an official enquiry and a memorial service in London that I attended with Megan and little Ffion, your mother. Such occasions for a country woman like me can stand out with startling clarity, when all the days that surround it have faded into confused obscurity. Megan had to spend time in London, there were so many things to be settled. Ffion stayed at home here with me.

I look back on those days when your mother was growing up as the happiest time of my life: my second childhood I used to call it. When you are growing up yourself, if all goes well, you take it all for granted. This time I was an observer as well as a participant in the golden age. Your mother was an enchanting child, and enchanted too. She could weave spells. She was not merely beautiful to look at. She was at peace with herself and absorbed by the natural world around her. In that gorgeous summer at the end of the nineteen fifties, I saw her once lying in the garden with her arm outstretched and a newly hatched chaffinch perched on her finger. She was quiet and undemanding and yet she had a retinue of friends who used to follow her. I liked to be in the shop around four o'clock in the afternoon after school, to watch the eager way two or three of her little friends would troop after her to her playroom. She played the piano and the fiddle and she danced. She sang and she learned verses. For three years in the sixties the chapel flourished because we had so many children in it. Ffion was every bit as clever as her mother. Cleverer, Megan said. You can imagine we both doted on her when she became the ideal Head Girl at school. I don't need to try too hard to draw a portrait of your mother. An old friend who was in the assembly when you graduated, wrote to me that you would only need to look in the mirror to find what your mother looked like.

Towards the end of the sixties the tempo of our lives quickened, no doubt because the times were changing. There had been a moment earlier in the sixties when one of Ffion's friends came running to the shop crying because some children had told her the world was coming to an end at six o'clock. That would have been the Cuban missile crisis. After that, when it didn't happen, I think our little community breathed more easily. But it began to dwindle. International crises came at regular intervals. It is a feeble conclusion to arrive at, but families only succeed in being happy to the extent they can isolate themselves from the trials and tribulations of the great world outside.

Once Ffion had gone to college we had to run to keep up with her. She had chosen to go to Aberystwyth because it seemed to her to be an active centre of the language struggle. Ffion told us it was the time for revolution all over the world and Megan and I listened with our mouths open. 'We've got to be extreme, remember,' she would say, 'so that you can go on being moderate!' I'm sure you will know all about their adventures and misadventures since your father and your step-mother were involved as well. For a year or two or more, it seemed they were all in and out of prison more often than they were in college.

I've wondered a great deal about those heady days that may seem long ago to you, but for me remain my most piercingly immediate yesterday. Why that great surge to defend our language and way of life, after decades of indifference and neglect? It wasn't Ireland of course. There were no bodies lying in the street in pools of blood. And yet it must have been an uprising of some sort: a people determined to hang on to their separate identity even if it meant defying the comforts of globalisation as well as the shock and awe of iron-fisted authority. I think that is how communities are the world over, not just us. If our family is anything to go by, we have always needed a cause to embrace. How I wish you and I could discuss these things face to face, even across the generation gap.

When your mother brought your father to Pentregwyn for the first time, we thought he was a poet. He had long hair down to his shoulders and his trousers were more flared than a sailor's. I think he thought Megan and I were old fashioned country women and he was very quiet, very unlike his friend Seth ap Tomos, a medical student from Cardiff. Seth said he took to Pentregwyn from the word go, like a duck to water. As a group they took to using our premises as a centre of temporary accommodation while they climbed television masts and went on interminable protest marches, rallies, missionary journeys, or public fastings. They left a van here filled with English road signs ready for the moment when they could tip them outside a magistrate's court. I'm sure you must know, Bethan, that your father fell in love with your mother when his father, your grandfather the judge, sent a bunch of women to prison for contempt of court. For Ffion that was something to laugh about in the end. After the marriage she got on very well with her father-in-law. That was the thing about her really. She could charm anyone when she put her mind to it.

It is plain enough that our lives went down hill after her death. At first we were all so devastated that your poor father was only too relieved to leave you here with Megan and myself. I never saw a man so stricken down with grief. At least for Megan and myself looking after you was some form of consolation. I'm not suggesting he held you in some subliminal form of blame for Ffion's death, but in your first years, his visits grew less frequent. A routine established itself. He had a career and we were only too pleased to have you here. All the same we had our suspicions about some form of serious neglect at the exclusive Nursing Home in Cardiff, that had led to her death.

When your father and his second wife insisted on taking you away from us, a real rift opened. Medical friends of Doctor Seth were of the opinion that Ffion's blood pressure had not been properly monitored and that led directly to a brain haemorrhage eight days after you were born. During any birth, life and death are always in precarious balance. The consultant who part-owned the Nursing Home was a friend of your grandfather's: they belonged to the same club. Of course nothing could bring her back but we believe the neglect that had taken place was hushed up. It was even put about, these medical friends told Seth, that Ffion was afflicted with some obscure genetic defect. We believed in those days that when influential lawyers and doctors got together they never found it difficult to stitch things up to suit themselves.

You could say we were bitter and unforgiving. No doubt we were also troubled by the thought that we had colluded in a cover up. That Nursing Home went unpunished. Step by step we seemed to be retreating from the world. It is equally true the world was retreating from us. Supermarkets opened in market towns within convenient distance of Pentregwyn and our former loyal customers were spoilt for choice. There was a story in the local press of a 'tug of love' contest in Pentregwyn. This infuriated us. A television reporter with his cameraman turned up outside our shop. I wouldn't let them in. Megan was upstairs. She threw a bucket of cold water over them. They never bothered us again. We hung the bucket up in the shop as a trophy!

About that time Megan seized the opportunity to take a Crombie early retirement. It helped us out financially but it wasn't the wisest move to take. It gave her too much time to brood. She developed an irrational hatred of your father and mother which made any further reasonable relationship impossible. She also grew more violent. She took part in a protest at the foot of a television mast. She had a lump of lead in her handbag and used it to smash the window of the control room so that the young people could get in. We no longer owned a television set in order to avoid buying the licence. Megan said she didn't want to see the miseries of the world reduced to a domestic peep-show. For my part I had no desire to volunteer to be sent to prison for not paying the licence. The irony is that in her last years I bought a television and it was on all day in her bedroom in order to give me the time to get on with my work or some respite from my poor sister's morose meanderings.

Myself Alone

I felt like that when Megan fell ill and there was little hope of recovery to either physical or mental health. It was at this time that Doctor Seth came to our rescue. Megan at first was deeply suspicious of him. She saw him as one of the group that Ffion had belonged to and an ally of your father Alwyn Nichols. Ill health left her very confused and Seth kept up his visits even though she was liable to attack him physically at any time. People said I should have had her put away in a home. I could never do that to my only sister. By the end she spent most of her time in her room distrusting everyone except me; and I did feel then that I was the last of the Bowens of Pentregwyn and everything they had stood for seemed doomed to extinction. I was on the point of feeling sorry for myself and comparing my situation to that of the boy who stood on the burning deck in the poem they made us learn in Primary School. When Megan was still lucid she would explain to me that the lives of little people were blown about by great economic cycles like leaves in a gale. She would say that multinational corporations could be as merciless as any totalitarian regime. Village shops were in the same positions as third world peasants growing peanuts. In the long run she would say there wasn't all that much to choose between unrestrained capitalism and communism. She was bright and she knew about these things and that made her decline all the more heartbreaking for me.

It was when I was alone and feeling rather sorry for myself that one of those happy accidents occurred that restore your spirits and make you realise that life after all is a marvellous gift and something to cherish. Not that Curig would call it an accident if I understand him correctly. He says the will aspires but accidents determine. He says the margin between the planned and the accidental is very thin but it's the best place to be because it is the only source of the trace element that can provide inner tranquillity. He has a way of looking at things that has brought me great comfort. Mind you his life was in more of a mess than mine when I came across him.

His car had broken down outside our shop. He was curled up on the back seat. He hadn't eaten anything for days and he was in a fever. Everything had gone wrong. He had no job. His wife had left him. He said I took him in like a stray animal. As it turned out I think the advantage was all mine. You could say his problems and his presence gave this old place a new lease of life. He is a thinker of course. A man of great ideas. But I'm afraid too untidy and absent-minded to carry them out. So in one sense, we make a good combination. I may be a failed business woman, but I am practical and I like to see things carried out properly. Neat and tidy. It must be the methodist in my makeup. As Curig says, we all have talents that crave for fulfilment, but what we need most of all is faith.

My dearest wish is to see Pentregwyn General Stores restored in a new capacity as a living centre to a renewed community. We have already taken the first steps. Curig is what you could call an untrained architect and he has drawn up exciting plans to open up the property and divide it into areas devoted to communal activity: a library, an art gallery, an organic food centre, a coffee and tea bar, a book barter service, and even one of those cybercafes that are becoming so fashionable. Plans could be too ambitious and I know my health won't last long enough to see them through, so I thought I would match this chapter of accidents with my own firm will and intention: I leave this dear old place and all that goes with it to you dear Bethan, because you are your mother's daughter and the legitimate heiress (if one may use such a portentous word) and because you are you. As far as my romantic hopes for this little corner of the world are concerned, I am also taking a gamble, like making a bet that such a thing as family goodwill exists. That's what I like to believe. You could say I have lived my life in the belief that you would like to be like your mother. I also realise that I could be completely wrong, just as you could have grown up to be completely different. When you read this I shall be dead and gone and all I leave you will be my love and your freedom to do whatever you think best. My devotion to you was doomed to be distant, but now I leave you all that I have to leave.

Your great aunt

Sulwen

Nine

DOCTOR SETH opens the doors of the shop with a flourish and goes so far as to give me a wink. He is in merry mood, designating himself Master of Ceremonies. He is building himself into a clownish character who raises a curtain on a special occasion and still provides you with a witty aside.

'Do you think you should carry her over the threshold?'

His attempt at a friendly smile stretches the tight skin on his pale naked face too far. He is bent on dragging me into this murky business, making it mine as well as Bethan's burden. He is trying to squeeze me into some version of a happy ending of his own devising. He poses as author, actor-manager, and wants to treat me as a pliable member of the cast. He wants Bethan to settle down into her great-aunt's shoes with me alongside her, ready with support and comfort. He will manipulate us both from the shadows behind an illusory throne. This is a doctor inclined to treat his patients' ailments as a bit of a joke: the kind who pick up limp wrists and wink as they glance up from their gold watches to make such cheerful remarks as 'at least we're not dead yet'. He cannot be unaware of the turmoil in Bethan's mind: he just chooses to ignore it.

I can't. I have a queasy sensation that things are getting out of control. For two days and even worse two restless and uncomfortable nights we have been marooned in the bedroom of a mediocre motel behaving like a bewildered middle-aged couple instead of a pair of too long separated lovers delighting in and feeding off the golden opportunity of being alone together. Our intimacies are limited to rubbing backs and patting shoulders.

This infernal letter has thrown Bethan clean off her rational keel and it is doing me no good at all. I didn't rush all the way to Wales to get stuck over my ankles in a morass created by an old spinster's fevered sentimental memories. Bethan is treating that nauseating manuscript like a message from the Underworld.

Until we embarked on this ancestors expedition, I never found Bethan lacking in a critical faculty: she was certainly never a girl inclined to blame herself for things going wrong. On the contrary, perhaps because of the very nature of her chosen career she was quite adept in discerning the shortcomings of others and never in my estimation without good reason. The media world sometimes seems to be populated by fly-by-nights. If there is one thing we have learned to share, an inclination I believe enhances our loving attachment, it is a capacity for rational objectivity. This is not just nit-picking for nit-picking's sake. I look at it as an exercise in intellectual grooming. We have nurtured it as a control factor that allows us to endure living apart – suffering as it were, in order to improve our career prospects: or at least Bethan's. If we lose that ability, goodness knows what else will begin to unravel.

She is in a confused mess, being drawn down as I see it, into a whirlpool of ancestral emotions. I am being increasingly frustrated by my inability to pull her out of it: or even bring her consolation and comfort. It is as if her skin has turned sore and tender. When I try to embrace her she stiffens, holds her head away, moans and mutters things I can barely hear, such as 'I know this may sound stupid, but I feel I understand for the first time really what it means to be a woman...'

What the devil does that mean? Are there lessons here that I, a mere man, am supposed to learn? She is after all twenty-seven years old, determinedly independent with a well-cultivated will of her own. She can't behave as though she were approaching for the first time the mysterious transformations of puberty. What am I to understand? Is she referring to some mystique of womanhood beyond male comprehension? How can I become more loving and sympathetic than I already am? That miserable letter is thrusting up a barrier between us. She sits up in bed like a woman in a trance and I lie with my hands under my head numb with frustration and lack of sleep.

What is she looking at? Ghostly figures beckoning from a blank motel bedroom wall? She is seeking for evidence that is well beyond discovery. What was the relationship between the mother she never knew and the agreeable, affable, inoffensive father she thought she knew so well? Did I hear her mutter something about being a victim in the womb of time? The mother she never knew except for those crucial unknowable months in the womb. The fact is we were all once in the womb, otherwise we wouldn't be here and by that reckoning we are all victims. By that morose reckoning an utterly delightful, cheerful, singing creature ready for any adventure is being transformed in front of my eyes into a moody, sulking woman paralysed by her own imaginings. In the daytime, instead of getting dressed and in spite of the spring sunshine outside, she pores over the pages of that interminable letter as though she were scanning Holy Writ. When she gives me pages to study I find my Cymraeg is inadequate. I don't have my lexicons to help me and when I ask for elucidation I disturb her meditative concentration and become liable to be snapped at. I become sulky myself. I have things to say about myself I would quite like her to hear.

When I was growing up I used to ask my mother why simple sentences in sacred texts needed volumes of explaining when their meaning was so patently obvious. God is Love. Well there you are then. She would smile at me and say that simple things were never that simple otherwise the world wouldn't be so consistently getting itself into a mess. Our side Good. Their side Bad. That sort of thing. And here I am now a grown man, holed up in a dull, colourless room, the sun shining outside like an order of release attached to my loved one by a sulky mucilage. The best I can do is take a shower.

When I emerge, prepared to be refreshed, she is immersed in a new theory! 'It's all a punishment,' she says. 'A curse on my head for being the source of conflict. I should never have been born.' This is more than I can stand. 'That's absolute melodramatic rubbish!' Even if it costs a row between us it's got to be said. 'I mean if that were true, nobody should have been born. In which case you could argue the world would have been a better place and got on very well without us.' Bethan accepts this absurd proposition without a murmur of dissent. This lack of response unnerves me. Those pages strewn over the rumpled double bed are subversive creepy crawly creatures dragging her down into a whirlpool of dead people's obsessions. Her so-called devoted great aunt has become a queen of the underworld and this common-place motel the mouth of Avernus.

We need to get out. I suggest we go for a long walk to clear our heads. She waves me away. She has a fresh bout of reading to undertake. As I see it, that letter has the impertinence, the nerve, to imply that its contents are more important than our relationship; the joint existence that is our reason for being. It is the basic assumption of lovers that they were born literally for each other. This elaborate account of other people's past is like an elephant trap designed to make all our future collapse into it. I take the path alongside the river glittering in the spring sunshine where we should be walking hand in hand. Pentregwyn improves the further you walk away from it. Places may be trapped in their own past and perhaps that is as it should be: but persons, individuals, should be free to come and go and, most of all, to escape and make a fresh start. I thought that was an axiom accepted by us both. That letter has changed everything. She is beginning to view her whole life as some kind of drama leading to this: and this doom or whatever else it is, supersedes a heart-warming delightful comedy: I mean if we are in control of our own affairs it is up to us to make the whole thing work.

I am so uneasy the sunlight on the river brings me no comfort. I am appalled by the disloyal thoughts that swim unbidden into my mind. Is it possible this girl is not at all the unique special person I took her to be? These thoughts are worse than disloyal. They are downright treacherous. My obvious duty as a lover is to rescue the damsel trapped in a dark tower. What other function do I have and what other purpose does my degree of independence serve? Crises occur in the course of any relationship and my value in this instance is my capacity to resolve the problem. If necessary cut the Gordian knot. Let us say thank you very much to all concerned and put the damned shop and all that goes with it on the market. I hurry back to that miserable bedroom and put my solution to her. I try to be as bright and breezy as I can. It seems the best way to reduce a mountain to a molehill.

She crouches against the headrest of the bed and studies me with doleful eyes. I have the cold sensation of not being aware of what exactly she sees; a stranger on the doorstep trying to sell her something she doesn't want.

'Sell it!' I say again. 'Offer it to the executors if they are so damned keen on it. Or put it on the market. And let's get away from here. It's all very well in its way but we don't belong here, do we?'

The way she looks at me suggests that she thinks I certainly don't. I came along as some sort of safety net and witness to the power of impartial common sense, and all she hears is the patter of some travelling salesman.

'How can I?' she says. 'If I did, her ghost would come to haunt me.'

She shuffles sheets of that damned letter between her fingers like a string of prayer beads. Can this be the delightful independent free spirit who crawled into my bunk on the Paris Express, who roamed the globe with her camera in search of wonders? What can a man say to make her see sense?

'Who the hell believes in ghosts?'

She makes no answer. My words reverberate in the box-like room as though everybody did. Is she listening to me? Momentarily she appears to take my distress into consideration.

'I'll do something with it. Something worthwhile. I told you about Jens's studio in the middle of Jutland. That could be a possibility.'

And so we submit to her predestined place in her great-aunt's scheme of things. I bend my neck as I pass through the shop doors like a captive passing under the yoke. Doctor Seth's smile is still stretching the skin of his face. If his spectacles had rims it would all look less naked.

The interior of the shop is even gloomier than it appeared when we first peered through the crack in the blinds. It looks like an extended exercise in inanimation: all those empty shelves and that galvanized zinc bucket glowing in its own grey gloom. Doctor Seth stands in the centre of the wooden floor and stretches out his arms.

'It's a disguise,' he says. 'We left it empty like this to discourage intruders. Nothing here to steal, except the bucket. These days you can't be too careful, even in the depth of the country. Last year I had thieves from Birmingham using their chain saws in the middle of the night stealing trees from Coed y Glyn Wood. Roaring away in their lorry. The get-away! That's the world we live in. Sometimes I think civilisation will be snuffed out by an excess of transportation.'

He expects us to nod and in theory I suppose we should. But all I feel is a twinge of guilt that only deepens my resentment.

'However, Miss Nichols and Mr Lloyd, there is more to this place than meets the eye!'

The corridor that leads to what appears to be a network of store-rooms is darker than necessary. I reach out a hand to touch Bethan's shoulder and she follows the doctor with uncharacteristic docility. Could that be because of his devotion to her birth mother? Has he secured his position in her new iconography? Am I to assume that takes precedence over my devotion to her? The world has become a fragile construct held together by a gossamer network of devotions. The doctor flings open a door and we are confronted by a room in darkness. Lights are switched on and a large room is revealed furnished for an impromptu party and people standing around start clapping. I can only assume that Bethan is being made welcome by a reunion of Sulwen Bowen's customers. More devotion. What am I doing here? I feel out of place.

A red and white check cloth lies over a length of trestle table displaying plates of sandwiches, little sausage rolls, cakes and scones. There is a copious tea urn and behind it a large loaf of a woman in a flowered hat with plump hands raised ready to go on clapping. By an upright piano a harp is parked and standing by it a muscular female and seated two schoolgirls clearly waiting to sing. There is further evidence of local artistic activity. At a glance I judge they are amateur watercolours, landscapes and flower pieces, of the kind Bethan would ordinarily hold in contempt. With her the word amateur is a term of abuse. At the back of the room looking well washed and shy I recognise the graveyard twins. Ifan, the dry-stone waller has composed penillion in the strict metres and the schoolgirls are already clutching their copies. The thin creature moving so close to the wall he could almost merge into it is introduced to Bethan as her tenant and to me as the recently Reverend Curig, 'as in Capel', by the ebullient doctor who is not discouraged by my effort at fastidious rigidity. Curig's wan smile is a fixture and obviously a substitute for verbal communication. My distaste for the place and the occasion increases by the minute.

This is a public occasion, however small the scale. For the first time I observe Bethan in a collective context and I am not pleased with what I see. She is behaving with the simpering modesty of a schoolgirl accepting her first prize on a Speech Day in front of the whole school.

Mercifully there are no speeches. Only the two girls tweet-tweeting those traditional verses of welcome and then the tea where the erstwhile customers fall upon their own concoctions. Bethan is surrounded by excited ladies and I am left to study nondescript watercolours for lack of any more rewarding occupation. Curig the outside kitchen anchorite observes me from the corner of his eye just as I keep an eye on him. In this agitated atmosphere we already seem to be shaping up as rivals. Doctor Seth stands a little apart, his hands clasped behind his back, surveying his handiwork and finding it good.

The doctor's revels are not yet ended. There is no relief available and no release from his clutches. When most of the company has dispersed and a group of the faithful ladies are still washing up, he wants to show us what he calls The Workshop. This is a large shed in the rear of the buildings which Sulwen had allowed him to convert into a wood and metal workshop - 'and stone,' the doctor adds, 'if we ever get around to it,' where local youth could be initiated into the mysteries of craftman-ship. 'Diversification,' he utters with a wink and a roguish raising of his index finger. I never thought I would ever so dislike the sound of that cherished word.

I am mildly appalled at the transformations I am being obliged to witness. This dubious doctor's confidence is growing by the minute. Bethan looks mesmerised by his manipulations. He treats her like visiting royalty, a consti-tutional monarch so to speak who has transferred her authority into his disinterested, altruistic, but culturally competent hands. He is getting away with it. And that sanctimonious shadow Curig Puw traipses in their wake nodding his superfluous approval like a second rate shaman. Myself, I am dumb with disapproval.

'Now then,' says the doctor, dry-washing his hands. 'Shall we go upstairs and take a look at Sulwen's Room? We have tried to keep it as she left it.'

We walk up the stairs so carefully you might think we were afraid of waking somebody up. The room that was occupied once by Bethan's grandmother was stuffed with ancient furniture and relics that Sulwen Bowen could not bring herself to throw away. Somewhere in there we imagine are the scales that Bethan and her mother had played with in their turn, and the celebrated wheelbarrow that had been specially made for her. There is a small blackboard and easel that for one awful moment Bethan threatens to recognise.

In Sulwen's bedroom she moves about as though she were in a trance. The hermit and the doctor watch her closely, an audience captured by a performance. She opens the bureau like a priestess approaching a holy relic.

'There were notes, weren't there?'

She speaks so quietly I can barely understand what she is saying. The hermit and the doctor have an advantage: they are more familiar with the language of the liturgy.

'For the history of the parish and the family. That sort of thing.'

The hermit knows where they are kept. The mahogany chest of drawers is stuffed with them. And there is a bookcase reserved for volumes related to the subject. There are so many nods and sighs and smiles of gentle understanding I am obliged to shift backwards and take refuge on the stairs. I already hate this place. The faint yellow light from the bedroom casts my shadow on the wall. I raise my hands in despair. My mood is such that my own shadow is distorted into the shadow of a hanged man. I cheer myself up with gallows humour. The deserted shop is a desert. I recall legends of desperate proprietors taking out insurance on properties and having them set alight. I would take no exception to seeing this ugly structure burnt to the ground. Humour exhausts itself and I begin to contemplate how many rungs there are on the long ladder that reaches down into the depths of despair.

Ten

'WHAT ABOUT the clean slate?'

We are sitting, Bethan assures me, under the great rock where Bendigeidfran once sat looking out across the sea towards the Irish shore, with every intention of wading there with a minstrel strapped to his back. She has taken pity on me after another restless and fruitless night. She has put away the dreaded letter and we have quit the motel for what she has designated a day of sight-seeing for me and of meditation for her. The weather isn't all that marvellous: there is a stiff breeze from the south west and cloud shadows are scudding along over the sea. This café smells out of season and I don't feel as warm as I would like to be. The coffee is anaemic and my suspicion that Bethan is contriving to link these mythological associations with her newly acquired property is growing. My question is directly related to keeping her feet firmly on the ground, whatever happened to those singing birds and giants and exiled princesses.

'You have to admit he is distinctly weird... '

She seems reluctant to agree. This is all such a delicate business. I need to bear in mind all the time the natural affection she has for her native language and her country. I would never want her to suppress or even subdue it. What we need to do is channel it. There is the vital element of her creativity in which, in our separate ways, we both have a vested interest. For my part, I have to contain my impatience with my imperfect understanding of the nuances of the local dialect and hold back an urge which I can only characterise as a muted longing for the neutral expanse of the great wide world. In Pentregwyn I am aware of the uncomfortable sensation of other people's fingers all over what should be our private affair. Even being under the great rock of Harddlech overlooking the sea is only a limited relief. In this country even myths can be disturbingly intrusive.

'He has things he believes in,' Bethan says.

Does that mean believing is a virtue in itself? I don't put the question. She is looking at me rather searchingly as if she is about to ask me to own up to whatever it was I believed in. I wouldn't want an inquisition that went in that direction. I have a distinct recollection of having said, 'Love and do what you like' on more than one occasion in our over-punctuated past and of hearing her agree wholeheartedly: once certainly in Freddy Helmut's chalet: and once in the moonlight under the Pont du Gard.

'Whatever they are,' I say. 'The mystic Puw could still believe in them somewhere else surely?'

I have my own deeply felt and cherished creed, and it had been my intention to lay it bare at her feet during the excursion I had planned to share with her in Languedoc, before giving everything up to respond to her appeal for help in coping with this benighted inheritance. I believe in the family life that I was deprived of by the vagaries and exigencies of my father's capricious later career. I wanted to acquire the sound of children's voices and the bright seasons of childhood that were denied to me when I was forced to loiter for what seemed an age or at least days on end in hotel corridors. Belief and purpose are tied up together and I want her to understand that I am more than a convenient agent of supplementary perception. She has an obligation to me that should go further to balance my unstinting devotion to her. I'm more than a nice chap. I am a hungry animal with appetites and needs that call for some attention. I am a creature at this moment plagued with a confusion of desires. I have a dream of a family life of unadulterated satisfaction, and it has to be realised within a reachable future.

How and *where* is what we need to drive towards. We are talented and flexible. I have my small private income.

Among our options could be a modest villa on the shores of a lake; Annecy or Lago di Maggiore have figured in my dreams; but in reality anywhere would do so long as we were together and there was sufficient space to bring up children. I wouldn't object to a place in Brittany or Wales if her roots drew her in those directions, but we need a fresh start: a place of our own choosing not a redundant general store.

'I've been thinking.'

Bethan's hand reaches across the table to cover mine. I am immediately touched by how small it is. Hard to believe she is capable of so much arduous exertion. When she has a certain shot in mind nothing on earth will restrain her. I shudder to imagine her hanging out of a helicopter in what I was told was a flimsy harness.

'I'm being thoughtless and unfair to you. I've been so self-absorbed I've forgotten what a sensitive person my Eddie Cynddylan is really. He's the real artist in this combination. He's got the right temperament. I'm just a misplaced shopkeeper.'

I feel as if the clouds are lifting. We are on our way back to our old level of light-hearted communication.

'I don't know about temperament,' I say. 'Thin-skinned maybe. Certainly as far as you are concerned.'

I hold on to her hand as she is about to draw it back.

'I don't know what you'll think,' she says. 'But I've decided to move into Sulwen's room.'

She is watching me closely for my reaction. I don't know which it is I have to hide: disappointment or disapproval.

'There is so much I've got to think about,' she says. 'Ways of breathing new life into the place. It's so easy to get overtaken by events. There's got to be a pause. I must take time to think. I have to tread carefully of course. These people are so devoted to the place.'

What place I want to ask. I see no sturdy working class or those pentecostal singing proletarians Labour politicians like to rhapsodise about on their way to Westminster and Brussels. Let it all lapse into a wilderness. Turn it into a wildlife reservation. Diversify back to the Stone Age! Why should I care?

'New life...' I say.

I try to suppress the whinge that creeps into my voice.

'What about our new life?'

I say 'our' but judging by the way she is looking at me it sounds like 'my'. This is becoming worse than a debate. Separate dreams are emerging in open conflict. An old woman's soured past is threatening my glowing future. I am compelled to put my cards on this cold table. I have gambled and now leave myself totally exposed.

'You know I want more than anything for us to get married and have children. I've tried not to go on about it and not interfere with your career. But all this is diversion. Where can it lead to except a dead end?'

'Dear Eddie.'

The softness in her sympathy unnerves me. There is so clearly worse to come.

'There's plenty of time. People don't get married so young any more. You know I have this selfish need to achieve something. Maybe this will be it. I've just got to work things out. You've got to give me time.'

And that was it. I had a distinct impression of a door closing quietly but firmly in my face. My wish to escape to the wide world has been granted sooner than I expected. The chains of freedom have been restored and in no time at all I am back in the office at F.A.O. and having my back slapped by Freddy Helmut.

'You are looking rather down in the mouth, old fruit, if I may say so. Things not going to plan?'

I take evasive action. The wound is still too raw to have anyone poking around inside it. At that stupid tea party before I left Pentregwyn I suddenly had the nasty sensation of being only one in a three horse race, the doctor and the outside kitchen anchorite were paying her such close attention. And she was absorbing it all as though she had been doing it all her life. 'Seth' and 'Curig' she called them and the names dripped off her tongue with the ease of birdsong. In that pseudo-nineteenth-century cottage parlour she presides over the teapot as if she were taking part in a costume play.

It was one of those uncomfortable occasions when you are liable to be assailed by awful thoughts. The doctor saw her as a reincarnation of her mother. He was not too old to be tempted to try his luck a second time. He seemed unwholesomely pleased with my imminent departure and even had the temerity to add that I was leaving the remarkable Bethan Mair Nichols in good hands. As for the anchorite, he was delighted at the prospect of being left in possession of his outside kitchen. I had to wonder why Bethan so lightly brushed aside my argument 'for a clean slate' and getting rid of the creature. She was treating him kindly and he responded with an all-too-visible desire to please.

He approached me with raised shoulders, that could have been a demonstration of diffidence, on the subject of translation. He was struggling with an adaptation of a German philosophical prose poem into Cymraeg: by a Jewish writer called Buber. I had to admit I had never heard of it. It was all about the 'I and thou' experience. Then he corrected himself. 'Not experience,' 'relationship.' That struck a chord. Something to chew on. Unfortunately Bethan interrupted by suggesting I should give him a hand. Out of politeness I had to agree but I quickly added that that sort of writing was not really my cup of tea. And in any case I was going away, 'When you come back then,' she said, giving each of us a brilliant smile.

I was so wracked with suspicions I had to speak out before I left. Bethan just laughed and hugged and kissed me. 'Listen you silly old Swiss roll, we are used to separation and we can stand it because we trust each other.' I was still uneasy. 'And love each other,' I said, not without a note of timid challenge. 'And love each other of course,' she said.

For several days I behave like a prisoner resolved not to break down under interrogation. There is a great deal of work in the office to catch up with: not to mention the usual repercussions of office politics among the higher-ups liable to trickle down and effect everyday practice among the foot soldiers and labourers at the coal face, or in the vineyard, whichever cliché happens to be in favour at the moment. Accusations of corruption and nepotism are never far away in an international institution where interest groups of one sort or another are forever burrowing away like rabbits in an outsized warren.

Then there are the pleasantries, and irritations, of everyday life in Rome. At my own pace I allow myself to be drawn back into the routines of the social circles that revolve around the organisation that employs me. I suppose I fit in best with Freddy Helmut's circle because he is my immediate superior. I acknowledge this is a sign of weakness and an inability to strike out on my own. I blame, if I even bother to think about it, a series of fiascos, conspicuous among them the faded memory of Rosie Lorenz and the embarrassment of that Paola Something-or-other's mother looking at me down her nose.

On a Saturday morning over a Campari soda on a terrace facing the Parthenon Freddy introduced me to Alison. Alison Fettle. A very nice person, he says in his expansive way before she arrives. 'English, Eddie old boy. A compatriot of yours.' 'I'm not English.' It's an automatic response I seem to have used before. 'Well, British then. Or Welsh. Or whatever you like to call it.' 'I'm not British.' He is amused by my stubborn but decently subdued surliness. 'International,' I say boldly even if it sounds absurd while I say it. Freddy chuckles away while he makes up a witty response. 'Born in mid-ocean?' he says. 'Or was it in an aeroplane?' I don't think it is a matter I could take so lightly. Why should there not be a new breed of international civil servants unencumbered with nationalistic luggage? It is at least a proposition worthy of serious discussion and not just the raw material of badinage.

115

Alison I found charming and sympathetic, responding with polite restraint to Freddy Helmut's boisterous welcome. He invites her to sit next to me because he says we have a lot in common. He looks mischievously mysterious as he says this and orders another Campari soda all round. What we have in common apparently was we were both at Cambridge, she of course, I insist gallantly, after my time. All the same her face looks more worn than her body. She marches along with a sturdy ballet dancer's walk but I detect a certain sadness in her exopthalmic gaze, and her generous lower lip tends to hang down. She is a specialist in paper restoration and at present she has a commission in the Villa Julia that will keep her in Rome for at least the next five months. Documents and letters and so on. She finds it very soothing. My comment, that the world seems to be governed by documents and letters, seems tangential but she smiles just the same. It is quite agreeable to converse with a sympathetic woman not connected with the U.N.F.A.O. Freddy Helmut rather spoils it later by slapping me on the back. 'None of my business, old fruit, but it will do no harm to exercise a bit of freedom. Speaking as an independent observer I would say the Alison lady quite fancies you.' When he gets bored with statistics and estimates and logistics, he quite likes playing a jovial Mephistos to my naïve Faust. I resent being so transparent. How did he gather things weren't going all that well between Bethan and me?

He calls me a square with an inclination to brood. When things are not going so well in the office his criticisms always grow more personal. Maybe I am stiff and square. It has to be my inbred reaction to the haphazard flamboyance of my father. I am attached to lexicons because they are so much more reliable. I have to admit to a thirst for certainties. Then again that outside kitchen anchorite Curig Puw could well be on to something when he mutters on about that 'I and thou' business. My shortcomings are all to do with intimate relationships. When you feel trapped inside yourself you need an outlet. Bethan seems to have cut herself off from me: become absorbed in that shop that from this distance looks more like the yawning mouth of a pit. Does a place like that appear preferable to her than living with me? If I can't relate to the woman I love how can I ever confidently relate to other people?

Alison is an agreeable young woman. She has a soft and pliable manner. We enjoy parallel interests so that we can attend concerts and exhibitions and visit museums together. I estimate that as our friendship ripens I may be able to take her into my confidence and perhaps gain the advantage of a woman's point of view on my stalled relationship with Bethan. Well before that, I am aware that she has troubles of her own: born in Croydon the daughter of a bank manager and a school teacher mother, her parents were appalled when she went to live with an Arab called Aziz whom she had met in an Islamic Art exhibition in the British Museum. He was apparently extremely courteous and attentive. He was a scientist with a degree in some specialised aspect of metallurgy that she admits now she never quite understood. It appears she never quite understood Aziz either.

They had been married a year before she discovered the machinery he exported were armaments. Early one morning he set out for his office in the East End of London and she never saw him again. There were police and Foreign Office enquiries, and she was told Aziz had at least one wife and a family living in Kuwait. There was no record that he had ever rejoined them and the probability was that he had been killed. In any event the effect on Alison had been shattering. She found the world such a dangerous place that she retreated into her restoration work. To this day she felt happiest and most secure in the basement of a museum patiently piecing fragments of paper together. She speaks with a nervous self-deprecating laugh that I find the most attractive thing about her. We seem to belong to the same delicate species that is easily hurt as it flutters against the unyielding iron bars of limited experience.

Rather sooner than I anticipate or indeed would have wished our friendship developed into a comfortable routine. In some curious way Alison has begun to assume that I am a new friend eager to be of service. It could be that Freddy Helmut has in his genial way encouraged her to think in this direction. He was vastly amused when I rejected his offer of the chalet in the vineyard for a weekend of relaxation with Alison whom he described as 'my new admirer'. I was shocked at his insensitivity. Without indulging in high-flown phrases that is a bower sacred to the presence of my still-beloved Bethan.

By the same token, as my friendship with Alison progresses, I find it too difficult to take her into my confidence over my difficulties with Bethan. I adopt a pose of quiet despondency that verges on world-weariness and Alison takes it upon herself, as she puts it, 'to broaden my aesthetic horizons.' I might possess a range of talents as a linguist and statistician, or even pianist and mechanic, but these were techniques that bordered on the mechanical. The world of art, she insists, offers infinite consolations of which I appear to her to be barely aware. Since I am naturally inclined to be self-critical I accept her gentle admonitions with good grace. For instance, I listen harder and more carefully to Mahler and it is true this way I find the music more coherent and beautiful.

Alison takes my hand and I feel bound to squeeze it in gratitude. She rewards me with an understanding smile. Later in her small flat which I find overheated, she introduces me to Goethe's *Römische Elegien*. How could I possibly live in Rome and not be aware of them? I behave suitably crestfallen. It could be that there is a whole sphere of artistic experience that I have never encountered. 'Aber die Nachte hindurch,' Goethe sings, 'keep him busy in a different way. Even if he is only half instructed Love will make him doubly happy.' Alison moves closer to me. She murmurs there are feelings we could safely explore together. Aziz had been a dangerous lover with a sado-masochist inclination that had aroused in her sexual desires she had no idea existed. What she needs is a gentler man who could satisfy her without any frightening overtones of brutality.

It must have been at this point that my deep attachment to Bethan stumbled out. She listened sympathetically her bulging eyes fixed on my face as I struggled to be as truthful as I could. Even as I spoke she grasped my trousers where they were loose around my thighs and drew me towards her. She had a compelling need and it was my duty to satisfy her. For her it may have been a feast at a golden table, but I very much doubt it. For my own part I was overwhelmed with guilt. Not so much as having been disloyal or even duplicitous: this had been a curious incident in the night that Bethan need know nothing about. My problem was how to disentangle myself from a murky involvement with Alison Fettle without being brutally frank. At such close quarters I found her unattractive if not downright unwholesome. And yet she continued to treat me as some kind of Galahad who had arrived in her life at a crucial time when she was about to give up all human contact and lock herself away in some monastic museum basement. I had a role to escape from that felt like a rope around my neck.

Freddy Helmut is highly amused when he catches me making discreet enquiries about the possibility of an overseas attachment. There is a food distribution in the Sudan that is in need of the services of a statistician and something similar in the Eastern Congo that also requires fluent French! 'What's this? What's this? A sudden urge to move closer to the sound of gunfire? Isn't Rome exciting enough for you old fruit? Or is it a case of Potiphar's wife making a snatch at our Joseph?' I don't need to do more than smile. Freddy is always the most appreciative of his own heavy-footed humour. My embarrassment rises like a temperature as the days go by. I do not wish to reach the stage when I will be crossing the street to avoid her.

Bethan has taken to writing lengthy e-mails. 'More satisfying than broken conversations.' She says that in

Pentregwyn she has more time to think, and she has been delighted to discover that Sulwen's papers are fascinating. In the fifties and even earlier she had kept a diary which gave a fascinating picture of a unique way of life that had virtually vanished. She was greatly tempted to edit them for publication. Something in the native tongue along the lines of Kilvert's diary. What did I think? Was she being ridiculously ambitious? There follows a sequence of snippets of the precepts and perceptions of Sulwen Bowen. All this Bethan writes, as the great world goes rumbling and rolling on in the distance. And how soon would it be before I could get away and visit her? She missed the cool calm of my conversation, and the poor old Land Rover stood in need of some specialist attention.

I treasure her e-mails of course even though what I really want to hear is that she can't live without me. I add the e-mails to an old rosewood box, the little box of keepsakes and talismans, like the nail file with a pearl handle she left behind and the small photographs which are rare because she insists she always prefers to be on the other side of the camera. In my quiet way I am suffering quite a lot and there is no available comfort in reality. Alison Fettle, poor thing, was a false trail and all that episode has left me with is an extra burden of guilt. Is it all that unmanly to dream of domestic felicity? If Bethan won't respond to my pleading, which is now in the open and which she knows all about, perhaps I would be better employed in Sierra Leone or the Sudan than mooching about Rome feeding my self-pity.

A shaft of unexpected relief arrives in the shape of an urgent message from Juan-les-Pins. My father is in hospital and needs to see me as soon as possible. I make hurried arrangements at work and take a couchette on the night train to Nice. For some reason, whenever I make this journey, it always seems to be raining and I am always inadequately prepared. I arrive in the hospital wet through and I find my father sitting up in bed looking exceptionally pleased with himself.

'Ah, my dear boy. Nothing to worry about. Good news in fact. They've turned me inside out and declared me fit for further use. You will be delighted to hear I'm about to get married. I thought you'd like to attend the wedding!'

Eleven

'I THOUGHT I WAS going down hill pretty fast, I don't mind telling you. All alone by the telephone and all that sort of thing. And along comes 'Daisy Green as was' to pick me up and make me feel like a million dollars. Quite literally as it happens.'

He grins like a cat eyeing a bowl of cream. I am amazed, myself. It is as if his two worlds of fantasy and embroidered fact had suddenly merged to leave him sitting in the nursing home day room like a monarch on a golden throne listening to the invisible chorus of a heavenly choir celebrating his triumph. There is absolutely nothing wrong with him and his whole world is blooming. Through the window we have a view of the palm trees and the porphyry rocks in the cerulean sea and I am supposed to admire his sparkling new blue dressing gown and soft leather slippers and say how well he looks. He is the great actor granting a frank interview to a reporter not a father talking to his son.

'Amazing business really. I don't know what I was doing in Aix to be honest with you, let alone in St-Sauveur. I've got a vague recollection that somebody or other hadn't turned up. The fact is St-Sauveur turned out to be my saviour. Old Pinky Grosvenor used to say if you wait around long enough something is bound to turn up. Actors' superstition you could say. There they were anyway. The batteries on the Ambassador's motorised wheelchair had run out and dear old Daisy was having a hell of a job trying to push it. The fact is I offered to help before I recognised her. But she recognised me all right. There you are you see, dear boy. Fame has its own residue of rewards.'

He looks unbearably pleased with himself. I begin to wonder how many things can happen in this world when you're not looking. Or should I say when a father and a son share an equal lack of interest in what either gets up to? Would that be classified as lack of caring? Why should the fault seem to be more on my side than on his?

'She played small parts in several things I was in. A real trouper though, small part or no small part. I used to call her Dinkie. Dinkie Daisy. Very light on her feet. Anyway as she tells it now, she had her eye on me. And it may well be I gave her some encouragement. A perfect figure I remember. Very beautiful in her own way. No doubt about it.'

He gives a small wave of the hand like a connoisseur of female pulchritude viewing in his mind's eye his extensive collection.

'This American chap selling grease paint and sun lotion fell in love with her. After my time it must have been. Not quite rags to riches but by dint of hard work I imagine he rose to become Chairman of the Corporation or whatever they call it these days in the Land of the Free, and ended up being an Ambassador in one of those South American republics. Uruguay or Paraguay. Can't remember which. You'll have to ask her. She'll be along in a minute. Trouble is old Eugene was a heavy smoker. Sixty a day man who couldn't kick the habit. Business stress to blame poor old chap used to say. And in the end the old lungs packed in. Very decent chap. French descent you see. Very civilised. Unlike most Yanks. Always grateful to me for giving Daisy a helping hand.'

He gives a sigh of satisfaction and folds his hands across his chest, a picture of virtue rewarded. Role playing, I see it. Which part this time, a royal opportunist or a nimble god flying down from his perch on Mount Olympus? In the day-room, which he seems to have monopolised for his private use, he throws out both arms in a theatrical welcome gesture almost before the ambassador's widow enters. She isn't at all what I expect: not one of those bedizened dowagers he usually consorts with, rattling their jewellry and gold bangles and masked in thick make-up. Daisy Carriere doesn't bustle in, she just appears, thin and thoughtful in a dark trouser suit relieved by a row of pearl buttons.

This is an ambassador's wife accustomed to both formal and awkward occasions. She could easily pass for the well-preserved headmistress of an exclusive girl's school, herself schooled never to make a display of her great wealth. She is so polite and gracious I am compelled to respond in kind, wondering all the time what on earth she sees in him. He basks in her tender expression of concern like a performing seal. It appears there are one or two tests to be declared before he can be discharged. In the meantime Daisy Carriere, soon to become Daisy Lloyd, invites me to lunch with her. With an uncharacter- istic humility Orlando administers a sequence of benevolent waves and I am whisked away in a dark, discreet limousine and we are delivered to a dark, discreet restaurant of her choosing in the Haute Cagne. Everything about Daisy Carriere seems dark and discreet. Years of practice perhaps as an Ambassador's wife. She shows a deep interest in my work. So deep I am unable to resist the temptation of exaggerating its importance. Or could it be that I want her to realise that her intended's son is not a creature to trifle with? To demonstrate the vital impor- tance of the smooth transportation of food relief, I find myself dressing up anecdotes from my own experience to emphasise the significance of my role as well as illustrate the point. Did I really lean out of the open end of a Hercules aircraft to judge the accuracy of the drop? Did I really have a child soldier as a self-appointed personal guard in Mogadishu or did I just see one gesturing at me through the window of our heavily guarded hotel?

The way she listens loosens my tongue. I notice how little she eats. Just a mouthful before she pushes the plate aside. What is she exactly? A thin febrile woman living on illusions, or a practical matron with her feet on hard ground as she treads the wards of this world? How am I to tell? Not by busily presenting an acceptable portrait of Edward C. Lloyd. To steady the compass of my understanding I force myself to keep silent.

'He's very proud of you.'

With quiet skill she brings my father to the centre of the stage. She has a wonderful smile. It radiates guileless goodwill and a youthfulness that defies the approach of old age. The type of woman that looks designed to live for ever.

'We don't know how long we've got, do we?'

I tremble at the realisation that she could be reading my mind as she looks at me across the table.

'I'm determined to give him a good time as long as it lasts. And I think I owe it to you to tell you why.'

I look around the restaurant. All the diners are absorbed in their own expensive meals and conversations. An aspect of my father's past is about to be revealed, a great secret of no consequence to anyone except myself.

'He was a star, you know. A real star. He should have been knighted. He would have been had he taken himself a little more seriously. We all adored him. The thing was he really liked people. The audience and the cast and the technicians. Everybody. His critics used to sniff that he washed himself in people. Maybe he did. They liked it and so did he. As far as I'm concerned, he saved me at a time when I desperately needed saving.'

Looking across the table at the ambassador's widow, so cool and self possessed, I could hardly believe it.

'He doesn't really remember it and I still haven't decided to jog his memory. There was a most disagreeable director and he had taken into his head that I wasn't good enough. The rehearsals were a torment. I may well have been hopeless of course but he seemed to find satisfaction in making me cry. Ridiculous really when you look back at it but at the time it seemed like the end of the world. He decided I'd have to go. "I'm sorry, Daisy. I'm afraid we'll have to find somebody else." Your father put down the newspaper he was reading. All he said was, "Hang on,

Jack. You are being too rough on the girl. If she goes, I go." Then he went on reading the paper. And that was it.'

She is giving me a captivating smile and I realise that it is a reward for being the son of my father. The absurd notion flashes through my mind that she is more my type than his: quiet, sincere, thoughtful, inclined to be fastidious. What on earth did she see in him? If I knew it would be a seismic explosion, like the finite moment that brought about the Big Bang: another man in another universe. A selfless hero with a universe rotating around his selflessness. What gibberish am I reading into her radiant smile? Have I been looking at him through the wrong lens all these years?

'Of course I loved him then. He was so beautiful quite honestly. And so charming. Loved him from a distance you could say. A star-struck girl. And now I can love him by looking after him.'

It is as much of a marvel as a mystery to me that she could have stored her love for this man my father in ecstatic silence for all those years: a living thing in her heart when all the traffic of history went trundling by and she moved around the world from church hall rehearsal rooms to palatial embassies. A vision of constancy that compels me to examine myself. Could I have done it? Does it mean I have to stop moaning about Bethan's reluctance to leave that damned shop and come to live with me?

'I want you to approve if you can.'

That smile holds me in thrall.

'Of course I can.'

Her hand reaches across the table to touch mine. Her hand is thin and cold and I am moved by so much spirit and fragility. As I am by the quietest of quiet weddings in the mayor's parlour. There are more flowers present than people. I am the chief witness. Chairs are provided for the happy couple in view of the bridegroom's weakness after his days in hospital. There is Mario, Daisy's chauffeur and Hortense his wife and her maid. They are devoted to her and they show it. Three or four of Orlando's chums and his number one bridge partner, old Monique Townsend-Tully who I fancy when I look at her from the corner of my eye, looks more disappointed than pleased. Is this her reward for putting up with all his overbidding over the years? Life for Orlando was always a game, or a ceremony or a performance. If he was on the right track what have I missed?

We sip champagne after the ceremony. It seems the happy couple are about to embark on a tour of Spain in the comfort of Daisy's limousine.

'Let the good times, roll!'

Orlando is in high spirits as we clink glasses. He has acquired a rich wife who is determined to give him a good time as long as it lasts: and more than ready to forgive him for the occasional display of vulgarity. He looks like one of those simpletons who waves an overflowing glass at the television cameras after winning the lottery jackpot.

Before they leave he still has a private joke to mutter in my ear.

'No need for those trips to Geneva any more, Eddie, dear boy. It's all yours with my blessing. Along with the old rabbit hutch in Juan-les-Pins. See if you can persuade your little maid of the mountains to come down there and share it with you!'

I can't make out whether it's a blessing or a malediction, but in his eyes it seems no end of a joke. I am receding into a face in the crowd; one among the ranks of an admiring audience who applaud the great actor's glittering performance. To smile approvingly and even clap is the least that I can do. And then after all the muted excitement, they are gone. I feel like a schoolboy who has been abandoned by his parents, left to face life in a new school all alone. I even hear myself mutter, 'They didn't even offer to take me with them.' There was enough room in that vehicle. Mario sat smugly at the wheel with his little wife Hortense alongside him and, inside the cavernous interior, my father and his new wife doubtless still sipping champagne. I am still something left behind.

Being abandoned is the theme tune of my life. I can hear it surge up once again somewhere in the depths of my consciousness.

I retreat to the apartment in Juan-les-Pins, and I have to admit I find it strangely empty. I have never minded fending for myself. It's what I've long been used to and I never used to mind having this place to myself when he went off on one of his hedonistic excursions. There was quite a pleasing shape to his absence and it was a relief not to be pestered by the petty details of his likes and dislikes, the fuss and the grumblings when things were not exactly as he liked them. This time it is different. As if I were shut up in an apartment belonging to a stranger. Even the smell is different. Perhaps the *femme de chambre* had taken to using a different brand of furniture polish?

I am drawn to those green scrap-books that I always felt took up too much space in the overcrowded living-room. This time I find they are insufficiently well ordered. They are not in strict chronological order. The reviews are particularly haphazard. Some appear more than once if they praise but even then they are difficult to date: a long career, endless cuttings, innumerable photographs, in and out of character, casual, social and professional… he had all the leisure in the world. Why on earth had he never catalogued them properly? For the first time ever the thought occurs to me that he might have been expecting me to do it.

I engage in a frantic search for any pictures that could belong to the time when he rescued Daisy Green from a humiliating dismissal. Just how attractive or beautiful as she put it, was he in those days of his success? Just when was it? He seems to have been successful for a much longer period than I have hitherto imagined. In the end I am driven to put the stuff away because it all raises questions about myself and not about my father. He is my closest living relation and yet it seems I am inadequately related to him. If I'm not related to my own father how can I be related to anyone else? I roam about the spaces of the apartment, on and off the narrow balcony, trying to answer these accusations. Every now and then I hear Freddy Helmut's voice in its richest mocking mode: 'Come on now, Eddie old fruit. How do you define your self? Hmm? Well now, let me tell you. There's only one way. You are defined by your relationships. You only mean what you mean to other people. Otherwise you are nothing more than an instrument of consciousness. And since no one has ever been able to define consciousness, in isolation you can't be defined. Outside your relationships old fruit, you are an empty vessel that makes no noise at all.'

Twelve

DEAREST OLD EDDIE; how marvellous! You've acquired a stepmother. Now we both have one in a manner of speaking and we can compare notes! It sounds quite a story and after all he is a charming old rogue if you'll pardon the expression. And why shouldn't old people fall in love and all that. They've lived long enough to appreciate the pleasure. Good luck to them…'

Yes! And what about us? I have a nasty suspicion that girl is beginning to patronise me. I don't know what's happening to my back-bone, if I ever had one. I am degenerating into some form of invertebrate and I should do something about it. But what. Who can I turn to? I don't get any encouragement from the mirror.

Darling Eddie: I'm sitting in the walled garden, walled and wild I have to admit, at the back of Pentregwyn Stores looking at the high white clouds riding in the blue sky and I'm lazy and unspeakably comfortable, dear Eddie, because I've slipped back into a context where, for some inexplicable reason, I belong. This is the real world. I'm happy to stare at the bees in the untidy flower beds and the butterflies in the buddleia without rushing off to find my camera to photograph them. Like the garden I'm running to seed and couldn't care less. I should be doing this and that, but all I do is purr like a cat and lie back in this ancient deck chair. In fact I do have a cat as well as a home of my own. I've just pushed her off my lap to scribble this note to my dearest Eddie. She's called Sheba. She's quite old. All black with a white face and she loves to roll over and have her belly tickled. Curig says Sulwen was very fond of her. He says that in the cat's world I have taken her place...

I never thought I would live to envy a cat. And I am livid and green with jealousy to think of that Curig creature taking my place and dancing attendance on that girl: which means I'm angry with her too and even contemplating some form of revenge before turning around to see there is no form available. I get up in the morning hoping to receive one of her letters and I cling to them and treasure them but in the end they do little to raise my spirits. My only available refuge is dull routine.

My very dear Eddie: things haven't changed. You are still my closest friend and chosen lover. It's just that I'm here, instead of being here, there and everywhere! I think you have rather taken against my poor old shop. The truth is I am attached to the place and can't see myself giving it up in a hurry: but I am here for you whenever you can get here. I'm ready to welcome you with open arms whenever your career allows it...

My career! I didn't know I had one. I would be less disheartened if our signals crossed the void between an empty flat and an empty shop. That shop is far from empty. It seems to be buzzing with ever more life every time I speak to her. My world revolves around the time arranged for a call, but every time it ends becomes a miniature heartbreak. Ever more excitement in a nondescript shop at the heart of a nondescript village and I sit in my office translating and summarising papers concerning the urgent needs of entire populations; and then, avoiding the social gyrations of Freddy Helmut for fear of running into Alison Fettle, slink back to my solitary existence in Via

Baldassare Peruzzi. I seem to be trapped in a web of my own making.

Darling old Eddie: talk about writing the history of a parish! I've made the most exciting discovery. Sulwen had a lover! I'm keeping very mum about it. So far I haven't told anyone about it, (except my Eddie of course.) It all happened a very long time ago, and I'm putting the evidence together piece by piece. In those diaries she was so shy about it she could barely confide in herself. There are even bits of poems, always unfinished, that I suspect must be about him. Things about eyes speaking instead of the tongue, and opening and shutting doors, and secrets of the heart. What a different world it was and yet not so long ago. They had to be so circumspect. Convention ruled, not contraception! I think some of these diaries must have spent some time hidden in a damp place. They are mildewed. Then I came across this sketch-book. That was pretty damp too but I could just about recognise her. A long-faced girl a bit like those dreamy grey girls in Gwen John's paintings. The sketch-book belonged to an Adam Wilde. Just the right name. She refers to him often in the diary for 1949. She calls him the night painter. He liked to paint the world in the moonlight, she says, because it is a better place when everyone is asleep. Whatever went on I calculate it came to an abrupt end well before her father hanged himself. I find it all so mysterious and unfathomable. Not just their secret lives but the way traces remain after they've gone, lying there on the landscape like lichen on the stone walls. A.W. as she calls him lived in a cottage in a little green cwm hidden among steeper hills. Well away from people. He may well have been shell-shocked, or saw something terrible in the war. He was very nervy anyway. She says that. They allowed him to use the piano when he came down for supplies. Her father said it was the least they could do. She could hear him playing Bach from the shop and it lifted her heart. Maybe the lover bit is my imagination but it is quiet clear A.W. meant a hell of a lot to her. There is evidence they met at night. I've started exploring. She mentions the path that goes beyond Hafoty Fach. There is a ruined tyddyn up there that could have been his, hidden in the rowan trees and the brambles and the nettles. He could have been tubercular. There is a mention of him going to a sanatorium. Or could he have gone off his head?... My researches continue...

At least it's me she confides in, so far at least, and that cheers me up a little. Once away from work, I've got more time than I need really for brooding. All the aesthetic beauties of Rome that Alison used to enthuse about make me feel inadequate. I feel I should go in for some more abstract form of intellectual exercise, since I'm supposed to be intelligent. The more I do that the more I realise I don't have an original thought in my head. I was designed to be a man of action. My mother used to whisper, 'At least try and do a bit of good in the world while you're in it,' as though she had failed to do so herself in spite of her obvious gifts. And the would-be man of action sits in an office translating and summarising other people's cogitation and making statistical records usually to prove that not enough has been done. If only I could break this spell perhaps I could apply for a mission and achieve a piece of useful field work.

Dearest Eddie: We may be a bit lost these days. The reason is there are so many things we need to find out. I agree we should make a greater effort to help each other and my first aid is to tell you to stop denigrating yourself and your capabilities. You are my best friend and chosen lover and I hope I am yours. Isn't that an achievement in itself? Or a plus at least.

Our paths crossed and we have made them criss-cross and one fine day they will join and we'll be together, that is if you can put up with all the baggage I have accumulated on the way, like all the stuff I'm collecting here. I am still on the track of Sulwen's secrets, her 'inwardness'. Curig goes on a lot about 'inwardness' so I am beginning to get a glimpse of what he means. He calls it the burning bush inside us. That had me sneaking off to look it up in one of Sulwen's Bibles. I say one of them because I've never seen so many about a place. Leather-bound and crumbling some of them. It's all in Exodus, chapter three if you want to look it up Professor Cynddylan. And take off your shoes when you read it. I did. And would you believe it, 'the place on which you stand is holy ground!' And quick as a flash it occurred to me that in a sense it was Sulwen's shop! I think it's time you came here to sort out my mystic muddle.

Mind you I have come to one or two conclusions as I contemplate my next move. We live by what appeals to us. You appeal to me because of your tenderness and understanding for example. And this place appeals to me because it makes me understand better what it is my family down in cosy Cardiff have been making a fuss about all my life, i.e. it isn't just the language and all the protesting and raving that goes with it: it's the way it's related to the landscape. You need the native words to express just how beautiful the country is – so there you are. Rain or shine in my ramshackle shop I'll sing it. Love me, love my Pentregwyn Stores! Oh dear, I can hear you laughing all over the Alps…

Sometimes this girl appears so completely turned around I don't recognise what I'm looking at. Except of course that I'm not looking at her. That is the great privilege denied to me as I thumb my way through a massive lexicon of Serbo-Croat. My taste for language exploration is somewhat blunted. Bethan is getting positively preachy. Do we just seek a world like a fairground through which we can pass like tourists looking for pleasure and avoiding responsibility? She was the free spirit, I was the desk-bound bureaucrat and still am. She is the one who is changing and I am the fellow running to keep up with her. Which is strange enough since she seems determined to tie herself to that one place. I have to wonder how long it will last.

Dearest Eddie: help! Alarm bells are ringing. I got up this morning and looked through the window of my bedroom above the shop and what should I see before rubbing my eyes but a BMW parked on the road outside the shop and a man and woman inside arguing. My father and my mother no less. Dear old Alwyn was clinging to the steering wheel as if he were refusing to get out and the fearsome Lowri you could say was remonstrating forcefully. It was a bit early to drop in after all. I retreated from the window before they could see me and took my time to get dressed and get my mind adjusted and prepared for any eventuality. When I did open up they were all over me. At least Lowri was. I had forgotten how overwhelming her presence could be. She's a big powerful female in every sense of the word and her good intentions can be quite overwhelming. I have to make a special effort to prevent myself from stiffening up and becoming stubbornly unresponsive.

She is full of what she calls the Spirit of Reconciliation. If the shop is what I want and all that goes with it, then that without any question on their part is what I should have. Peace and Love all round and forgiveness like the balm of Gilead. But, and within less than a couple of hours, Lowri's 'but's start flowing. There is the whole question of economics. Ideals are well and good and she is all for them, but where is the capital coming from to achieve them? They are here to help. They want to play a part, because in spite of all the painful differences in the past, in the end, we are all on the same side are we not?... Oh dear. Eddie my love I am in danger of being suffocated with assistance. I wish you were here. I devotedly wish. I need the cool clarity of your reasoning. I really do. Is there no chance you can get away?...

She doesn't seem to understand that the cool clarity of my reasoning has long since evaporated. It's not just a case of what appeals to me either. Male and female, Madame Bethan Mair, are constructed to complement and not to compete with each other. The bliss of domesticity, which is what appeals to me, depends on mutual aid and moral support and physical compatibility. The last is very important, and wholly delightful, but has no permanence without the other two elements being constantly active and available so what we share Madame, at the moment, when you get right down to it, is a clash of wills. All that holds us together is what is pulling us apart. We are stretched as washing drying in a desert wind between the two poles of our separate wills. You want me there and I want you here. If this moulding mother of yours is taking over and doing all the things you approve of and agree with, why the devil not leave her to it. And why can't I summon up the courage to put this simple conclusion on paper: even in the form of an ultimatum? The answer is simple too. The greatest fear of all is the fear of losing you.

My dearest old rock, Eddie ap Cynddylan: things are hotting up on the Pentregwyn Front, and that's putting it mildly. The mighty Lowri my moulding mother has resumed the dangerous practice of mothering me to bits, and I have to make a constant effort not to relax into a sulky rebellious adolescent. About everything it seems I was always right and she was always wrong. She is more 'me' than me. So how am I supposed to cope with that? She has extracted my teeth before I can bite! She talks about going back to square one. That means, I think, picking up the revolution where it was left off when my birth mother died. Everything from now on will be for the glorious memory of Ffion and all she stood for and of course for dear old Sulwen, who has made the miraculous resumption possible. I don't know whether to laugh or cry. She has quite forgotten the nasty battle she must have fought over my head when I was a three year old 'little princess' playing with the toy scales on the floor of this shop. She talks quite freely about 'dear Ffion' and 'dear old Sulwen' in a way I never heard before, and she's taken to marching around the place as though she had taken possession of the title deeds of their blessed memory.

The fact is she is taking over and I've got to devise some means of checking her without causing her to storm off in a huff likely to last years rather than months. My cowardly father has fled back to Cardiff on the excuse of having vital work to attend to. The National Assembly could never get along without him. He has retired to the peace and quiet of his administrative bunker. And Doctor Seth has done a bunk too. He claims he has an aunt in Eifionydd in urgent need of his medical attentions. Lowri and her renewed enthusiasms are just too much for him. I think there is more to it than that. She knows enough about his past to hold an easy upper hand. He seemed unnaturally subdued in her presence, reconciliation and all that, or no. She is making waves and stirring up things in the calm or even stagnant waters where he fished peacefully to his own satisfaction. He still sighs for the days when Sulwen gave them tea and presided over their abstract discussions. Many were the happy arguments they had, the jolly carpenters of song, over the rival merits of strict and free metres, of Kibbutzim and Danish Folk Schools and Amish communities: all of which Lowri treats with sniffy contempt. Was there ever a people, she says, that were so ready to accept the word in place of the deed.

Before she turned up I felt positively relaxed and comfortable in this place. Very ready to live on nostalgia and vegetate for the time being: and there was every prospect of 'for the time being' lasting for ever or unless until you turned up and maybe found it in your heart to like Bethan's little shop. All I want is my former General Stores divided into four: the book shop and lending library; the refreshment corner; the organic fruit and veg section and the crafts and picture gallery. All in the best possible taste. And upstairs my darkroom and studio. I don't want grants from the County Council, or from Cardiff, or Brussels, all of which would be necessary to launch Lowri's great co-operative project that would include a large chunk of the parish.

She proposes a Friends of Pentregwyn Society and that legal Olwen Caradog-Jones is all for it. They have rather taken to each other. They worship together at the shrine of Ffion my sainted birth mother. And I suppose I do too. The Society declares our language is the only effective weapon we have for the defence of our homeland and we need to sharpen the weapon and use it aggressively since the best defence is attack. Who could disagree with that? I mean I agree with all Lowri's principles: it's just that she's trying to run before we've learned to walk. I think my mute mystic Curig agrees with me but he won't speak up. I don't think it's because he's afraid although you could quite easily think so.

Yesterday we had a comic interlude at supper. He declined one of Lowri's vegetarian dumplings. She was quite hurt and annoyed. In that outside kitchen he lives on bread and cheese and strong tea. He says he'll eat anything so long as it's always the same and he even went as far as to suggest we had too many principles and not enough faith. Huh, says Lowri, faith isn't much good without works. She thought she'd settled the argument, but he came back with an answer he looked very pleased with. Nobody has ever made a picture of the invisible, he said, but that doesn't mean it isn't there!

Oh dear, oh dear Eddie. Am I anything more than what Lowri made me? I'm feeling quite overpowered these days. I find it easier to define my dead mother than my living self and you can't be more unsure of yourself than that. I need you like a child learning to ride a bicycle needs stabilisers. Come and stabilise me, my darling. I need my scrunchy Eddie to be here to comfort me…

That silly word scrunchy convinced me that something had to be done. Somehow or other we had to get back to each other. Life without our ecstatic embraces was no life at all. In the office when I judged Freddy Helmut was in the right mood, I broached the question. I knew how busy things were and so on, but was there any possibility of my applying for leave of absence, without pay, of course. A matter of three or four months along the lines of an academic sabbatical. Whatever his mood might have been, he responded with a frown that was on the verge of a scowl. 'Eddie old fruit,' he said in a way that he knew I would resent, 'have you never heard the story of brother Stalin and brother Trotsky?' Whether I had or not, he was determined to tell me! 'Trotsky kept on dashing off. Stalin never left the office. Trotsky ended up with an ice pick in his skull. End of story.'

When he felt I had been sufficiently discouraged he went on to belabour his point.

'Eddie, you and I are Europeans. The last of an old breed. The world is no longer Eurocentric. Neither are our jobs, old fruit. You ought to see the application forms.

There are Indonesians and Indians and highly qualified citizens of Bongo-bongoland just lining up to take them over. Elegant French is no longer an essential qualification. Go away for three months and there is no guarantee your job will be here when you get back.'

It was his attitude that shocked me. It showed the true state of affairs underneath our pretence of friendship, comradeship, unbuttoned intimacies. I was his henchman, a dependent he was ready to indulge and from whom he expected unswerving loyalty. I was his private jester taken on to listen to his jests, the necessary foil in the office charade of youthfulness that kept this ageing *roué* going. He would exercise whatever power he had to keep me in line. The pleasures of the chalet by the lake, the illusion of a country residence, were nothing better than rewards or bribes, and related to the exigencies of his existence rather than mine. The upshot of this cold douche of analysis was an overwhelming sense of isolation. It seemed to bring the whole of my existence into question. I had always justified a close collaboration with a man I did not altogether admire with the conviction that at least the work we were doing did some good. The simple truth was that it could be done equally well and probably even better by somebody else. Our so-called gifts and qualifications were distinctly peripheral. We had never been more than names on application forms transformed into convenient cogs in an international machine.

Thirteen

THE FACT IS in this world everyone wants something and it shames me to confess that when I was told a Father Afonso from Portugal was waiting to see me at Reception, my intelligence was instantly exercised trying to work out what he wanted. The moment I saw his fresh honest face and shook his hand I was forced to a conclusion that quite humbled me. This was a man who wanted nothing except the warmth of friendship and the opportunity of doing good. As ever he radiated unstinting goodwill. He had penetrated the F.A.O. fortress like an angelic visitor from a more cheerful dispensation. He was a temporary guest at the Irish College and on his way to East Timor and in his expansive open-hearted way asked if I would like to go with him.

It was a characteristic pleasantry rather than an authentic invitation, yet even as we laughed, I began to take it seriously. He was the kind of man who tended to make things happen. He had friends and collaborators all over the world. The Order he belonged to was an organisation so much more venerable and in so many ways more flexible than ours. The Franciscans, like the poor, had always been with us and they did not suffer from our politicised millennial fever that claimed all the world's ills were curable if only we hurled sufficient technological advance at them. There was no doubt that he would be as interested in looking at the headquarters of the organisation I worked for, as in renewing our friendship. With that ease of unencumbered procedure that had astonished me at Evora, he had acquired the use of a speedy Alfa Romeo.

In no time at all, in spite of the usual strangulations of Roman traffic I am sitting alongside him as we turn off the Appian Way into side roads he is familiar with.

'I love Rome,' Afonso says. 'But I can't wait to get out of it!'

His Italian is better than his English. He explains it was his years of living and studying in Rome that had first awakened his interest in anthropology and prehistory.

'The weight of the Eternal City,' he says. 'Here you can get crushed by History. The only way I found to escape was to retreat further back. Further and further. To get face to face with the original bare bones of the human situation.'

In those days he used to love to get away to the Alban Hills: I Castelli. He would take me now to the café on the square at Ariccia where students used to toast each other's health in the Pope's wine. Once again I am the travelling companion of a man of the black cloth, schooled in rigorous religious routine, celebrating mass every morning before sallying forth into a waiting world, ready for anything, exuding his own brand of carefree pilgrimage. I have always been inclined to envy Catholics the trick of finding a dark box where they can go and spill the beans to a complete stranger. With a good friend and companion, such as Father Afonso so charmingly offers himself to be, if I unburdened myself to the depth of my discontented being, there is a danger he would cease to respect me. A small man always has his dignity to think about. The more insignificant the more dignity required.

'And how is our good friend, dear Call-me-Bethan? Shall I see her perhaps?'

'Call-me-Bethan' was a feeble joke made when we first set out on our trips together. The memory of those first rapturous days in the Alentejo came flooding back.

'Alas,' I say. 'She is far away. Hidden in her green Welsh hills.'

'Is that so. You looked so suited to each other, if I may say so. I half expected to find you married by now...'

'If only...'

I am lost to find an appropriate answer. I am so

shaken by the conjunction of his expectation and my own yearning. He is tactful as ever.

'Priests and old maids. Always so curious in these matters.'

I attempt an account of our chequered love affair that will not render it trivial in the sight of a man whose whole way of life is a concern for the poor and the sick. My complaint could well appear nothing to complain about. Our affair would only become of consequence if it were stable and responsible. Flighty infatuation would mean little to a man whose day was pivoted on private devotion followed by service to others. I pick out a picture that is more than anything a defence and apology for Bethan's behaviour and mine.

The road Afonso takes winds through groves of chestnut and oak to reach Nemi above the lake. Everything looks calm and golden in the evening light. Terraces from princely palaces descend steeply to the lake lying like a polished mirror in its deep hollow. We sit at a café table and we seem to have come high up the slope to marvel at the immemorial beauty of the landscape.

'Love is a great mystery!'

I doubt whether Afonso is still concentrating on the relationship between Bethan and myself. It seems more likely the view has inspired him to think of the world in general. I suppose for him, in a sense Rome has to be the hub of the universe. In my little case, the hub of the universe is wherever Bethan happens to be which means Pentregwyn Stores, an establishment for which I have more antipathy than affection. Afonso waves a hand at a world suffused with the golden glow of a Roman sunset.

'It's wonderful,' he says. 'The world is wonderful. It should be enough. But it never is.'

Perhaps he is contemplating our strained relationship after all. Lovers apart have nothing more than the idea of love to keep them going. He has the religious love which is sacred, we have ours which is profane. What does profane mean anyway? In our case a heathen rite, worship of a physical body. He would see our abstinences as something to put up with not to complain about.

'You think we are restless and ungrateful? We never have enough?'

I fancy a cheerful response in the polemical manner we had enjoyed in the Alentejo but I hear myself being plaintive. I am bewailing my loved one's absence, longing to view the world through her lustrous eyes.

'We demand magic,' he says. 'We require it. We can't live without it. I've always wanted to write a book on the subject. I do not imagine I ever will. There are practices in East Timor that need to be recorded before they disappear for ever. Taboos that keep robbers away. A house where nothing can be touched. Reserved for the dead. We need to record them before the whole population settles down to watch television. Usually from America or Australia.'

I am curious about East Timor. I know it is a small country that has been through a lot. A Cause. But now it becomes a Place because my friend is going to work there, restoring schools and hospitals and churches after civil war. He is a man to admire.

'I've got a sermon about it,' he says. 'About magic. I call it "The only magic that counts". It goes down well. In Portuguese at least. I can get to East Timor in twenty-four hours. That's magic. As the song keeps telling us we live in a wonderful world but we torment it and we torment each other and ourselves with our appetites and our greed. And these are multiplied rather than modified by the magic of technology and science. So that is black magic. So we need a more powerful magic to escape.'

He is smiling at me waiting for me to respond. I am tempted by say 'abracadabra', but in this place at this time with the sacred lake disappearing in the shadow while the sky is still burnished with sunset it doesn't seem appropriate.

'For me, as a good Catholic, Transubstantiation. The magic of Christ's blood. The mass that is available to me every day. The magic formula for harnessing the power of

God which we believe is the power of love and the reason for our existence.'

A cool breeze rises from the woods. Like the strength of his conviction it makes me shiver slightly.

'There's my sermon for you. It goes down well in Portuguese. After all, the fifth most widely spoken language in the world.'

I determine to be bold.

'What if the magic doesn't work?'

'Well, that's up to you, when you take it in. That completes the magic. "Does the trick," as they say in English.'

We agree it is time to go and eat. He knows just the place in Ariccia.

'Back to technology Mister Eddie Lloyd. Just think, a hundred years ago we would have hired a donkey and been famished before reaching Ariccia.'

In his company I am relaxed and more cheerful than I have been for a very long time. Life can be very pleasant even when you don't get what you most want. After all, that must be the condition in which most people live, so what have I got to complain about? Afonso has this gift of creating a happy atmosphere. I don't know whether the proprietor of this family trattoria remembers him but he treats us as honoured guests. A special wine is produced, the meal is a lamb speciality of the house and the proprietor hovers around waiting for signs of approval which Afonso duly delivers in his usual genial style. The wine loosens him up and he is all set for one of those wide-ranging discussions he always enjoyed so much.

'Technology and science, my dear friend, are wonderful, but I don't see how they can ever change the human condition in the way that magic can. Of course they can create a virtual reality, a sort of cyberspace in which plastic souls can circulate for ever like the damned in the circles of Dante's Inferno. But in the real creation we have to be willingly circumscribed by Death and the Laws of Thermodynamics. No death. No fertility. They know all about it in East Timor. And so did our remote ancestors when Diana accepted their worship in the sacred grove down there. But I tell you what. We can enjoy a bit of technological magic!'

From his pocket he extracts a glistening new mobile phone.

'My companion,' he says. 'I never go anywhere without it. Next to communion, communication is all! Call-me-Bethan, old friend: what is her number? Let us give her a call and tell her we are thinking of her and wish she was here.'

I am not so sure this is a good idea. He would be a third party intruding on a very delicate stage of our tangled relationship. And how am I to behave? With coolness and restraint or collapse into a self-pitying whine. And how would it look to her? A pair of inebriated diners enjoying an after dinner joke? I give way to his unrelenting benevolence. She takes some time to answer. I don't believe she recognises his voice until he explains who he is and where he is and who he is with. Once they have exchanged benevolent greetings there's little more to say except that he is passing the little handphone to me.

'Eddie my love. You won't believe this. Or perhaps you will in the company of dear old Afonso. Who do you think has turned up here? None other than the great Jens. Jens Strangerup. He is quite bowled over by the story of Sulwen. He wants to make a film about it, called Sulwen's Room. Isn't that wonderful? And of course it throws everything here into the most tremendous turmoil. I'll write to you about it. All very amazing. The sooner the better you get here, darling Eddie. Love to you both! Bye now!'

I hand back the technological pest to its owner. Afonso is looking at me expectantly. What emotion am I expected to display? Joy at the sound of the loved one's voice of course: a single sound swimming in an ether of undiscriminating affection. This man is too good for this world or for my little world anyway which is seething with suppressed jealousy. What can I begin to tell him?

'It's all go there apparently,' I say. 'Some people have turned up from Denmark. More film people. Disturbing the peace as usual.'

I feel my voice is croaking with the effort of appearing rational and self-contained. I launch out on a description of Bethan's inheritance which is critical and yet as cool and objective as I can make it. The girl is torn between her creative ambitions in the flimsy uncertain film business and her local attachments. Pentregywn is an economic backwater living on memories of a more prosperous past, on illusions, and on a living language which is perhaps all they have really got and is stubbornly refusing to die. Afonso listens eagerly. 'Interesting,' he keeps saying. 'Interesting' – with the studied enthusiasm of an anthropologist viewing an unusual case. He is trying to fit in all this with an overall view of the European condition, which seems to be dominated, we think, by the twin dynamic of technology and American wealth and military might.

I urge him to drop me off on the Aventino. I say a walk home will help me to digest the pleasures of our trip. A gust of wind from the Circo Massimo sends red dust swirling around the street lighting giving a dim ghostly tinge that suits my discomforted mood. Was there a threat behind the excited impatient voice on the mobile phone? Whether she meant it that way or not this was an exercise in female power. Diana of the Woods had taken up residence in Pentregwyn and it was up to her worshippers to follow her there. My suspicions and my misgivings multiply by the minute. So he thinks, does he, this Danish genius that I have never set eyes on, that the story of Sulwen and her shop would make a fabulous film? Assuming that is the case, which I very much doubt, how in the hell did he hear the story in the first place? How indeed except though her, which can only mean she has been in regular contact with this Jens creature all along. I thought I was the only one to share the secret. The truth is I may be only one of a legion of her correspondents. She sits with her laptop all day long, leaving her mother to do the work, dispatching e-mails to a whole circle of admirers and suitors.

They probably include the winsome and willowy Barry Parrott. He has a certain physical attraction. She said so herself in the early days of our friendship. About this Jens she said, I remember her saying, 'He's hairy and as ugly as sin, but some women find him irresistible.' The recollection of her most casual remarks acquire a nasty capacity to sear my mind with the sizzle of a burning brand-iron. 'Jens is so intense and dedicated, he trembles all the time. Mind you, he can be inspiring to work with, but I keep my distance, especially after I overheard him say, "That Bethan creature is the most beautiful female since Venus De Milo had her arms sliced off!" Why should I remember such a daft remark?'

Why indeed. Oh why? So much of her charm lay in her habit of disparaging what I called her beauty. 'Thank heaven you love me for my idle chatter, Eddie darling,' she would say. What do I really know about this girl? I need some reassurance that I am something more than another collector's-item. Another trophy. The mere sound of her voice on that mobile is enough to make me question what exactly all the words we have exchanged mean. And that must mean questioning even the meaning of my existence.

Dearest Eddie: I'm doing my best not to get over-excited but it is the most thrilling and unexpected thing to have happened. You should see my mother's face! Dear old mother Lowri doesn't know whether she is coming or going – most likely going, I suspect. I heard her whisper 'Who is this hairy monster?' and in a way I can quite understand her confusion. Jens doesn't care at all what kind of impression he makes. He is convinced he is 'the most talented film-maker of his generation' – someone wrote that about him in one of those Danish film mags and he firmly believes it. It does make you realise you've got to believe in yourself before you can get anything worthwhile done. Anyway he was bowled over by the story of Sulwen and her shop and he's here in all his trembling and shivering assertiveness determined to make a film about it. He is roaming about the place with a video camera making his own kind of reccy that he can study while he makes up his mind what exactly he wants to do. He says he loves everything about the place, laced curtains, old ladies, locked chapel, empty shelves and dirty outhouses and over-grown churchyards... the lot. Coming from a flat country he stares at the hills and the wooded valleys and the shapes of our deserted slate quarries as if they had been thrown up just to astonish him. That's the secret of his talent, I think.

You'll think I've been bitten by the film bug again and I suppose I have but I'm determined to manage it in a more measured and crafty manner. I think I can promise that! Meanwhile, dear Eddie, I am the very interested spectator of a power struggle between the great film-maker and my mother who tends to regard Jens as an overpowering and irritating visitor from outer space. She says rude things about him to me in Cymraeg and he declares he needs complete creative control, as he calls it. While he is making his mind up how to proceed absolutely nothing should be changed. Tensions are rising by the day. Lowri says whatever form his film takes, documentary, romantic fiction, whatever it has to be in Cymraeg otherwise it would be an insult to Sulwen's memory. Jens wants to keep all options open and wants peace and quiet to think as he marches around the place. He sees it all as an unique opportunity and I just about think I can see what he means. War threatens to break out on the playground before long between a pair of 'wilful little beasties' and I shall be compelled to exert my school ma'ma-ish authority. That's all for now. Further bulletins from the front to follow, your devoted Miss Bethan, Form one...

How can she face the same old carry-on again, the same old filmic confusion: the parabola of plans, prospects, projects and the downward curve of conspiracy, double dealing, collapse, dismay and heartbreak. I've pointed out the pattern to her more than once and more than once she has accepted the analysis; until another white hope appears above the horizon, another will o' the wisp for her to chase. Then she inclines to laugh at me and accuse me of bourgeois inertia and lack of vision and enterprise. It's not a source of salvation that has blown in to Pentregwyn from across the North Sea, but yet another nordic wild goose and I suspect it is my job to shoot it down.

I am lost in thought as I sit on a marble bench in the shade of a cypress tree. It is a favourite little park off the Via Quirinale. A troop of Horse Guards in all their finely polished breastplates and plumed helmets canter down the street in perfect order en route to a ceremonial occasion of state. A motorised dust-cart follows in their wake cleaning the roadway of steaming horse-dung. It appears a convenient parable of earthly glory. I feel an urgent need at least to consult and even confide in the so un-self-absorbed Afonso. Is it possible I could summon up sufficient strength of character to ask him to allow me to accompany him to East Timor in some useful capacity? Would she think better of me if I were engaged in some more challenging enterprise: and what would he suggest? Should I in some vague and genial fashion declare I am in need of his advice?

He invites me to join him on a visit to an orphanage next to an Abbey on a hillside not far from Terracina. Orphans of different races and shades of colour are dressed in uniform dark play-aprons. They crawl around the polished floor like day old chicks looking up at the supervising Sisters of Mercy for crumbs of affection. Afonso explains that most of them have lost parents from H.I.V. or T.B. I am touched by both their beauty and their condition. I chide myself for being so absorbed in my own trifling trouble. These children face a lifetime searching for warmth and tenderness. It is too shaming to find myself on their level, isolated and crawling in search of affection in spite of my education and all the qualifications on my application form. I'm not equipped to face the rigors of East Timor. I have still to grow up. A humiliating truth. Too humiliating to mention to Afonso.

My own dear darling E: the latest from the front! Lowri has beaten a retreat. Which is not to say that she is beaten. Gone off to Cardiff for rest and refreshment and to regroup and even seek reinforcements. She says she'll be back as soon as this nonsense is over. 'Nonsense' shocked me a bit. Mothering or no mothering, it showed what she really thought of what was, and perhaps is, my chosen profession. As the saying goes, the unintended word unlocks the heart. Lowri's sole aim in life, to give her full credit was to restore the supremacy of Cymraeg, and in her heart of hearts that involves sacrifice and more sacrifice. Cinema and Television she considers opium for the people disguised as candyfloss. I can't be cross with her. Not for long anyway. I'm trapped, you could say, in the toils of her affection.

Anyhow Jens has seized on a key concept. The form of the film would be based on a soul from the future meeting the past in a continuous present. That's the rather pompous way he puts it. I think sometimes he loves the theory even more than the practice. That's what we are doing at the moment, puffing away at enchanted cigarettes and admiring the smoke rings. One way would be to have an actress playing something like me, wafting around the shop as it was when Sulwen was taken up with her artist, and foreseeing events such as the hanged man without being able to do anything about it.

He is much taken with the notion of recreating the life of the shop as it was in different stages of its existence: even going back as far as the days of Griffith Ezra Bowen – Griffith the Great as Jens calls him. Doctor Seth has returned from his self-imposed exile and Jens has roped him in as technical consultant. Seth doesn't let on, but I know he is absolutely delighted – Jens has made flattering remarks about the décor of his cottage and Seth can see his nineteenth-century obsessions bearing fine cinematic fruit! Jens also toys with the idea of some kind of conversation going on between a hermit in the woods (surprisingly like Curig!) and the wraith from the future as they follow the doomed affair between the young Sulwen and her artist lover.

I can see you smiling a faintly sceptical not to say cynical smile, Edward Cynddylan! All I can say is that the plots of most films sound like kitsch when you slam them down in outline. I've heard you say as much yourself. Think of all the weird and wonderful things the Greek gods got up to. In any case I'm putting it all down however wild and woolly so that you can pick holes in it for me. If you can't get away and come here to join in the fun at least you can help me with your customary cool and calm critical analysis.

Of course the other proposition when all this ambitious dreaming comes to a stop, is a plain and simple honest-to-God documentary. In one small section of my heart of hearts that is what I favour. Something I suppose I could undertake myself. But while the great Jens is so taken with the Sulwen story and rampaging around the place I hold my own little scheme in reserve. Would you call that devious?

More to come soon. Be patient with your ever-loving Bethan.

Fourteen

FREDDY HELMUT is in high spirits, rubbing his hands.

'The office trip to Saturnia, Eddie old fruit! The weather forecast is good. Should make a very rewarding weekend. Health-giving and all that. Refreshing the cockles of your cockle! Let's set it all up shall we?'

That 'us' means 'me'. As though I didn't have enough on my plate! There is a report on the economics of child labour in the leather industry in Pakistan to be summarised in French and in German. Why on earth he doesn't undertake the latter himself I've no idea: and there has been a mysterious but distinct downward shift in my prestige that makes it unnecessary for him to tell me. Either he has gone up or I have slid down. That could be related to his outburst on the insecurity of our tenure. Somehow his has become more secure and mine has become more dependent on his good will. This at a time when my self-assurance is dented by sleepless nights and torrid dreams about those bloody Danes getting up to all sorts of mischief in Pentregwyn.

'Let's get going, old fruit. Up Guards and at 'em. There's a time for everything. A time to dither and a time to dance. I've got itchy feet already.'

There is something ridiculous, verging on the obscene, in a man over fifty dyeing his hair and behaving as if he were under twenty-five. I have to ask myself why should I be so censorious? My father perhaps. Not that he ever dyed his hair but he took immense care of it, tended always by expensive hairdressers. There are people who would rate my secret longing for serene domesticity and the voices of children as equally absurd. Problems of this sort I would want to explore with Bethan, however absorbed she may be in her revived film ambitions. It should be all part of mutual comfort and support. I know what I want. My dilemma is how to prioritise it, as we say in the office, among the clamour of other people's urges. Why should a man need to scheme to achieve the natural consequence of life-giving love?

We have made this excursion before and it is pleasant enough if you can put up with secretaries giggling and Freddy's raucous jests about the aphrodisiacal benefit of the sulphur springs. He has his chosen spot near a ruined mill where the waters foam and eddy around the white rocks before entering a rough and stony pool where you lie and get what Freddy calls incalculable medicinal benefits. He is always very vague about their nature relying on the traditional lore that he claims stretches back well before the Romans. What good it does me I have no idea. Freddy gets cross when car-loads of fat ladies arrive and squeeze themselves in and out of their swimming costumes behind the open doors of their motor cars.

We spend the night afterwards in what I suspect is an unsuccessful health farm converted by its dubious proprietors into what they call 'our private hotel' Fortuna. Below there is an overgrown volcanic hollow which contains the remains of yet more medicinal baths. The proprietor and his wife treat Freddy Helmut with an obsequiousness that has to be seen to be believed. They seemed to be agreeing with his every utterance before he even opens his mouth. In the old days I used to follow the goings on with some amusement and, as it were, join in the fun. I suppose it was to please Freddy and counteract what he described as my excessive academic detachment. 'People are more than specimens and statistics, old fruit.'

Of course I always knew that. What does he bother to notice about me, since my transformation through love? After all, he has seen Bethan, he has duly admired her, and even gone through the motions of giving our relationship his blessing. But he has never registered the depth of change it has engendered in my character. I may look the same as ever: the self inside he used to be so fond of speculating about has changed for ever. Either he is too self-obsessed to notice the worn fragility of my protective covering or he is too far gone in supercilious indifference himself to bother to take it into account.

In the private hotel Fortuna a merry night is working itself up into a saturnalia which I am not willing or able to join in. Freddy and his followers are allowed to do what they like. They take possession of the place. To avoid the sweat and the noise and the music I wander out of doors and down the hollow to admire the ruins in the moonlight. I soothe myself with the banal thought that, cloud permitting, the same moon will be shining down on Pentregwyn. When I get back to the ballroom of the hotel, to my astonishment and alarm I am attacked by a burly forestry specialist from British Columbia, George Albert Bright. We had always been on the best of terms. He had a powerful handshake and was apt to say things like 'Howdy' and 'Bright by name and bright by nature'.

Tonight he is drunk and he is poking me in the chest with a robust finger and accusing me of breaking the delicate heart of Alison Fettle. But for my nauseating presence she would have been at his side at this very moment enjoying the health-giving freedom and fresh air. This as the dancing is in progress and Freddy Helmut is working his way through three reasonably attractive secretaries, exercising his own middle-aged version of the Judgement of Paris, and observing my confused response to the untoward attack from the corner of a bloodshot eye. I am unwise enough to protest my innocence. I am not responsible for Alison's agoraphobia or whatever else she could be suffering from. I even go so far as to mention my attempts to rebuff her advances. For this I am rewarded with a punch in the mouth which floors me more from surprise than the force of the blow. I sit there on the floor looking at the blood from my lip on my hand while the noise and the dancing goes on and George Albert staggers away in search of more to drink.

It becomes clear that the disastrous trip to Saturnia and, more precisely, Freddy Helmut's continuing and ill-concealed amusement, are leading me to a decisive moment. I have been my own Hamlet for long enough. It is too easy to regard one's own existence as critical, doom-laden, potentially tragic: and all others as comic or trivial. The fact is, unless I can quickly develop a skin as thick as an elephant's pachyderm, my living in the same office as Freddy Helmut will become intolerable. I am, after all, a man with modest but secure private means. I have academic qualifications to be proud of. I am a linguist, I even have a pedigree of sorts that Bethan seems to think counts for something.

The time has come to deliver an ultimatum to myself. I have to break out of a stupor of inactivity and compose a letter to Bethan that exposes my situation with startling clarity. It's not the kind of exercise that can be dribbled out on a laptop keyboard where the fingers are liable to do the thinking and race away with breathless conjecture, trifling complaint and interminable digressions and an entire battery of ifs and buts.

It has to be thought out, reduced to the clearest possible terms and then recast in a form calculated to reach her heart. It is perfectly simple. I am convinced that our love has infinite potential if only it is an established fact, a solemn union. Therefore marry me right away or at your earliest convenience or else I'm off to East Timor on refugee work for an indefinite period. That gives me only temporary relief. What if an answer comes shooting back, 'Very sorry to lose you, but if you've got to go you've got to go. Good bye and God bless.' In any case it is an empty threat until I put my case to Afonso and he accepts me reporting for voluntary duty at his side.

This in itself is anything but easy. Our friendship is a calm but superficial affair, as though we were two members of the same club who share an interest in antiquarian matters; detached, genial, without obligation or further attachments. And time is running out. We sit together in the belvedere on the Pincio admiring the view of the eternal city in the evening light. He gives a little sigh. He admits he always gets sentimental about Rome when he is on the point of leaving it. I struggle to control my inward turmoil by looking at the world through his eyes. For him this must be the headquarters of a 2,000 year old effort to give the world and human existence a civilised meaning. At this time of day it seems particularly eternal: those green masses of gardens, the domes of churches catching the light, the darker green of umbrella pines guarding the classical ruins, the overall triumphant presence of St. Peter's.

Generations of the sons of pious peasants from the west of Ireland, the extremities of Brittany, and Galicia and the Algarve have travelled here to be trained. His grandparents sold top-soil from their smallholding in Monchique for the construction of golf courses on the coast so that he could be educated and dedicated to his vocation. He cited this disturbing fact as an instance of the complexity of late-twentieth-century living: the not so mysterious forces of a global economy driving technological bulldozers tearing up the top-soil of people's lives. When Afonso contemplates history it always seems to shape up into the form of a sermon. He sits so still in the evening light he could be part of a religious tableau: he could model for an oleaginous memorial to one of those stubborn sixteenth-century Franciscans who insisted on travelling all the way to Japan to be martyred. What can I say to him?

'Do you think I should come with you?'

I spoke pleasantly without any note of desperation in my voice. After all he made the offer when he first dropped in at F.A.O. It was his usual brisk and cheerful invitation. At this moment there is a certain sadness in his smile as if he were confronting one of the minor life crises that make up the human condition.

'If you did,' he says. 'It should not be a form of escape.'

It is an abrupt shock to realise how much he must understand my condition. I must be more transparent than I ever imagined. My attempts at camouflage are thin and ineffective. Father Afonso, the apostle of a higher form of law and order sees through me just as easily as that malevolent Lord of Misrule, Freddy Helmut. I am a sitting target, like a pheasant squatting to conceal itself in an open field. Can I bluster my way out in some sort of doctrinal dispute?

'In this day and age, Afonso, marriage is a contract between equals. The very thing that gives a woman genuine equality in a relationship is contraception when you come right down to it. What has the church to say about that?'

I am mildly piqued that he looks so unconcerned.

'The Christian church teaches "thou shalt not kill." All the statesmen and politicians in the world spend most of their countries' wealth on armaments. Does that mean they should all be excommunicated?'

He is not taking my talent for disputation at all seriously. He shakes my arm as a token of fraternal friendship.

'You should let love decide your fate, Eddie. You have already made your choice and it's nothing to do with East Timor. Your kingdom is elsewhere. It's not the kingdom of heaven, remember, but in one way or another you must take it by storm. If you abandon contraception you might even found a dynasty! Think of that.'

In any case our discussion ends in laughter and a new level of comradeship. We go off to eat together at the table he has booked in dell'Orso. We eat guinea fowl and drink Velletri and he regales me with anecdotes of his travels to and fro, wherever the Portuguese flag may have flown. I listen appreciatively, realising that is the only payment he really requires: someone to listen to his *poésie de départ* before he goes out again on his lonely mission. Maybe it's the wine but I sense a surge of love and gratitude welling up inside me, that there are men like Afonso in the world. By their fruits we recognise them. Whole tribes and orders of humans in the jungle who are that much better than me. Afterwards of course that whisper that clings like a bat at the top of my skull asks 'grateful to whom?' in a lexical variety of languages that end up with Bethan's: *diolchgar i bwy? I bwy?*

Fifteen

AFONSO DEPARTED on his mission.

'You must have faith,' he said. 'Faith in yourself. Faith in Bethan. You know why don't you? "Faith indeed is the foundation of the things we hope for…" Magic Eduardo, of one form or another…'

And he was gone, leaving me in an emotional limbo. He had gone, taking his mission with him and my little problems were no longer a part of it. My ultimatum remained unwritten, not because I couldn't find the words; because I couldn't find the will. I was overtaken with a strange inertia, due to more than the summer heat. What in the end was all the hurry? The decision in any event would be hers and for the time being she was preoccupied with this film project that with each successive report seemed to reach new heights of absurdity. What possible advice could a minor bureaucrat offer when the participants are so mesmerised by a filmic phantasy in free fall?

Early on a Sunday morning I found myself wandering in a pleasurable daze among the ruins of the Forum. It is so easy to be trapped in a routine and to ignore the great monuments of the past at the heart of the city. I just felt like being a latter-day Gibbon and indulged in a contemplation of the rises and fall of Empires. From the point of view of my masterly inactivity it was only a matter of time before the walls of the Pentagon would be in the same state as the five broken aisles of the Basilica Julia. By extension the whispers and rumours that rolled through the corridors of a delegated power where I worked were little more than plots and plans to reduce the Future to a less menacing prospect. In truth, rumours of internal changes, promotions or redundancies cause more of a flurry than fresh schemes to relieve drought or famine or flooding.

Events determine the Future and Mr Gibbon assures me that in spite of all the shock and awe of military might and Star Wars, we exercise less control over them than over the weather. Mistakenly as it turns out, I conclude that the way to insulate yourself from the malign power of events is not to initiate them. I have an urge to wrap myself in the consolations of complacency; pass the time analysing the parallel follies of ancient and modern history and close my ears to the hidden threat of catastrophe that provides that rumble of urgency lying behind the monotonous music of the daily news bulletins. Afonso should still be here so that we can debate with fierce friendliness to what extent we can detach ourselves from History and what obligation if any we have to try and improve it.

It must have been while I sat on the warm stone in the shadow of the Basilica that my father was struck down by a stroke. In the spirit of never ending holiday they were attending a fiesta in a village outside Valdepenas when he decided to have his photograph taken in the saddle of a wooden Rozinante. He had grown a pointed beard which Daisy said suited him. Anything Daisy said had become the eleventh commandment, chiefly because she gave him anything he wanted. They seemed to have settled on spoiling each other as a way of life. He wanted a better picture taken. On a real horse. In a more heroic setting among the rocks. Always felt it was a part he could have played. By the time it was all set up and he was wearing imitation armour the heat became too much for him. He collapsed trying to get on the horse.

They rushed him in that luxurious limousine to the nearest hospital. For a day and a night he lay in the overcrowded Emergency ward, struck dumb among all the screaming and groaning. There was barely room for Daisy to squeeze between the beds to hold his hand. She was wonderful. She swung into action with the skill and resourcefulness of a natural commander. I suppose you could say her wealth too was a help. And Hortense and Mario were in constant devoted attendance. The moment Orlando was fit to move she hired a private jet and he was flown to a clinic outside Lucerne. There was a view of Pilatus through his window.

'Your father has this stroke, and so it's difficult to understand what he's saying...'

Daisy's voice was indistinct but calm and controlled.

'He's asking for you. Can you come Eddie? I need you too.'

I must have appeared pretty stricken myself. Probably more with guilt than with grief. Freddy Helmut became extraordinarily sympathetic. He went out of his way to arrange immediate compassionate leave. The unworthy suspicion did flash through my mind that he might be a trifle over-eager to get rid of me. I had become a long faced ghost around the place, too ready with the grimace of reproach, the silence of disapproval. To my surprise, before I left, George Albert rumbled up and muttered 'Sorry to hear about your pa', tapping me briefly on the shoulder.

The faithful Mario picked me up at the airport. Behind the wheel of the gleaming limousine in his austere grey uniform he was an unlikely candidate for the role of Sancho Panza. At the same time he expressed taciturn disapproval of my father's excessive exuberance. 'A mistake,' he muttered. 'And for what?' The luxurious interior still smelt of Daisy's discreet perfume. In here they had driven around in a prolonged haphazard honeymoon determined to make up for what I imagined could have been interminable years of separation. It could well be that she had fallen in love with his glittering stage presence even before I was born. And now this same dark discreet vehicle could be destined for a leading role in a funeral cortège.

I make a strenuous effort to contemplate my father's life and become mildly shocked to discover that I find it impossible to detach it from the troublesome shortcomings of our relationship. Hearing Daisy's voice saying he was asking for me was enough to establish with a sudden sharp recognition that I am flesh of his flesh. I never aspired to his transient triumph or even wanted to be like him, but I am his all the same. I have the same way of turning my head, and our hands make the same unconscious gestures. Something of him moves whenever I move. A diluted version perhaps, but a version all the same. It becomes painfully clear that a residue of jealousy has lingered in the sump of my consciousness possibly from birth. My mother always put him first. Even when she was cuddling me she would set me aside, however gently, quite swiftly, to respond to his slightest whim. He had to be fed on demand and fed first. Even the love of my mother, which sustained me all my life and through all my academic trials and petty triumphs, had its source and origin in the extent to which I reproduced the characteristics of my father's younger days: which means his enduring presence must be part of the elusive self I have always either searched for or tried to escape from. If there is no such thing as a separate existence why be so bothered to look for it?

And there he is, in the physiotherapy room of the exclusive clinic, being hoisted by a wooden contraption with his arms stretched out until he looks like a blasphemous caricature of a Christ on a cross. Judging by the almost imbecile smile on his slack mouth he is aware of the comparison and is even formulating some pseudo-Shakespearean lines in his head to grace the occasion. They could be tragic or comic according to the expectations of his audience: should he play the Son of Man or Don Quixote? To the very end, I can't prevent myself from thinking, a crowd pleaser.

Except of course that Daisy is determined that this shall not be the end. All the resources of the latest Swiss treatments will be engaged in restoring him to sufficient health so that she, as she says herself, 'can go on spoiling him to bits.' I smile of course to demonstrate complete approval and gratitude: there is also a brief surge from the old source of jealousy that this father of mine could inspire such unconditional devotion. Why is it so many people love him, except his only son?

My dearest Eddie: how awful about your old dad. You must be so upset. I only wish we were near enough for me to comfort you. And he looked so well too and so full of spirit. I'm so sorry. Give him a big kiss from me. And my love to your lovely step-mother. She sounds a wonderful person and there are not so many of those around are there? Not from where I'm standing at the moment.

The wretched Jens, genius my foot, has imported what he calls his team. Since when has he had a team I'd like to know? He sees himself as a pocket Napoleon. Anyone would think he was D.W. Griffith and my poor little Pentregwyn is infested with his hangers-on. Curig keeps muttering Sulwen would turn in her grave, and a creature Jens calls his production assistant has tried to turn the poor boy out of his outside kitchen. Says it would make an ideal production office for her. I sent her packing with a flea in her ear. There are two conspicuous villains in the piece let me tell you, like a pair of body snatchers, Burke and Hare I call them, and you could say we are engaged in mortal combat. Burke you could say is Brendan Trembold, an outsize pseudo-Irishman with podgy little lips that mourn his fantasies all day long. He had a successful career in Hollywood, or so we are told, specialising in action thrillers but now he wants to go on to some-thing more ambitious and artistic and he believes Jens will be the next big thing to come out of Scandinavia. Who, I say to myself, is kidding who?

And then Hare is Harold Cunard-Cohen – (he loves his hyphen) a hairy East End barrow boy who claims to have access to untold millions provided he gets hold of the right scripts, and it bears his stamp of approval! So what started out as a perfectly simple sincere project, a piece of filmic art that could be shaped and moulded out of a modest budget, has snowballed into a fantastic monstrosity. I am just about holding on. There is a battle going on you could call the War for Jens' Ear. He goes for long walks and you can see him in the distance waving his hands around his head as though he were being attacked by a swarm of bees. Which of course is what's happening. Harold talks about market forces and Brendan comes up with the proposition that the Sulwen story be transferred to Jutland, where Jens could so to speak work from home, and the figure of the secret lover be transformed into a resistance fighter in hiding during the Nazi occupation!

This is where I put my foot down. I told him if the film wasn't based firmly on the fact of Pentregwyn and the true character of Sulwen, they could all get the hell out of hcrc. I was not going to tolerate amy more of B&H's muttering about box-office poison and who would want to know about a place like this unless something sensational happened here, either an earthquake or a virgin birth! Dear Eddie, I'm so fed up with the whole thing, but I do beg you not to say I told you so. I'll give it another two or three days at the most, and if they don't come up with something I can accept and agree to with a minimum of enthusiasm, I'll send them all packing. Jens included, although I have to add I have not lost my basic respect for his undoubted talent.

And that's enough of that. You've got troubles of your own, and you don't want to listen to me going on and on about mine. Just believe I love you and think of you as my rock and the idea of our being together again the greatest if not the only comfort. Bethan.

'I'll have him walking again and talking again. No question.'

Daisy is as quietly determined as ever. In her own discreet way she has been doing battle with a pair of consultants who had concluded that my father needed long-term institutional care.

'Their institutions of course. They have great diagnostic skills. Especially on bank balances. I mean it's all a bit of an act isn't it, when you get down to it? Strokes are unpredictable and unfathomable and that's the beginning and end of it. I've got all the time and the money needed, and I shall have the pleasure of lavishing it all on him myself.'

We are putting on a brave face, and my father nods his approval. All he needs is for Daisy to hold his hand from time to time. He can grunt but he can't speak and the distortion of his mouth makes it appear that he is smiling all the time. I want to look at him affectionately but I have to look away from time to time. Daisy is amusing him by calling the consultant specialists Doctor Freud and Doctor Jung. I haven't studied them long enough to decide which is which.

'Ham actors,' Daisy says. 'That's what they are. I should know. Nothing like an unsuccessful actress to make a successful ambassador's wife.'

We travel around the bays and inlets of the lake in search of suitable properties to rent or even buy: suitable that is for what she describes as my father's determined march to recovery and comfortable convalescence.

'It may take a long time,' Daisy says again and again. 'But I've got all the time in the world.'

And we do have a style of going around the place as if she owned it. Mario is her chauffeur and I am her interpreter. She is only moderately impressed by my linguistic fluencies. She has long discovered that money combined with English can get you more or less anywhere. In the smart magazine scale of values, her late husband James Eugene Carriere, may only have presented his ambassadorial credentials to minor rank countries, but he did represent the world's one and only superpower, and in the smaller South American republics the voice of big brother was listened to with rapt attention. Ambassador Carriere was a devoted husband, Daisy gave me to understand, but a stern proconsul. He liked the upper class English accent she had learned in her London drama schools because it was still very acceptable in diplomatic circles.

'Poor old Jim,' Daisy said. 'I only called him Jim when there was no one else around. He was a stickler for protocol I expect just because he had come up through the rough and tumble of big business. And as he used to say, it could be "pretty damned rough". Protocol! Oh dear! I didn't really care for it but I walked through it like a play on provincial tour. Charm and correctness on all occasions and the more clottish the people, the more smiling and gracious formality. I used to get so bored. "If only my old dad could see me now" has limited satisfaction. He was a pretty unsuccessful jeweller in Southend-on-Sea. Never mind. All that's over now. Pull up here will you, Mario.'

We are in an overgrown drive leading to a vacant villa on the lake-side. Daisy pops into the bushes, half concealed, and comes back adjusting her light summer dress.

'That's better,' she says. 'I was nearly bursting. You've got the keys have you? Lets go and take a look at this place without having the agent sniffing at our heels.'

My sweet old Eddie: I've turfed them out. I can't tell you. It all became too much. When I say turf them out, Burke and Hare had already slunk off: Cunard-Cohen could see no prospect of a block-buster script and Brendon Trumbold gave up after a last ditch attempt to get Sulwen transplanted to the West of Ireland. I know it sounds ridiculous beyond words but these creatures live and breathe in their own phantasmagoria. (I never really understood what that word really meant until this lot turned up in such force.) Jens, his intrusive P.A. whom I could not stand, and a great hulk of an electrician who he brought along as a bodyguard and equipment humper, stayed on because Jens and I were engaged in a fierce theoretical argument on which everything seemed to hang. This electrician, a gorilla called Bjorn, got into trouble in the Half Way Tavern down on the Wrexham Road, and that also delayed their departure. What was the theoretical argument? I hear you ask (as a connoisseur of course). It boils down to very little really and leads me to suspect he had some other more devious aim in view. My point was that faces and fates in a place like this are moulded by the landscape or were anyway in old Sulwen's lifetime. I wanted a film about a place, a person, a people seen from the inside and rooted to this one place. Jens argued that the camera studied the outside and it was the director's job to provide the inside vision and that you could perfectly well have a complementary setting in Denmark, New England, Ireland, almost anywhere, so long as he held on to the inner vision and found the means to express it. Not very profound or original when you boil it down like this but I can remember raising my voice to the edge of a prophetic scream and shouting what is the point of trying to conquer the hostile universe when we seem intent on destroying the only base humanity has got… and I think he gave up. Hysteria seemed to have taken over. Now I hang about the place like a deflated balloon and Curig and Seth creep around with secretive smug smiles on their faces. Any chance of you coming here, when your dear old dad recovers? I miss you so much. Bethan.

And so you should. Reproach. Reproach. You brought it all on your own head. Who else put the bee in that Danish genius's bonnet except the beauteous Bethan Mair? Where do these spiteful voices come from; spirits rising from the nasty deep. When a skull is buzzing with the sound of so many of them whispering across each other, how can there even be room for anything designated the essential self? Nothing left except the unsteady pulse of desire. Now Bethan wants me something like as much as I want her. That is a fact from which one of the buzzing voices draws a nectar all of its own.

She needs me and I have this unworthy demeaning urge to inflict on the delicious girl I am supposed to be so deeply in love with, a measure of punishment in payment for the sustained painful anxiety her ridiculous film adventure has imposed on me. Petty schoolroom spite no doubt. There is still a whisper in the bone echo chamber, Cynddylan's empty hall, muttering 'a perfectly natural reaction.' Active love remains in abeyance while the abstracted debate goes on. I have an excuse to persist with inertia and masterly inactivity. My father needs me.

I am enjoying Daisy's company. She looks on me with approval, which is more than I can say for myself. In such a short space of time we have become close in the way of two people involved in the same crisis. It could be more than that even. It is still possible to discern what an attractive young female she must have been and it is clear that in women of this calibre the attractiveness lingers on. Even with limited imagination it is possible to envisage Bethan Mair at the same age carrying herself with the same ease and confidence. Daisy has no difficulty in inspiring a certain devotion because she makes no attempt to do so. It's not just her wealth and practised charm and outbursts of frankness and unstinting benevolence; before the wedding my father had lost no time in drawing attention to what he called Daisy's dulcet tones. 'It's a young girl's voice' he said. 'And a young girl's eyes too wouldn't you say?' He was drawing attention to the great prize he had won. At the time I found his infatuated enthusiasm a bit sickening: but here at Lucerne I can quite see what he meant.

'I'm not your mother of course. But we get on pretty well, don't we? And that's what matters.'

She confesses that all her house hunting is a bit of a

charade to pass the time between concentrated spells of ministering to Orlando and seeing that all his needs are meticulously attended to. There are nurses who come on and off duty; a timetable for physiotherapists and speech therapists; schedules of consultation and much talk of progress and patience. I watch her transfer her critical inspection of the patient's treatments to picking out the shortcomings of prospective properties. She is as fit and agile as the mistress of a corps de ballet. While she trips around empty rooms and up and down staircases I am able to amuse myself by examining the lavishly illustrated brochures and analysing the way the three, or more usually the four, languages contort themselves in delivering swathes of euphemistic information. Part of the condition of great wealth is being spoilt for choice.

'He's my baby you know. Your dear old Papa. He's the baby I never had.'

We sit together on a bench watching the stately progress of a white ferry boat on the blue waters of the lake. I am eager to be taken into her confidence. It comes like something I am in need of: establishing a link between trust and openness.

'I had an abortion the year after I came out of Drama School. You mustn't tell your father, Eddie. The man in question was a friend of his. Not a friend perhaps. A fellow member of the Garrick. He came up behind me in the street one day outside the Haymarket Theatre. He whispered my name in my ear and took me out to lunch and I suppose you could say swept me off my feet. The young are so susceptible. I was anyway. He was doing well and he had a wife of course. I wanted a career. He arranged the abortion and paid for it. I paid for it by being unable to have children.'

The ferry boat dwindled in size and moved into the shadow of a forest that seemed to come down the steep mountainside right to the water's edge. Sadness and sympathy moved me to silence. Daisy took my hand and shook it vigorously.

'Your Papa thinks you are too sensitive,' she says. 'I think he could be right about that. "The dear boy is too fastidious. Makes him damned intolerant at times".'

This time her imitation of Orlando's theatrical drawl only made me smile faintly.

'I'm a boring young fogey, I know,' I say. 'And a goodie-goodie to boot.'

'Rubbish my dear. In any case we all have to try to be good, don't we? Run the straight race and all that. Besides where would be the thrill of falling over if there wasn't a race in the first place?'

She has this gift of reassuring people. Maybe I'm not as mean and petty-minded as I think I am.

'You should realise he admires you enormously. Sometimes we never notice things that are too close to our noses.'

The days pass so pleasantly by. We wander from pâtis-serie to pâtisserie through the ancient yet lively streets in search of delicacies that will stimulate Orlando's appetite. Not that it needs much stimulating. His stroke has done little to impair it. Some speech articulation is returning. Enough to allow him to go through appreciative motions. It is possible under Daisy's gentle tuition I am learning to look on my father with a more fitting degree of respect and affection. If she finds him so precious and wonderful it is up to me to search for those trace elements in his nature. A man only has one father and this is the least he can do to honour him.

In this summer by the lake Daisy has become the fount of all wisdom. I have to tell her how things stand between Bethan and myself. I tell her about the great film fiasco from my point of view so that we can laugh about it. Daisy has her own views about the rival merits of theatre and film. For her, theatre is the higher art form; as far as I can judge, on the grounds that Orlando was at his best on the live stage. On film, actors are no more and no less than the director's puppets. I was intrigued by her other conclusions, ideas that had not occurred to me before. In a world which was unevenly divided between the halt, the maimed, the sick, the poor and the under-privileged on the one hand; and the cruel, the cunning, the avaricious and the power mad on the other, the only hope for perpetuating civilisation was to treat life as a ceremony and the theatre as a critical echo that could say whatever it liked through the mouth of the mask.

'There you are, young man. A failed actress disguised as an ambassador's widow, speaking. Now what about this girl of yours? What is her problem apart from being much too pretty?'

I find it difficult to get across the problem of Bethan's inheritance. The complex mixture of family squabbles and culture conflicts, Daisy says, is less easy to follow than the ins and outs of Paraguayan politics. If you had an inheritance surely the best thing was to grab it and enjoy it, 'Look at me for heaven's sake!' In the wisest possible way she tells me to stop splitting hairs and being paral-ysed by diffident hesitations and imaginary scruples.

'Do something impetuous, for God's sake. Be unpre-dictable. Go wild. Get her out here. Kidnap her or something. Women need handling you know and it's a woman that's telling you! Whatever you do, I'll back you up.'

I think by that she means cash no object. Lying in bed that night I decided to surprise Bethan by arriving at Pentregwyn without previous warning. Plane or hired car. No expense spared I would pull that old shop bell and wait on the threshold to be invited in. There and then, in the flesh, I would present her with my ultimatum. Something awful like, 'Marry me or you'll never see me again.' I thrilled myself with visualising a giant clash of wills and both of us overcome at last by the sheer power of love. I hear Daisy's voice again, either saying or singing, 'You can only remain buoyant in the sea of life by filling your lungs full of love.'

In the morning, bright with resolve and determined to act impetuously I join Daisy at her reserved table in the breakfast room to tell her my plan. As I approach, her hands are already raised eager to involve me in a brilliant notion she has worked out with the speech therapist.

'We could use the scrapbooks you see. We can get him to explore his memory and put the pictures into words. Nothing wrong with his memory. It's just a question of getting the words out. Occupational therapy too. Putting them in order. The thing is, Eddie dear, will you do me the most enormous favour? Will you nip down to the apartment in Juan-les-Pins and bring back your Papa's scrapbooks. All of them I think, don't you?

So I set out, but not in the direction I had in mind. The apartment when I get to it is infinitely depressing. The *femme de chambre*, who has her own key, has not been in to clean. Her cat has been ill and she has spent hours in the vet's waiting room. And the mistral has given her headaches. Her excuses are vigorous and fluent. Meanwhile a melancholy veil of dust lies over everything, especially the green bindings of the scrapbooks. I can't wait to get out. Memories of old discontents lie around like dust in the still air. I have better things to do than packing awkward scrapbooks into boxes. I suppress resentment and get on with it, until the mission is completed to Daisy's delighted satisfaction. 'You are such a good boy,' she says. And there is a glittering reward in a message from Bethan.

My dear old Eddie, I surrender. I've given it a lot of thought. I'll marry you if it will set your mind at rest and of course if you still want me. There's too much freedom flying around anyway. A rootless human race will soon vanish off the face of the earth, dusty nothings in meaningless orbit. Mind you, and in the same breath, I'll need to live on the end of a long leash. Now I can't wait for you to turn up my dear old darling! Journey's end in lovers meeting and so on. Come and get me. Bethan.

Sixteen

JOURNEY'S END in lovers meeting? It's never that simple. Daisy claps her hands and makes expressions of girlish delight; my father, resting against his mountain of pillows nods his head with slack-mouthed approval. I grin until my cheeks ache, but inwardly I am seized by a shameful nervousness. Capitulation or challenge? I need to see her face with my own eyes to see exactly what her words mean. How could the vicissitudes of this wretched season of being apart, of intermittent, unsatisfactory communication, have strengthened her attachment to me, when it has done everything it damn well could, including her wild flirtation with abortive filming, to undermine my devotion to her? Why should I be behaving as if I were still lurking among the losers instead of being on the point of grasping the long coveted prize?

My father wants his leather-bound copy of Shakespeare's sonnets. They have been a lifelong standby for special occasions. I never hear them without the echo of his theatrical modulations. His lips are moving and Daisy can make out 'Let me not to the marriage of true minds / Admit impediments…' She is moved. There are tears in her eyes. His finger trails along the lines and a strange noise issues from his mouth.

Daisy speaks without lowering her voice.

'He was just as mellifluous as Gielgud you know. And much better looking. More masculine. A matinee idol if ever there was one…'

My father is smiling as though her judgement meets with his modest approval. My love story is dissolving into theirs. Their lips are going on about an ever-fixed mark as if they were engaged in a thrilling duet before the curtain falls at the end of the third act. The whole world is their stage and I am their designated solitary spectator. My head and my smile are rigid to prevent myself looking away.

Daisy has sensed my unease. To explain it away I search out my grammar and my lexicon. My studies of Y Gymraeg have lapsed due to other pressures and I need a crash refresher course before I venture boldly into the heart of its territory. Words after all in this kind of situation are weapons. Language is all. My nervous speculations mean nothing at all to Daisy.

'Do they have another language? I never knew that. Come to think of it I know more about Paraguay than I do about Wales. That's what comes of being brought up in Southend-on-Sea. Come to think of it I don't know much about Scotland either. Have they got their own language too? They were two funny bumps on the map in the schoolroom. Unknown parts of the Empire. Anyway, rejoice! She's had two mothers, and now she'll be getting a mother-in-law who always longed to be a fairy godmother! Just made for the part!'

Her house-hunting hobby along the lake is given a new impetus. She wants to give us a Swiss home as a wedding present, where we can bring up a whole tribe of brand new Cynddylans. The brochures are reopened and her enthusiasm takes wing. There is one property that she previously disapproved of because it had too much land, too many lawns and gardens. Now it has other possibilities. She has heard of rich patrons of the arts who have built small concert halls and museums even in such gardens. Why couldn't she build a little theatre and call it The Orlando Theatre in honour of my father? And when they have, as the phrase goes, passed on, Bethan and I would be still around to keep it all fresh and a vital memorial.

'All in good time I know,' Daisy says. 'But you just tell her, "my people shall be thy people and thy God my God…" or is that the right way round? Anyway you know what I mean. I'm so excited. I'm spelling it all out for your

Papa and he keeps nodding his approval. We'll all be one big happy family. A positive nest of singing birds!'

She tears herself away from my father and his scrap books to see me off. We ride to the airport in her limousine and I study Mario's patient back as if it were a fixture. Daisy says she wants to share in the excitement; makes her feel young again.

'Don't you go calling yourself boring Eddie Lloyd. You are a knight in shining armour! Not that that girl of yours is a damsel in distress. She sounds a bit of a terror to me to tell you the truth. But that only makes things all the more tasty and exciting. Maybe you'll have to pin her down by giving her a baby! Listen to an old witch talking. Anyway whatever you get up to I'll always be around to help out! Oh dear what fun!'

Why is my elusive self always drawn to positive, strong-willed women? It's not elusive at all, just plain weak: and do I need to work out why that should be so? It seems since my mother died a certain type of woman ceased to exist: the patient ones, tied to hearth and family, ready to suffer and even smile at grief. I can't see Bethan and Daisy posing as Ruth and Naomi among the alien corn, Swiss or otherwise. But as my mother used to say: don't chase after difficulties. They'll come to you.

On the flight to Manchester I try to calm my nerves by studying my notes on the aspirate mutation. It's a delicacy of the language I am inclined to admire and it reinforces my idea of Bethan and the sound of her voice. Next to me a football fan, who has been left behind by his companions, sinks inside his seat belt in a sulky stupor. Sometime in the future his misadventures will be a source of much merriment in the club, but at the moment he is groaning with self-pity and I am distracted by the fear he might vomit all over the place. He holds a sick bag in his podgy nerveless hands. I wonder if he is capable of accurate aim. He gives me a vigorous nudge to indicate he wants to get to the toilet and I'd better get out of his way.

I am on the way to join the woman I love and my head

should be alive with appropriate music. That should make me more than a speck of consciousness riding at thirty-five thousand feet with a random collection of similar specks held together in a technological marvel engaged in its daily chore of abusing the environment. Colour my thoughts with the sunlight of recollection: explore our physical relationship back to its miraculous source in the Alentejo: register and re-register the joyful details of each reunion: picture her swimming in the lake and lying with me in the chalet and air-brush Freddy Helmut out of the picture. The more rigorously I think of those occasions his shadowy figure is liable to appear in the role of either a grinning Pandar or a smirking Peeping Tom.

The weather is, as they say, unseasonable, but the hired car is waiting for me to collect it. I need to consult maps and remember to drive on the left. Everything should be where it was, but the season has changed. This is meant to be August and hot summer. Instead it is raining and the low clouds shroud the hills that in popular song are supposed to welcome me. They look miserable and forbidding and I fumble with my maps afraid of getting lost. I shall need the warmest of welcomes to compensate for the trials of the journey.

It is with enormous relief that I pull up outside Pentregwyn General Stores. I have to look twice to recognise it. Scaffolding has been erected and I need to walk under the ladders to pull at the shop doorbell. The place is still a bit of a dark tower to me but inside I shall find the great prize I have come looking for. I need to ring a second time. A hefty female with a crown of grizzled hair takes in the presence of a stranger at the threshold. She appears to be in a nervous state

'What is it? Who are you?'

Her Welsh is abrupt and hostile. I make my reply in my best Cymraeg.

'I am Bethan's friend. She has sent for me. I flew from Switzerland today.'

The stiff figure in front of me, softens: crumbles even.

Her head begins to tremble. At any moment the tears will flow.

'The poor little girl. I am her mother, Lowri Nichols. She was attacked you see. Savagely attacked. And that poor boy Curig Puw was seriously wounded trying to save her. It's been a terrible shock!'

My heart is pounding in my chest as I follow her through a shop that is in some process of renovation. I was never ready for this. Was it thieves broke in here? This place that I had never liked has suddenly become the end of the world.

'How bad is it? How bad is she?'

My linguistic skills descend into a stutter.

'Can you tell me?'

The woman turns to look at me with doleful suspicion.

'We don't know yet whether she will be permanently disfigured. The doctors are particularly worried about her left eye. Whether she will lose the sight.'

I am too appalled to move. Those wonderful violet eyes on which I have doted from the first day I saw her. My bright-eyed photographer. She wanted me and I wasn't here.

'And that poor boy... Do you have anything to do with this film business?'

She stares at me sternly ready to pronounce me guilty by association. Everything she says sounds like an accusation.

'I warned her, but she would take no notice. And now it's come to this.'

She leads me to a sparsely furnished study that Bethan has made for herself with the lingering atmosphere of a bohemian art student's den. Her husband is in there seated on a high stool. They both look out of place. Lowri and Alwyn Nichols. It seems more than possible that she has never told them about me. I am acutely embarrassed. I want to be with her, not them. I came all this way to be reunited with her, not to be faced with this. The husband is far more amiable than his wife. He looks deeply worried but he manages a charming smile. There is just the faintest resemblance to his daughter.

'Ah,' he says. 'Edward Lloyd. You must be her friend that works in Rome. I'm sorry you are met with such bad news.'

He offers his hand and I take it and feel a little better. He seems my type of human being or at least I feel an instinctive alliance. There is a solitary red leather sofa on which they invite me to sit. He is the one who offers me a cup of tea as some kind of comfort to my state of shock. In this combination it is the wife who does the talking. Her account of the events is a judgement, a verdict I am expected to accept.

'They contaminated the place you could say. That huge Danish electrician, "the Ape" Bethan called him, spent his time drinking in the Halfway on the Wrexham Road. There was nothing else for him to do. He started boasting about rich Hollywood producers spending a fortune on a film in Pentregwyn. The shop became a treasure house loaded with gold. There are gangs you see that operate up and down the North Wales coast. It's hard to believe, in such a quiet innocent place as this. The word gets around the criminal network. And there's the drug culture too you see. Both worlds touch each other. Co-operated you could say. Like a cancer in a sick society you could say.'

'Lowri,' her husband says. 'Don't preach. Mr Lloyd needs to hear the facts.'

'The weather changes so quickly. It was so warm a few nights ago. Bethan sleeps in Sulwen's room. She heard a noise downstairs in the shop. She came down and they pounced on her. These two men. She was wearing so little. It was a warm night. She fought. She struggled and shouted. Curig heard the noise. He tried to save her, poor boy. They turned on him. They beat him and stabbed him. Then when they saw what they had done they panicked and fled. There is one of those alarm buttons still by Sulwen's bed from the time when she was ill. Bethan managed to reach it. I can't think how. She thought Curig was in danger of bleeding to death. Seth got the emergency call. It had been fixed in Sulwen's time. The ambulance came and rushed them to hospital. Just in time to save the poor boy's life. Or so we hope. So we hope.'

She breaks down with the effort of reliving the dreadful event. Her husband takes her in his arms to comfort her. I press my hands into the red leather and bend my head as though I had taken a blow myself. Her father drives me to the hospital. We seem to understand each other enough not to make artificial efforts to speak. What is there to say? The disaster had happened and neither of us could have done anything to avoid it, and yet our distress has to be tainted with guilt. We feel responsible. How much do you have to do to protect your loved one? Everything and yet in the end it will never be enough.

I barely recognise her. She could be any battered young woman in a condition you can hardly bear to look at. How can I relate the creature in the bed to the bright and beautiful image lodged in my memory?

'It was a nightmare.'

She has difficulty in speaking. I tell her not to try. Her lips are so swollen. Her cheeks bruised and battered. Her left eye is bandaged still. They want to save the sight if they possibly can, but they can't promise anything. What kind of animal could do this to her? Her face and her beautiful body are bruised and disfigured. The bruises on her body are made more horrific when you think of beauty being blown away to be replaced by the form of butchery that precedes decay. Life is so precious and so short and so precarious. She presents a vision that I don't want to see but have to look at.

'I thought they were going to rape me. I had so little on. It's the kind of thing you think could never happen. But it did.'

I try to make a soothing noise. I bring my head closer to hers. She is shivering with the effort of speaking but she insists on making the effort.

'I screamed as hard as I could. And he hit me and the other one held me down. He just kept hitting me and telling me to shut up.'

She is squeezing my fingers with all the strength of her pain that she wants me to feel too.

'Go and see him.'

She wants me to go and see Curig.

'Intensive care. Look through the glass. Tell me if he is still on that life support thing.'

I don't really want to leave her side or to see the poor chap in his desperate condition. I don't really want anything any more. Except help perhaps. Except learn how to give help and not be so helpless. All this is bringing me face to face with my own inadequacy. What is the point of falling in love if it leaves you as useless and as helpless as this?

He has an oxygen mask on his face and his eyes are closed. Apparatus attached to his arms. Intravenous drips. Blood transfusions. I am ashamed to remember how I felt about him. Based on jealousy: some ridiculous sense of rivalry. I chose to think his hermit-like habits, his asceticism and gnomic utterance were all pose. Now what I am looking at is a hero in the proper sense of the word. He saved Bethan's life possibly at the expense of his own. What greater love could a man have? I am ashamed to stand looking at him through a glass. I need to go somewhere to heap sackcloth and ashes on my own head. As I am about to move away a nurse appears to remove the oxygen mask. His eyes open. He sees me. Recognises me, even smiles and raises a hand to give me a wave. I can only lift a hand and smile back and then bow my head, and long for some form of absolution.

Seventeen

IT FEELS AS THOUGH we are being tested to destruction. Bethan caught in a random squall of violence, a vicious outburst of which I was completely unaware. In my mind we were already married from the moment she tapped out her surrender. On the journey here I had concluded, much to my own comfort and satisfaction, that whatever problems there were to face, it would be so much easier to face them together. I composed jokes in my head about the abortive Danish film project so that I could enjoy the engaging sound of that rueful giggle she would give when contemplating her own impulsive adventures. 'We have to try don't we?' she would say. 'Otherwise what on earth are we good for?' Laughing together was our standard source of strength. Now I have to endure a strange silence. I am cut adrift from the one being who drew me here. This poor creature Curig Puw has appropriated an heroic role that should have been played by myself. All I am left with is the exercise of a sour mixture of guilt and patience and the nagging question of how well I would have played that bruised role myself.

Bethan was discharged from hospital too soon. It is true they have saved the sight of her left eye, or as the Indian specialist put it if I understood his clotted accent correctly, her eye was allowed to save itself. It was assumed she could more or less do the same for the rest of her person. Since her mother was at hand to take care of her and nurse her tenderly until her disfigurements took their own time to fade. This hardly took into account the overwhelming effect the attack was having on her whole personality. She could not bear to be looked at, let alone touched. Shadows frighten her. She had suffered criminal assault and battery and there should be more professional guidance available. It is not enough for her to retreat like a damaged chick into the shadow of a mother hen's capacious wing. For myself I am unqualified and helpless. My desire to comfort her makes no connection and I am left helpless, superfluous, a species of well-meaning bystander liable to get in the way.

Her one concern in the world is for Curig Puw. His condition is still serious and I make it my daily duty to keep an eye on him and report back at frequent intervals. Had his kidneys indeed been ruptured and how transitory would be the bruising of his spine: what was the condition of his spinal cord? He remains in that side ward under close observation and as he lies there, his pallor and his patience give him a saintly look.

I am assigned to occupy his quarters in the outside kitchen. It has been converted into something far more clean and comfortable than when I first set eyes on it, but it remains in the shadow, spartan and gloomy. 'Ideal for storing potatoes,' Doctor Seth says in one of his demonstrations of dry humour. I have been obliged to revise my hostile view of this man too.

He has been the nearest thing to a touch of comfort in this crisis. His helpfulness is restricted it appears to me, by the residue of resentment that Mrs Lowri Nichols feels towards him. She dominates the situation. Even her husband is reduced to no more than furtive signs of friendship and gratitude to his friend the doctor, with whom he shared so much in the exhilarating days of protest now long gone when Ffion Locksley was their object of affection. Since our services are so little in demand Seth and myself turn to each other. I have come to accept him in his parochial context. After a crisis of this dimension all judgments are open to revision. It is clear that he does much good by stealth and that jealousy as much as anything else made me misjudge him. I have even learnt to enjoy his eccentric sense of humour. In the face of adversity he becomes resolutely cheerful. Part of his medical training, he says.

'Let me tell you, Edward Llwyd, civilisation is alive and well and is enjoying a quiet retirement on the outskirts of Pentregwyn.' He reveals that he is engaged in a history of the parish of Llanfair Iscoed. 'Picking up the baton where Sulwen left off.' He blushes as he says this as though he were confessing a weakness. 'From quite a different point of view of course,' he says. It will be something clinical and exploratory, free of any sentimental piety. He intends to begin with the neolithic cave on Y Garn, pick up a bone and carry it down the centuries right up to the present time, to join the bones in his legs which he keeps in trim by hill walking and modest climbing, an activity that gives him great pleasure and a sense of well-being, and in which I am more than welcome to join him. 'From the top of Y Garn you can see the Past in the shape of mountain tops whichever way you care to look. Displaying their strength to the unstable Present. I've got a poem about it I must show you.'

The savage attack has galvanised the whole community. Even before Bethan returns from hospital Pentregwyn Stores has become something of a shrine, a place invested with a degree of awe. Flowers still arrive at frequent intervals and I become aware of the awkward creaking motions of an organism gathering itself together to try and repair damage to its fabric. Seth sings about a breath of some sort animating a valley of dry bones. It is something I have never encountered before. I was never more aware of myself as a foreign body, or more eager, once I recovered from the shock, to find ways to integrate myself into what was going on around me. I develop a hunger to acquire more of my new language and the life that goes with it. For the time being this is part of my love for Bethan, free to express itself, while she shrinks away from me. I cultivate the habit of listening to other people rather than listening too intently to the voices inside myself.

The young generation that congregates two or three times weekly in what Doctor Seth called the Workshop decide to put up a conservatory attached to the sunniest wing of the outbuildings. It proves, Seth says, that they can do something more than sing and muck about. The resolve is to work day and night to get it ready for Curig's return. It will be his sanatorium and sanctuary. An older generation of craftsmen join in, 'for the good name of Pentregwyn,' they say. The criminal intruders are said to have fled to Merseyside, but the burly plumber is confident they will be caught. He shakes his head and blames a lethal combination of alcohol and drugs for their savagery. He has things to say about broken families, lack of discipline, lack of training. While the place is a hive of activity, construction and reconstruction, I can only listen and watch, lost in admiration. Merely walking about has become a form of exploration. I begin to detect a powerful connection between the spirit of the people and the spirit of the place. There is more than meets the eye here to everybody and everything. The work goes on in spite of the objections Lowri Nichols makes to the noise and chatter. Conversations are conducted in hoarse whispers when they feel she is about to appear. Her policy would have been to carry Bethan off to their comfortable home in Cyncoed, Cardiff. Everything would be so much easier to manage there. Bethan won't hear of it. She wants to be within reach of Curig. For my own part my most vital function is to keep her in touch with his progress and learn to appreciate his remarkable qualities. She has come to look on him as the corner stone, you might say, of Sulwen's legacy; the essential spirit, if such a thing existed, of the Pentregwyn General Stores.

Subject to the vagaries of the weather and as an exercise in patience as much as anything, I take to walking further afield. I don't find much ease and comfort in the local pub. It's busy enough but I find it divided into cliquish sections and even subsections. There is an area of English-speaking newcomers. 'Settlers' as they are known locally. At the other extreme the Cymraeg speakers; divided between the young and vociferous and the middle-aged who don't have much to say to each other. In between are the casuals and visitors. If I have to sit with a solitary drink, give me a quiet spot on the Piazza della Maddalena any day. I determine to explore the length and breadth of the parish and beyond. The greenness of the countryside I find soothing: so also the people and my place among them. They listen with admirable politeness to my attempts to be fluent in their language. They accept the effort with a certain graciousness and I am made to feel accepted, even respected, and this I find, to my surprise, deeply satisfying. This would not be a bad place to live if only Bethan would make a greater effort to recover her spirits. The poor girl has been battered in the spirit as well as the flesh. She wants to move in the shadows and not be seen, and appears wary and suspicious of all attempts to approach her.

Walking down from the neolithic cave that Seth talked about with such enthusiasm I pass a pair of ruined cottages and in the long front garden of the last one, the elderly twins Ifan and Simon, are engaged in lifting the potato crop. They seem pleased with what they are doing and pleased to straighten their backs and talk to me. Simon it is who draws attention to the clouds over the higher hills and gives his opinion that rain is on the way. Ifan waits for his more simple-minded brother to go through the social motions before he deigns to speak. He has things to say of more abiding significance and it is my business to attend to him patiently while he assembles the appropriate words.

'We were born here,' he says.

He points at the ruined cottage behind them. 'Both of us,' Simon sniggers. His brother ignores the interruption. 'Who started stealing those blue slates I wonder? Terrible mistake to leave the cottage empty. How is that young girl coming along?'

I have to assume he is sympathetic and wants to be reassured.

'Nothing has been the same in Pentregwyn since Sulwen died,' he says. 'She was a good woman. A bit of a saint if anyone asked me. She kept the place together'.

'You were born here.'

I show a polite interest. It was the correct response.

'These you see were the joint cottages of Tan y Garth. My father was in charge of the horses at Plas Mawr. He followed the plough as they say. Small cottages. Big gardens. That's how it was, you see. Simple life. Happy times. Two mile walk to school in all weathers. Next door was Griffith Griffiths the shepherd. We used to watch him shave with a cut-throat razor, once a week outside the back door. Strongest man in the parish. And a bad temper too. Until he broke his leg you see. It never mended. He had to take to a wheelchair and we used to take it in turns to dig his garden and push his chair. Happy days. That would be sixty years or more ago. And here we are. Still digging.'

This was a cue for merriment. I realise they are even older than they look.

'My mother lived to be ninety-seven,' Simon says.

He is beaming with pleasure and Ifan condescends to give a frosty smile.

'That's why we never married. Even though he is a poet.'

Doctor Seth calls Ifan Dafis a hedge poet. Not without affection. He says his dry-walling is much better than his verse, but both activities are welcome. They contribute to the wellbeing of the parish.

'What's the difference between a hedge poet and a carpenter of song, anyway?... The degree of competence? The depth of perception? In Pentregwyn let a hundred flowers bloom.'

He is eager for me to engage in disputation of one sort or another. I have to take Curig's place as his sparring partner. It becomes a pleasure as well as a relief to visit Seth's cottage for tea and a talk. I have a lot to learn and his scones and blackcurrant jam are always tempting and tasty.

Daisy rings up full of goodwill and sympathy and

anxious enquiry. 'Oh the poor little thing. Bring her out here as soon as you can, won't you? We'll lavish all the care in the world on her.' I explain that Bethan is concerned with the man who saved her life and for the time being cannot be moved. 'Have you shown her a picture of that delightful house?' It seemed inappropriate at this time to mention the fabulous wedding gift my new step-mother has offered to make. As I explain the situation, Daisy becomes disappointed to the point of petulance.

'Why not bring him along too? They can't have better clinics out there than we have here in Switzerland surely.'

I put forward a hurried excuse that Curig is too dangerously ill to be moved and Bethan and her mother are still too upset and distraught to discuss anything rationally. She has to have the light on all night. Daisy's assumption that her windfall of wealth can solve anything becomes irritating. I suspect she finds my lack of initiative irritating too. I break what I take to be a disapproving silence with eager expressions of concern about my father's condition. Her cheerfulness, returns.

'He's so much better, day by day he improves.'

'How marvellous,' I say with all sincerity, and with relief at being able to change the subject. I am charged to ring again soon and to keep her informed. At the moment I have no inclination to do any such thing, or indeed anything else. Too much has already happened. Bethan barely ventures outside the premises until she has been assured that there is no one about to stare at her. She makes a daily inspection of her naked self in a long mirror upstairs. I am not allowed to be present. She mutters that a legendary process has gone into reverse. The fair maiden has been transformed into a hideous hag. This is far from the truth, and there is a limit to how many times I can contradict. So I express my whole-hearted willing-ness to abide by whatever restriction she chooses to impose. This vicious business has built up that wall between us we both swore could never exist. We talked more freely and frankly when we were a thousand miles apart than we do now under the same roof.

I am prepared to lie low in Curig Puw's outside kitchen and wait to be overtaken by events. There is a desk and a book-shelf stuffed with books that appear to have belonged to Sulwen, including three different translations of the Bible into Cymraeg. I am able to check up on the Old Testament to get that quotation about 'thy people and my people' right. I have to admit that Bethan and Daisy don't fit at all into the image of Ruth and Naomi. Still, it does my knowledge of the language no end of good to mull over the different versions of familiar passages.

In his desk I find a copy of Sulwen's famous letter written out in Curig's childlike handwriting. It has become a text – he is working on a commentary. Now I have time to study it myself and am prepared to do so in the most critical manner possible. I carp therefore I am. I shall suppress all heretical and blasphemous fantasies and concentrate on analysing a text which, it seems to me, has become the basis of a cult. I want to prepare myself for extended discussions with Bethan on this delicate subject. The kind of things we should have been talking about when she first received the letter. I realise I need to wait.

Something of a jolt. A letter from Personnel in our Department in Rome has been sent on to me. The sort of jolt that throws a fresh light on any situation without making it any clearer. It is polite and formal. It includes an application form in which I am invited to apply for what is in effect the post I already hold. There has been a reassessment of contracts and conditions. A new efficiency drive which they are convinced will meet with universal approval. The rate and range of salaries and pensions have been revised. It might well be that some grades may go down and not up, and others disappear altogether. The application would need the support of the head of the office but the personnel department has no doubt that it would be forthcoming and enthusiastic. I lie back on Curig Puw's bed and I am cool and calm enough to realise that my career hangs from a fragile thread held in the hand of that grinning puppeteer Freddy Helmut. This is my chance to be as bold and impetuous as Daisy thinks I should be. The choice is a brief note telling them to stuff it: or preserve a masterly inactivity. It is not merely my habitual caution, or sloth which makes me opt for the latter. I have a heap of contradictions to sort out. Daisy's presence has made a difference to my attitude to my father. Are there filial obligations that I have consistently avoided, failed to fulfil? Do I leave Bethan to the tender mercies of her parents or does the love she once declared for me so freely before this unhappy hiatus give me priorities over theirs? Was her love a deliberate gift or a happy accident? You could say the same about life. Curig's outside kitchen is as good a place as anywhere to sort that out.

Eighteen

ALWYN NICHOLS has a capacity for amiable passivity
that I find impressive. For a brief period before I arrived
on the scene he had leapt into fierce and concentrated
action, plunged into a fever of activity by the vandal
attack: now he has lapsed into his habitual mode. He has
a certain gracefulness about him that suggests whatever
he is doing, or even not doing, is appropriate to the occasion. At Bethan's age I imagine he was as attractive to
women as I well know she is to men. A mild air of having
been pampered underlies the calm he radiates. He has his
modest needs to be attended to by a wife who still
discerns the original attraction behind the middle-aged
plumping man. He remains the trophy she won, to be
regularly dusted and polished, even if it were at the
second attempt as Seth ap Tomos assures me. For
Bethan's sake I need to know more about them, understand them better, but I have to confess it is not a study I
would apply myself to, just for the sake of doing it. A
marriage should be a fresh start, not sinking deeper into
a quagmire of kith and kin. All I ask for is a Bethan recovered, not a caravanserai of relatives. As Freddy Helmut
was always ready to point out, I tend to prefer lexicons to
people! In some obscure sense I suspect that Alwyn and I
are kindred souls: all we ask for is a quiet life to pursue
our chosen hobbies. And this could be because we are
both the only sons of overpowering fathers; larger than
life figures, licensed to exercise their egos on the public
stage. Orlando would have enjoyed being a judge sending
restive elements of an audience to prison, having critics
clamped in irons.

I have the feeling Alwyn would enjoy a quiet chat with me and even a frank exchange of views: however he moves with caution under his spouse's watchful eye. He is given his meals on time, his daily paper and his pipe, when she allows him to smoke it. He has placed a comfortable armchair in a corner of Bethan's workroom where he can smoke and listen to music through earphones. Even without the music or the pipe, he is capable of chewing the cud mentally for prolonged periods of time. If there is any meaning to accidents that occur, he needs to go over the circumstance in minute detail to seek it out. He has settled on being agreeable as a way of life, although keeping a wary eye open for more unwarranted attacks. After all the initial distress, maybe he has been able to relax on the assumption that lightning does not strike in the same place twice.

The important point is that he has a soothing influence on his daughter more effective than mine. It seems a distinct step towards recovery when she taps the bald crown of his head as she leaves the table and returns to rest. He enjoys the momentary petting. While he is present I hover cheerfully on the fringe of the family, more than ready to make the best of whatever occurs. Bethan has become a priority for all of us – the sick child in the house – just as she insists that Curig Puw should take precedence over her.

A call comes from Cardiff and Alwyn springs to life. He is summoned to attend to some critical piece of devolved government. An unexpected glint of combat lights up his eye. The anonymity of civil service committee conflicts allows him to release combative qualities that would otherwise lie dormant. I know that feeling too. He goes so far as to shake my hand and say how glad and grateful he is that I should be at hand to support Bethan and her mother: then he is off in his BMW like a greyhound slipping its leash. What better release from primeval household emotion than a bout of cheerful office manoeuvres.

This leaves me face to face with Lowri Nichols. Her pent-up energies and urge to fuss and fidget are at a loss now her husband has departed. I still don't know what she sees when she looks at me. Something her daughter picked up on her haphazard and largely misguided travels. Not as obnoxious as Jens Strangerup, but a cause for unease if not suspicion. Too friendly perhaps with Seth? Another foreign body to watch out for? She may still be working out whatever it was the girl saw in me. My subdued geniality and sickly smile do not seem to appease. Why had the darling headstrong girl not discovered some fine upstanding Cymro with all the right ideas? Lowri is little impressed with my linguistic prowess. I feel she finds my utterance too precise and stilted. It could be I am over-eager in my anxiety to please. On the other hand if Bethan and I get married, which remains my firm intention, in spite of everything, this woman becomes my overactive mother-in-law and my tenuous almost ghostly intention to found a family will have to contend with this fact.

Lowri is well armed with opinions most of which I have to admit I have to agree with. This is some form of comfort. We are united in condemnation of the machinations of the American military industrial complex and its commercial power, and the manifest dangers of globalisation. Her indignation is fuelled with a shrill form of righteous resentment that often makes Bethan resort to claiming she feels weary and unwell and needs to go upstairs to rest. My own relaxation is roaming around the parish, up hill and down dale, observing the advance of a warm autumn and taking a benign interest in whomsoever I chance to meet. The pleasures of local life are an acquired taste and something I have never experienced before. I am much taken with the politeness of the older inhabitants particularly in the outlying farms and cottages. They seem glad to welcome a visitor who has made the effort to learn their language. Seth ap Tomos says I ought to wear a dog collar and assume the role of a nineteenth-century parson. Indeed one inclination all these agreeable people seem to share is a resistance to the forces directed towards the speeding up of Time with a capital T. Ifan Dafis, the dry-walling poet, moans on about some mysterious force he calls 'The English Tide'. He has a range of facts and figures about chapels closing and the steep decline in Sunday School attendance. 'What in the end,' he says with a gnarled hand in the air challenging me to provide an answer to his rhetorical question, 'What in the end is the hurry? Do we have to race each other to the grave?'

Lowri is not impressed with my new-found enthusiasm for village life. I am slow to realise that her disapproval was never confined to Jens Strangerup and all his works. Or to sour memories of the Past revived by the presence of Seth ap Tomos. When Bethan has gone upstairs to rest she gives freer rein to objections to Pentregwyn and its sluggish inhabitants. She makes clear to me she is opposed to Bethan's misguided attachment to the shop and her plans for its revival. 'Tinkering with the problem' she calls it. A waste of valuable energy.

'What is needed, you see, is a national change of heart.'

With Bethan out of earshot she grows more dogmatic by the minute.

'What is needed is a social and economic regeneration led from the front by a genuinely patriotic government. We are small enough as it is. What is needed is a national commitment. That is what is missing. That is the vital ingredient.'

I make no attempt to argue. My gestures suggest a confession of ignorance of the complexities of the situation, but unwavering goodwill notwithstanding. I have to show some gratitude for her at least taking me into her confidence. She is encouraged and we seem to come closer than at any time since we met. I conclude this must be a good thing. She doesn't know whether or not I would be interested, but she is a candidate for the next National Assembly election. It would do no harm at all if Bethan came to the constituency and showed her open support.

Once she had recovered of course. It could even be a form of therapy. Take the girl out of herself.

'Of course with Alwyn and me, Bethan always comes first. Always did and always will. I took on motherhood long before politics. That doesn't mean a woman can't do a good job of both.'

I sense that I need do little more than mutter 'Amen' to all her pronouncements to gain her approval: which is a prospect at once encouraging, but also a cause of unspecified unease.

'We have to recognise that Bethan does have this streak of being headstrong and unpredictable. But we know where that comes from.'

The way she glances around the place is revealing. This shop and the family that built it and owned it is a true source of a succession of woes, culminating in the terrible attack that almost destroyed her precious girl. For the girl to return and claim this tainted inheritance had been flying in the face of the very Providence that had placed Bethan in Lowri's loving care. I am expected to understand and even share these sentiments, whether spoken or unspoken, Lowri's prejudices become a factor in any decision for the future that Bethan and I decide to make. Meanwhile I continue to echo the mantra that 'Bethan comes first,' and to suffer all the difficulties of co-existence with her formidable mother.

Daisy rings up. She sounds bright and cheerful.

'Eddie! Your father wants to speak to you.'

His speech is slurred, not unlike when he had too much to drink. Just as cordial too.

'Eddie, dear boy. How is your delightful maid of the mountains? Can I speak to her?'

I hasten to explaining that she is sleeping and that I wouldn't want to wake her. She finds sleeping difficult. So it's best to get the best of it while it lasts. This could be a defensive mode but it feels like the sober truth as I am saying it.

'Poor little thing. She's taking a long time to get better

isn't she? Anyway, give her my love.'

'Yes. Of course,' I say. 'Of course I will.'

'I suppose you are going to get married still.'

'Of course.'

This time I sound a little cross. Why should he doubt it? He has so many romantic illusions about feminine pulchritude, it is possible he thinks of Bethan as damaged and the damage would be enough to make me change my mind. The bloom knocked off the blossom, the flowers discarded. Even worse, with his predator's understanding of female instincts, he may have judged that in the end this delicious creature would never want me anyway. I am stung by the recollection of how easily he was able to win Bethan's sympathetic attention when she stayed with us in Juan-les-Pins. He behaved more like a rival than a father. If there were pretty women around he had the automatic right to the first claim on their attention. My father has lost none of his ability to make my pulse race in the wrong directions for the wrong reasons.

'Good show. Good show. The thing is dear boy, it's getting a touch autumnal here. Mist on the lake and flocks of birds migrating. So we think we'll migrate too. To Marrakesh. Daisy has American friends there from the old Embassy days. Retired as you can imagine. Well now, why don't you two join us? It's a big house apparently. Room for all of us. Think of it as a honeymoon if you like.'

The burst of persuasive eloquence has exhausted him.

'What you need to remember, dear boy, is that your remote ancestors escaped from those damp hills as fast as they could. Here's Daisy to talk to you.'

'Eddie. Isn't it wonderful? He's almost back to normal, wouldn't you say? I'm so proud of him.'

As I express enthusiastic agreement I waver between remorse and outright guilt. A son should be more concerned about his father's well-being. My critical reactions are nothing more than bitter spurts of jealousy that can be traced all the way back to my mother's womb.

'It's the most wonderful offer. I'll certainly put it to her as soon as she gets a little better. Her nerves are still in a pretty ragged state, I'm afraid.'

'Of course they are. I am most desperately sorry and I do sympathise. But you put it to her, won't you Eddie darling? Your father is convinced she and I would get on like a house on fire. That's not the best of all similes is it, but he claims to detect basic resemblances. I don't know what you think?'

'Oh yes. Quite possibly.'

Daisy is laughing.

'After all, we have to admit he does know about women.'

I am obliged to laugh too.

'Anyway the road to Marrakesh is wide open and beckoning. No expense spared of course. The honey-moon is on me.'

I have to stutter profuse thanks and promise to do my best and keep in touch. And that was that.

My dilemma is whether or not to take Lowri Nichols into my confidence and tell her about this generous offer. She has been strangely incurious about my background. I have kept quiet about my new stepmother. It would not do for Lowri to know Daisy was the widow of an American ambassador. I doubt very much whether she had heard of the great Orlando either. And if she had, it wouldn't be a fame she would approve of. For her, Entertainment with a capital 'E' comes under a general heading of 'candyfloss'. I have taken in a range of her prejudices. 'American ambassadors are imperial proconsuls in disguise...' 'Too much wealth makes people capricious, especially women...' 'Rich gifts wax poor if givers prove unkind...' She is armed with quotations as well as opinions. She sees the world in uncompromising terms and so I decide not to tell her and add the offer to the load of secrets that are accumulating inside me while I wait for Bethan to make a full recovery. Part of me is wound up in a protective ball waiting for the girl to return to what she used to be, delightfully bouncy and full of beans.

Nineteen

THERE IS NOTHING quite like the aura of mystery that surrounds the person you long to possess. Through the long kitchen window I watch Lowri and Bethan engaged in the soothing processes of making blackberry jam and jelly. An unusually warm day in October. The smell of the wilder fruits of autumn hangs in the air and the sweetness of the decay of the season. It looks like an ageless scene of domestic harmony: a Dutch interior of mother and daughter working easily together. The concentrated silence seems appropriate and even congenial. It says nothing about what I perceive is the growing tension between them. Bethan turns to me increasingly as an outlet for subdued complaint about her mother. Not, alas, for making love. I am required to express tenderness and concern: an infinite gentleness as I touch her body but nothing that would have the slightest suggestion of male aggression. It is a sign that I am going too far if she begins to shiver. Then she will revert to snapping at me as if I were responsible for all her ills. I learn to keep my distance unless I am called for! The kitchen scene, in the sunlight and shadow alternating on the stone floor gives only a tantalising glimpse of a possible return to normality. Even though I have acquired a semi-detached affection for this place and its people, I would be at a loss if challenged to define what exactly normality here could consist of.

Too much seems to depend on the condition of Curig Puw. There is a symbiotic link between Bethan's rate of recovery and Curig's. Seth has taken pleasure in pointing this out more than once as though I were not already all too painfully aware of it. 'Isn't it odd,' he says. 'Your Bethan has merged miraculously into Sulwen's place as the presiding deity of Pentregwyn. It makes you think, you know. There's an awful lot in folk wisdom and magic. Provided of course it doesn't get caught up in the dogmatic machinery of religion. Marvellous to contemplate the transfer of half a creative relationship from an old woman to a lovely young girl. Do you know what I mean?'

I know only too well and I don't need him to tell me. There are moments when he poses as the Prospero of Pentregwyn, that I find very irritating. We get on well and I have no doubt he is well-disposed towards me, but at moments like this he appears to be over-privileged and under-employed. Early retirement and well-meaning rural pursuits are all very well, but we are told there is an acute shortage of doctors. There is plenty of choice among the slums and favellas of this world where he could be practising his art instead of waving his wand over this moribund parish. Of course, precisely the same criticism could be made of myself.

His admiration of Curig's courage and stoicism is unbounded.

'The old boy must have been in excruciating pain after what he had been through. And he still is no doubt. I don't know why I call him "old boy". He's years and years younger than I am. Child of old parents I am told. Probably born to be a guru. And there must be something in her as well you see. Deep calling unto deep.'

Now I know he is teasing me. I have to muster a weak smile. He has adopted a stance of treating life's triumphs and disasters as a bit of a joke: human behaviour to be observed with the interested detachment of the scientist puzzling over the antics of free radicals. He is forever looking for an argument on the subject. He wants to boast that his approach to life is governed by scientific principles and the rigors of his medical training. I hold myself back from bluntly pointing out that it is more likely to stem from his disappointed love for Ffion Locksley. When he thinks no one is looking, he gazes at Bethan as though she were the reincarnation of her dead mother.

There is no magic about it and Seth must know that as well as I do. He must have known all along that the aim of Sulwen's interminable letter had been to bring both of them together. Not so much the mystical fulfilment of an ideal but an old maid's romantic fancy. Everything written for future consumption is in effect a last will and testament; an attempt to control the course of events after the writer has left the scene; a pre-emptive strike on the future. In a place like this, that insists on being weighed down by History, the past can reach up from the ground to restrict all freedom of action.

'He must have been in agony most of the time. Sedation or no sedation. And yet completely uncomplaining. The nurses were telling me they had to look into his room every now and then to make sure he was still there. I wrote a hir-a-thoddiad about him. Nice little exercise in one of the twenty-four measures. Ends up with something like – "Floating above the world of wishes, listening to the music of the spheres." That is how he does it, I fancy. When he's out and about I'll tell the old boy to patent it.'

Seth is in a cheerful mood. He is taking me to visit Curig Puw in a brand new Convalescent Hospital built on a hillside overlooking a broad valley. I can see a distinct pattern emerging: a conflict going on between Seth ap Tomos and Lowri Nichols for influence over my Bethan. As she emerges from her nightmare and the protection of a mother's wing, Seth believes the balance of power will tilt in his direction. Before the atrocious attack, Curig's ascetic way of life never met with Lowri Nichols' approval, and even now she is cross and deeply irritated by his refusal to seek criminal damages. 'Who does he think he is forgiving?' she said. 'He is so naïve. Drug-fuelled thugs have to be punished. Does he think it helps if he punishes himself?' Seth thinks his friendship with Curig will be a key factor in future developments. He says this to me in so many words as though Edward Lloyd did not at all enter into the equation. He assumes that, all along, Bethan's wayward courses have been driven by a subconscious urge to fulfil Sulwen's will. I can derive no comfort at all from that absurd theory.

Seth strides over to the large window ready to admire the view across the valley even before he sees it. I pass two of the beds in the ward occupied by ancient males too weak to speak. Seth estimates they are suffering from the final stages of cancer. He remains resolutely cheerful. He is bold enough to manoeuvre Curig's orthopaedic bed closer to the window. In the oblique sunlight the colours of autumn he says are singing. The wooded slopes are great masses of green and gold and brown and yellow. The pattern of hedgerows around the trim fields with isolated oaks, the river winding along the valley in its own good time... 'All the air things wear that build this world of Wales'.

Seth warms to his enthusiasm and Curig smiles approvingly. Seth points at the patient.

'When Brother Curig is in his mystical mode, you know, every blade of grass means something!'

'Of course it does. You lie here for change, Doctor Seth. Studying the view. It will cure you of your worship of science and technology.'

'Who says I worship them for God's sake? Mind you they've helped quite a lot to make you better.'

They are happy for me to see them squaring up to each other. It's well practised and ostentatiously good-humoured.

'You want to watch out for him.'

Curig's voice quavers without being querulous.

'He hasn't got red hair for nothing. He's a real fox. Up to no good. Do anything to win an argument.'

'Curig tries to say too much technology separates us from God. I say it's worse than that. It separates us from poetry and separates us from the seasons.'

Seth points to a vapour trail in the blue sky.

'Think of all those aeroplanes polluting the upper atmosphere carrying pampered humans south like a load of stuffed birds to dodge the winter. It's a sin against the four seasons. The only poetry that matters is the poetry of place!'

Seth claps his hands. He has rounded off the performance to his own satisfaction. Curig Puw sinks back into his pillows, clearly tired but still smiling.

'We are going to get him out of here in no time at all. Up and about, engine running, raring to go.'

In the corridor of this brand new hospital building I suffer an abrupt sensation of being caught up in a web of circumstance not of my own making. By falling in love I never intended to sink into such unchartered waters. I wish the patient well and I also wish I had nothing to do with him. He was never a part of what I considered my scheme of things. How close did he and Bethan become during ups and downs of that abortive film enterprise? There was so much going on I never witnessed and I can no longer enquire about. It does me no good at all to think of him as a rival and even less to consider his wellbeing as a controlling factor in my life.

Seth and the lawyer Olwen Caradog-Jones invite me to join them for lunch in a restaurant near Olwen's office.

'Join the conspiracy, Edward Llwyd,' he says. 'The only way to regenerate a community these days. A conspiracy of the well-meaning who know how to get things done.'

He is in boisterous confident mood like a doctor walking the wards with all his patients making good recoveries. This is in some contrast to Mrs Olwen Caradog-Jones' beatific calm and the melodious whisper that emerges from her imposing frame. I can only attribute their close collaboration to their devotion to their native language and habitat. There is nothing like a Cause for making persons of disparate temperaments and attitudes work together. She smiles at resounding speech she would otherwise find discordant and even disorderly, and he listens patiently to her decorous whisper. They also share a tender concern for the welfare of Curig Puw that I find verges on the overwhelming.

'The poor boy,' Mrs Olwen says. 'I'm quite sure he doesn't realise he has been transformed from what was virtually a social outcast into a local hero. If only dear Sulwen were alive to see it.'

It is quite a sophisticated operation. For both of them the rehabilitation of Pentregwyn and that of Curig Puw are closely bound together. Rehabilitation involves restoring Tabernacle Chapel as a listed building: transforming the old village school into a community centre: Pentregwyn Stores and Sulwen's legacy to become a vital centre of village life and the flagship of the spirit of renewal. More than that, if Bethan approves; Sulwen's inheritance can become a stepping stone to claiming grants from various directions, most of which I confess I never knew existed. There was no reason in their view why Edward Lloyd could not make some tentative approach to Brussels to sniff out any grants that could be available from the European Union. In spite of these ambitious plans, the move that excites them most is to organise, out of sight of course, an appeal from the people of Llanfair Iscoed to persuade the United Free Church Council to call Curig Puw to minister at Tabernacle Chapel and possibly two other chapels still functioning in the vicinity.

'I tried to have a word with Lowri Nichols in this regard,' says Olwen Caradog Jones. 'To see whether she and dear old Alwyn could put in a word at Presbyterian headquarters. I'm not saying we are bosom friends, but after all we're all on the same side are we not? I'm afraid she was distinctly unhelpful. Discouraging in fact. She doubted whether such an unworldly and impractical creature could function effectively as a minister in this day and age.'

'Yes, well… where there is no vision, shall we say?'

For once Doctor Seth ap Tomos cuts the flow of his eloquence short. He is keeping half an eye on my reactions. I am a new recruit to the conspiracy and it is too early for me to witness his hostility to Lowri coming out in the open. He will want to test the strain a relationship with a prospective mother-in-law will have on me. I am infected with the atmosphere of conspiracy and beginning to think in distrustful Machiavellian mode. If battle lines are to be drawn, am I to be caught in the middle? My limited objective intelligence tells me that my position in any analysis of the situation would be closer to Lowri's than to theirs. I am after all some sort of international civil servant and my knowledge of the food and agricultural situation tells me that the ills of this world are on too vast a scale to be dealt with in this piecemeal atomised fashion. Seth may be interesting enough in his eccentric speculative way but in spite of all the good work he likes to imagine he does by stealth, his theories are too hopelessly utopian to bear serious examination. Olwen Caradog-Jones is in the grip of an emotional attachment to an ideal past that amounts to mental paralysis. The difficult Lowri could be right about Curig. He is so otherworldly, his feet barely touch the ground.

What about me though? I listen to their conspiratorial conversation and smile and keep my own counsel with all the guile of a spy in the camp. What should a spy do? This lovesick overprivileged private individual with his small but cushioning private income. How should he dispose of himself in a suffering world? In a state of some despondency I return to Curig Puw's outside kitchen and reopen the application form that has lain on his writing desk, alongside his notes and his copy of Sulwen's famous letter. 'Surname, given name, date of birth, career to date…' Oh dear. To begin at the beginning. I may as well swallow my pride and fill it in. Just in case.

Twenty

SETH AP TOMOS declares that Pentregwyn is bracing itself for celebration. He tells me that two hundred years of protestant non-conformity have inculcated restraint as a way of life; buried the medieval instinct for ceremony and most traces of Celtic magic. Pentregwyn is poised between Gwynedd and Powys so the greyness of slate is never far away and the rain is always ready to paint it across the sky. 'None of your proletarian boisterousness around here.' And so he goes on. He is so absorbed in his fanciful abstractions he never realises that I'm not a social anthropologist on a field trip. I came here to collect a bride and all I found was a defenceless girl struck down, lying wounded you could say on the bare floor of her inheritance. I'm not sure I can absorb or even take any more of Seth's machinations and theories. He treats me as a captive audience and I don't know whether he realises it, or even cares, but the effect on me is to increase the sense of alienation. I am only hanging on to the place to wait for Bethan to recover; to have her restored to her old self and our love reinstated. I resent the fact that even at this advanced stage the slow process is still related to the recovery of Curig Puw and the return of that reluctant hero.

Her mother and I stand by an upstairs window, above the shop, observing her progress down the village street, on her father's arm. She is using a stick and is covered from head to foot in hood and cloak, which I find excessively theatrical. Her recovery is far more advanced than that. There are moments around the house and in the shop supervising alterations when she can be quite sprightly. But she has mood swings and is liable to hide an urge to burst into tears by retiring to rest. Alwyn Nichols and his only daughter have emerged to inspect the decorations in the village hall and to listen to the cerdd dant choir, conducted by Olwen Caradog-Jones' cousin, rehearsing among other works, the chorus of welcome, with words specially written for the occasion by none other than the ubiquitous doctor. The bunting is out. Seth and his allies have been scuttling about for days. The young members of the workshop are all puffed up with their own importance. At the window Lowri Nichols is simmering with discontent and suppressed disapproval.

'So much talent,' she mutters. 'Such a gifted girl. She was meant for something much better than this.'

'My goodness yes,' I say to myself. 'What about Marrakesh for a start?'

The warm invitation remains wide open, repeated several times, until I wonder why I don't put it to her. What better place for a winter convalescence? Why do I lack the courage to suggest it? Because I know Bethan would dismiss a notion so inconsistent with her vision and accuse me of lack of commitment by daring to suggest it. What the loved one wants the loved one should get remains axiomatic. But the strain is telling. I am more capable of appreciating Lowri's misgivings with every day that passes. This shop and what goes with it is an inheritance fraught with booby-traps. I can sense her apprehensiveness about her husband too. He is wandering down that village street in search of his long lost love, the birth mother of the young woman with whom he is walking arm in arm. This was the blessed plot to which Ffion Locksley brought him in the first fine frenzy of their love. The self-appointed master of ceremonies, Seth ap Tomos, is deliberately manoeuvring the amiable Alwyn in that direction and as things stand at the moment, there is very little this active frustrated woman, alongside me at the window, can do about it. In the wordless silence I imagine I can hear her heart pounding. Or could it be my own?

It is the custom for a daughter to be escorted down the

aisle on her father's arm. For what other ceremony are they rehearsing? She is being led away from me. Whatever is happening, there is precious little I can do about it except exercise patience and wait. At mealtimes these past days I have had to sit and listen to Bethan outlining the extent of Curig's virtues to her father, with all the enthusiasm of a convert trying to convert a well-wishing sceptic. From a prolonged period of lassitude and feeble incapacity she appears to have revived her energies for the sole purpose of singing Curig Puw's praises. For God's sake is he so marvellous? He is hardly any more than one more faltering pilgrim plunging around in the gathering dark and that is a category very much on the increase in this age of confusion. A category common enough to include me if she cared to look. There is a detectable inverse ratio. The more attention she has paid to his condition the less she has paid to mine.

When father and daughter return it is Alwyn who declares himself well satisfied with the preparations. He is full of admiration of the cerdd dant choir.

'Such dedication,' he says. 'And there was a lovely new setting of old Waldo's words.'

He begins to hum. ' "What is love of country? Keeping house / Among a cloud of witnesses?" Very moving wasn't it Beth?'

Bethan doesn't seem to share his enthusiasm even though she nods.

'You can't save anything by singing,' she says.

While she commands undivided attention she intends to make her standpoint clear.

'You have to build,' she says. 'You have to act. That's what this shop means. A centre for action. And I'm going to build it that way. That means more than restoring it. It means giving it a new life.'

There is no discussion. She retires upstairs, dragging her cloak behind her. Lowri considers following her. Alwyn extracts his pipe and looks around for a quiet corner where he can smoke it with impunity and no doubt ruminate about the fading radiance of the past in Pentregwyn. I go out in search of a more tangible present. There is so much to avoid, I head for the iron age fort on Y Garn. I have resolutions to make. I set out resolutely enough in the warm afternoon light. When I reach the summit I am caught in a sudden shower of rain and need to jog home to keep myself warm in my wet clothes. It is chilly enough in the outside kitchen. When I change I realise that I am no nearer making any kind of decision at all. So little of what I do or say seems to be of any account.

I join the family for tea. Bethan seems to be in a better mood. It is as if the sun has come out. In this place her moods control the weather.

'Curig will want his quarters back,' I say. 'I'd better move out. Where do you think I should go?'

Lowri looks at Bethan as if to say now that she is recovered, she is handing back domestic command.

'There's the conservatory,' Bethan says, looking thoughtful. 'We could easily put up a bed in there. Or you could come upstairs and sleep with me.'

With more relief than resentment light breaks where no sun shines. I grasp that I am being teased and that she is laughing at me, and maybe at her parents as well.

'I've got promises to keep, haven't I?'

She comes behind my chair, puts her hands around my neck and places her face alongside mine as though we were having our photographs taken. An image in any case to develop in her parents' minds. I want to seize her and swing her about in my unbounded relief. Instead I am being held down quite forcibly and I have to smile about it.

'Here he is, my dear parents. The very man I am going to marry. Aren't you pleased? Isn't he a lamb? Isn't he a gorgeous pet?'

They recover at different speeds: a brief embarrassment is overtaken by more formal expressions of pleasure. It seems to come more easily to Alwyn than to his wife. She has a whole sequence of misgivings to contend with, from fears about Bethan's health and stability to my alien background and ambiguous behaviour. All I can do is splutter and make some demonstration of being both overcome and blessed.

That night in semi-darkness, not without moments of childish giggling, we undress together in what used to be Sulwen's room. Bethan sits naked on the edge of the bed and then to my alarm holds her head in her hands and begins to weep. I have to comfort her. To keep her warm. She buries herself in the warmth of my arms and I can barely hear what she is saying.

'I've been such a miserable bitch. I have. I have. Punishing you for what happened. As if it could ever have been your fault. Will you ever forgive me?'

'There's nothing to forgive.'

'It's horrid really, to have to admit it. You were the one I could strike at and know you wouldn't hit back…'

'That's fine,' I say. 'I wanted you to take it out on me. I was guilty anyway. For not having been there to defend you.'

The best thing was to reduce words to murmurs and the desire to comfort each other. There was enough to overcome. Everything between us had to be reduced to a tender exploration, a rediscovery, a search for renewal. We slept at last and for me at least the sleep was long and blissful. When I woke, Bethan was sitting at the window in her dressing gown sipping a glass of water.

'You sleep like a baby,' she says.

She smiles and I feel I meet with her total approval.

'I've been thinking,' she says. 'I got everything in the wrong order. It was such a mistake to plunge into that film business before getting this place properly set up on its feet. On a firm foundation. It was a catastrophic misjudgement. You would never have made it, would you?'

I am still in a daze. Unequipped to answer hypothetical questions. If I dreamt anything it was the sensation of one-ness as we had been on that first night in the couchette on the Paris Express with the blue light burning dimly and my heart fit to burst. Whatever had happened since then had faded away into a mist of dreamy inconsequence. I wake to just this. Here and now. Together again.

'I've been thinking,' she says. 'You've seen me in my true colours. You've seen how tough and how wrong and impossible I can be. Do you really want me? No. Not just me. All this that goes with me? Are you sure you won't be pining for those umbrella pines? No, I'm not really joking. If you want to pull out, darling, pull out now. I'm back on my feet and you've done your bit and I'm eternally grateful. I'd be heartbroken of course, but this place isn't your responsibility. Old Cynddylan the First died centuries and centuries ago.'

There is just one simple thing to say.

'You are my responsibility,' I say. 'I'm not going to let you go.'

She puts down the glass and prepares to come back to bed, an entrancing image of delicate submission. She snuggles into my shape and murmurs how nice it is to be together again.

Twenty-One

AND WE NEED TO go on insisting how nice it is. Being in love is a condition that requires perpetual renewal. I know some of my ex-colleagues who would say I was strengthening my resolve with simplistic conclusions. I have indeed said farewell to the pines of Rome as far as that job in F.A.O. went. My contract has expired, my Rubicon crossed in the opposite direction and my invasion boats burned. Every day that passes makes it clear however much comfort and delight we enjoy in our physical relationship, what she requires most of all is a partner that she can totally rely on. I need to cultivate an affection for this shop and all that goes with it. We'll set up a small language lab between the cyber café and the library. Teach the locals to become more independent and self-reliant by being European. Sounds good but, I have to confess it is hard to love a grey building that seems forever poised between a failed past and an indeterminate future. I just have to have as much faith in Bethan's vision as I have in my love for her. That becomes life's most necessary equation. So I roll up my sleeves to participate in the local life that surrounds it: not exactly a throbbing heart, but still beating faintly.

Participation is all. Seth ap Tomos takes me along to a bardic contest in Croeswen, a neighbouring village. The autumn season has begun and there is a three-cornered contest between rival teams. The village hall is full and there is an eisteddfodic buzz around the place. The audience listens attentively to the satirical exchanges in the strict metres, ready to appreciate verbal dexterity and even more eager to burst into laughter. It seems to me a higher form of light entertainment and I have to keep my wits about me to laugh in the right places. Seth tells me the teams take their rivalry seriously but the chief satisfaction is a general sense of fellowship and goodwill. 'It's the spirit of survival,' he says. 'In spite of everything, we're still here.' It is all very warm and laudable and I am happy to feel no longer a stranger in their midst.

There are patriotic undertones to everything that goes on around Pentregwyn these autumn days and in the midst of it all, a crowning event one might say, there is Curig's Welcome Home. Good old Curig. Fair play to old Curig is the general cry and I am well equipped with something to celebrate myself and very ready to join in any cheering. There are cultural and religious figures on the platform ready to place Curig's courage and suffering in a wider context. He was on the spot to defend the higher values of a better ordered society and the most effective reward we could make him was to listen more intently to what he had to say and make greater efforts to protect and encourage our unique language and the civilised way of living that went with it. The eloquence goes down a storm and I am delighted with my own willingness to relax and join in the applause. For once I don't need to keep my head above the waters, so to speak, and take in great draughts of sceptical air so as not to drown in the excitement. It is a new sensation and a special pleasure to discover I can swim with the shoal.

Alas it is old Curig himself who provides an anticlimax to the day's happy events. Young stalwarts from Seth's workshop escort Curig to the platform in a wheelchair. There is more applause than ever. He holds tightly on to the lectern and for all his height someone murmurs that he looks thin and fragile enough to be blown away. It is absurd that I go on calling him 'old Curig' when he could well be younger than I am. He is clearly pleased and grateful and smiling, but when he speaks it comes out in a barely audible murmur. It appears to be more than a modest disclaimer of any merit in his action: it amounts to a sober analysis of his own shortcomings, almost a public confession. It seems wholly inappropriate. Our audience, accustomed to eloquence, becomes restless and impatient. After straining their ears for several minutes one or two bolder spirits call out, encouraging him to speak up. Uwch! Uwch! He nods and smiles as though he were in total agreement with them about his own deficiencies. He manages something approaching a shout.

'I know! I know. I'm sorry and I apologise. What I was saying was, I can't change the world, but I can change myself if I try hard enough. There will always be things, important things, that we will never succeed in changing. But the one thing that always lies within our power is to change ourselves.'

And then he relapses into his mumble trying to qualify the sweeping statement. It doesn't seem the appropriate discourse and there is general disappointment and in the end polite applause. Another speaker attempts to fan the flame but the spark has gone and the only hope of a reasonable recovery is a hearty bout of hymn singing. I don't know the words and Bethan seems stiff with disapproval. As the meeting disperses she holds on tightly to my arm which makes me feel agreeably strong and indispensable. There are important persons around, including county councillors, who want to speak to her, and she uses me as a buffer zone and does her shrinking violet act which obliges me to suppress a grin.

'Such simple people.'

I can hear her mutter under her breath.

'What do they expect? Gladiators? Babes must be fed with milk.'

In between formal introductions and handshakes she gives me her version of Curig's chequered history before he arrived in the refuge of Sulwen's outside kitchen as though I had never heard it before and in this version it is a record of misunderstood martyrdom. She wants me to understand the fickle nature of public support. In her view people are like hungry sheep looking up to be fed, and in the end it is the job of people like us to feed them. That is more or less what she meant by feeding babes with milk. Curig, she insists, is a natural hermit, a guru, and should be accepted as such. All civilised communities should be equipped with such a creature. It's a crying need.

Seth has laid on what he calls a surprise party in the plâs. The New York Newts are not in residence at Coed y Glyn, and we assemble in the large sparsely furnished drawing room and look through the uncurtained long window at the floodlit lawns and shrubbery. The guests seem to have been carefully selected. People I imagine Seth and Olwen and their circle hope will exercise influence in favour of their plans. Curig is parked in a comfortable chair in the corner and supplied with a glass of orange juice. It seems to me that he is more avoided than consulted but that does nothing to diminish his aura of inward calm. Bethan is reluctant to help with the entertaining beyond handing out drink and bits that Seth's volunteers from the workshop have prepared beforehand. She sees to it that the chosen locals get their proper share. She takes particular exception to a loud voiced young man from either the National Trust or the Arts Council, who grows noisier with the quantities of wine that he manages to consume.

'Freeloaders. Networkers. Safe in their jobs. Do not disturb,' she whispers angrily to me. 'You'll never get anything out of this lot for the kind of projects we have in mind. They are so blindly optimistic. Seth especially. If you ask me anything, we have to prepare to be disappointed. Ourselves alone, dear Eddie. Ourselves alone.'

While I bask in her approval Ifan the dry-wall poet touches my arm.

'Big place, isn't it? I'd like to show you something'

I look around and ask him for the whereabouts of his twin.

'In the kitchen,' Ifan said. 'Washing up. One of the sons of Martha.'

I follow Ifan down a series of dimly lit corridors to a

bare room beyond the kitchen and the scullery.

'For you to know how things used to be,' Ifan says. 'Here there was a long table and the steward sat there in front of a big ledger and a cash box. The Colonel would march up and down behind him ready to tell anybody off. And when they'd paid the rent, the tenants would bow and back out like this, twisting their caps in their hands.'

So that I could, I suppose, fully appreciate the extent of their servility, Ifan went through the ritual himself in elaborate dumb show until he backed into a wall and burst out laughing.

'That's the kind of world it was,' he says. 'My father used to tell me. His brother was a tenant of the old Colonel and would run to do his bidding. Licking his boots as the saying goes. They were better than us you see. A higher breed. The master race. And now I'm here, messing about. Never been inside this mansion before you see. I had to see it.'

The locals. These are the people Bethan hopes to persuade to stand on their own feet. Are we talking about a race of sturdy stalwart independent-minded peasants, and where do we find them? All dispersed, in the colonies, on the prairies, in the outback. Are there any left here? Her missionary zeal looks beautiful, is beautiful; but you need to evaluate in cold blood the material you propose to deal with. It seems urgent to pick up these points with her. My sceptical breath has to be of some use. However when I get back to her side, she is ready to cut our evening short.

'Time to go home,' she said. 'Curig needs an early night. He mustn't be tired any further.'

So we leave in spite of the host and Mrs Olwen Caradog-Jones pressing us to stay. There was more music to come and her cousin, a noted soprano, had promised to sing. With me as a polite echo, Bethan says we would have loved to stay but our first duty is to give Curig his medication and see him put safely to bed in his cherished outside kitchen.

Bed will be our refuge too. The shop is strangely silent. An empty place of shadows that bear no trace of the triumphs and sorrows of more than a century and a half. It's difficult not to feel a stranger in a foreign setting at such moments, until I remember she has come to regard it all as part of herself. Alwyn and Lowri have returned to Cardiff to deal with a crisis in the domestic arrangements of his father the irascible judge. It appears that the old boy has dismissed the third housekeeper-slash-carer in a matter of seven months. Lowri I thought was glad of the excuse to escape the celebrations. Alwyn was more reluctant or more ready to say so. So we had the place to ourselves and the silence.

'He is so good.'

Bethan continues to sing Curig Puw's praises.

'You have to live with people for days on end through trials and tribulations to see how good they can be. Or how bad come to that. When Jens and his lot were hanging around the place they looked so superficial and cheap alongside Curig. So here-today-gone-tomorrow. He was so wonderfully patient and understanding. And so wise. I learnt a lot from him. I have to admit it.'

We are in bed and our heads on the pillow and she is still talking.

'I keep on saying it, don't I? Am I getting on your nerves? You are good too, my Eddie darling. And cuddly too. So that makes you twice as good.'

We take refuge in each other's arms from the silence of the shop, from the parish and the echo of the world's alarms. When we have made love it seems the moment to whisper in her ear about the charms of Lake Lucerne and the possibilities of Marrakesh.

'Tell me something,' I whisper. 'When shall we take our honeymoon? Before or after the wedding?'

'Um.' She is happy and relaxed. 'It sounds wonderful.'

I am not sure she has understood me. In no time she is fast asleep. I am not so lucky. When Daisy last called, the sympathy in her sweet youthful voice made me feel sorry for myself. She said she couldn't understand what all the fuss was about. A shop in the country was a nice idea, rather like hollyhocks around a cottage door. She had a dim recollection of taking part in a play about a village shop. That was old-fashioned even then. 'Hardly part of the modern world, Eddie darling, with satellites and e-mails and the world-wide web making the whole world just one big village from China to Peru!' I hear her voice so clearly.

'You poor lamb. Being in love is no joke is it? I've no idea about all that 'roots' business that seems to be troubling your little maid of the mountains. But I do know about being in love. I'm a world expert. Now listen Eddie. If cash would help at all, I want you to count on me. After all I am your step-mother!'

With my head on the pillow while Bethan sleeps I listen again. I can't sort out the difference between maternal sympathy and a siren's call.

Twenty-Two

I MIGHT WELL have dreamt of wandering around the walls of Marrakesh hand in hand with Bethan Mair. Daisy had mentioned that she and some ex-Ambassador's wife had taken up painting as a change from playing bridge in the afternoon. A glance through the window in the morning tells me it is raining in Pentregwyn. There is no way available to reconcile Bethan's world with Daisy's. In reality I don't see how they could begin to speak to each other. My father's musical comedy version of the beauteous Bethan Mair Nichols is so far from the truth, it amounts to a sour joke. He has absolutely no idea who she is or where she comes from and that means dear old Daisy will have even less. It makes me smile in a hollow sort of way to try to imagine what they would make of her mission to teach people how to improve their quality of life by living on less. It was the gospel according to Curig of course in the first instance, but he only applied this recipe for living to himself. Bethan's more drastic aim is to apply it to a whole community and so sugar the pills that she proposes to sell in her shop that they will smile as they swallow them. Sometimes I find the dynamic of her ambition taking my breath away.

Since her recovery she has begun to think of herself as a different person and she says herself she hangs on to me as a reality check. There are times when she becomes so preoccupied with her plans and her purposes, I have to give her a little shake to command her attention. On fine afternoons I more or less drag her out of the shop and the village to accompany me on exploring one or other of the

217

three valleys that converge on Pentregwyn. They are a great consolation. I make her bring one of her cameras along. This is a quiet little conspiracy of my own. There are so many quiet little conspiracies going on I need one of my own to prevent myself being blown about by the cross currents of other people's intentions. I need to reawaken her pleasure in film and the visual arts to take a little of the edge off the sharpness of her missionary zeal. There also needs to be more tender attention to the well-being of our romantic relationship.

Towards the end of Nant Cymun there is a waterfall and nearby a ruined cottage. The whole place is bathed in the golden light of an October afternoon: we are entranced by the sparkle in the cascading water and the abrupt stillness of the light on the water of the lower pool.

'I think that must be where Adam Wilde lived,' I say.

'Who?'

Bethan is concentrating on her photography. She thinks she has caught the blue flash of a kingfisher under the old stone bridge.

'Sulwen's secret lover,' I say.

'Oh him...'

It's not something she wants to be reminded of and I should have known it.

'It could be nice to restore it,' I say. 'Turn it into our private retreat. Wouldn't cost all that much.'

In my own mind I imagined asking Daisy for a small loan. Small in her dimensions at least. It is something I could bring myself to do without too much embarrassment. Bethan's little nose wrinkles with displeasure.

'Bourgeois self-indulgence! They're doing it all over Wales these days. Major hobby of the new well-to-do Cymry.'

She clasps her hands in mock ecstasy.

'Oh my dear, we fell in love with it the minute we saw it. Just had to have it!'

And that I suppose is the end of that. She has kept her promise or most of it anyway. We share a bed and a house and a shop and we are dedicated partners. Not a day goes by without her declaring how much she relies on my love, and I am satisfied with that even though the subject of a formal marriage seems to lie in abeyance.

Or at least it does until Alwyn and Lowri Nichols return in the faithful BMW full of cheer and good intentions. There is an unexpected warmth in the way Lowri is smiling at me. She has a habit of taking a deep breath before making a pronouncement. Bethan usually takes advantage of the pause to move about and contrive to be busy. She is bustling in and out now like a moving target. She claims to be expecting the representative of an information technology service to discuss the possibility of an installation in one corner of the shop where she plans the library to be.

'Tada was most impressed to learn that you were the son of Orlando Lloyd, wasn't he Alwyn?'

Tada means Alwyn's father and Bethan's grandfather the cantankerous and would-be distinguished Judge David Nichols. 'Austere', 'remote', 'self important', 'pompous': I derive the assortment of adjectives from the bits and pieces of information I have gleaned concerning the *odi et amo* relationship between my Bethan Mair and her grandfather who, Lowri has insisted on more than one occasion, dotes on her and still boasts about her brilliance whenever he gets a chance, and takes as much credit as he can for her achievements. I have come to understand that in the Nichols family, distinction and fame amount to a religion: but never, Bethan insists, her cup of tea. And yet I conclude not unrelated to her own determined pursuit of goals. Born to be a mover and shaker.

'The great Welsh actor, Orlando Lloyd,' says Lowri.

Well, I have never heard that one before. And I doubt whether the great Orlando would have been best pleased. He thinks of himself as a quintessential Englishman, which I suppose in every practical sense he is, Cynddylan or no Cynddylan.

Alwyn joins in.

'The old boy has always taken a great interest in the

theatre. Ever since I can remember. I think in the first flush of youth he fancied becoming an actor. Or so the rumour went.'

He smiles and stands back to display amiable tolerance. Everything is way back if you stand back: even the difficult father who sent the daughter of this shop along with a number of her comrades to prison for contempt of court. After all he became her father-in-law and the proud grandfather of her daughter. Time softens every story and turns a threatening monster into a harmless toothless tiger caged in the leafy comfort of a Cardiff suburb and snarling ineffectively at his keeper.

'Tada is so pleased,' Lowri says. 'I can't tell you. It's quite a time since we've seen him so cheerful. Delighted in fact. And excited. Isn't he Alwyn?'

'Jolly nice to get him off the subject of housekeeper-carers and their manifold shortcomings. Not to mention his aches and pains. He expects you to find every twinge and tremor utterly absorbing, poor old boy.'

'His imagination runs away with him...'

Lowri raises her voice to gain Bethan's attention.

'Nothing less than a great society wedding for his little Bethan. No expense spared. He'll pay. A big wedding in the Cathedral. And a massive reception afterwards in a Country House Hotel of his choosing. And he'll be sitting across the aisle to the great Orlando Lloyd!'

'Too bad.'

Bethan delivers her verdict over her shoulder.

'His little Bethan won't be there.'

'That's exactly what I told him,' Lowri says. 'But we have to be patient, don't we? Old people live in the past. Or at least they do in their own idealised version.'

I find I have a certain sympathy for Lowri since their return. She seems intent on closing an ideological gap between Bethan and herself. The enterprise of Pentregwyn General Stores is to be encouraged rather than denigrated: but built on sounder economic foundations. More often than not these premeditated approaches have the opposite effect. I have the impression that Bethan's attitude towards her Cardiff family background has been hardening from that fateful moment she opened her great aunt Sulwen's letter and came into this unforeseen inheritance. She feels free to indulge in her own line in spirited invective.

'He never had the intelligence or even the plain gumption to rise above the range of petty-minded restrictions he imposed on himself. His brain was suffocating inside his wig!'

And so on. Poor old Lowri meanders around the place trying to demonstrate goodwill but increasingly as time goes on Bethan treats both her parents as well meaning obstructions getting under her feet. Before they leave Lowri cannot resist returning to the subject of a wedding.

'For the sake of your friends, Bethan darling, not to mention your family. You've no idea, Eddie, how popular she was in school and all around really. A quiet affair in dear old Bethania our family chapel. And then a nice reception where old friends can meet. There are all sorts of people who never stop enquiring about you, wondering what you are up to. She is already a bit of a legend in her own time you know, Eddie. And friends are important aren't they? You've always thought so and I'm sure you were right.'

'Right then!'

Bethan lowers her head and slaps the palm of her hand on the table.

'This is the way it's going to be, family dear. On the shortest day of the year, which will give the happy couple the longest night, B.M. Nichols spinster, and E.C. Lloyd bachelor will be united in holy matrimony by the Reverend Curig Puw if he is able to stand up long enough. If not he can sit like the Pope and we can kneel. This moving ceremony will take place in the parish church over there not more than a stone's throw from that tottering memorial to Griffith Ezra Bowen. And it will take place after the Plygain, the traditional early morning carol service. All candle-lit of course. And the bride will be given away by her lovely papa if he's willing. She and the bridegroom will be tastefully dressed in tracksuits and fleeces because the church will be unheated. And here endeth the lesson.'

And indeed that was the way it was, almost to the letter. A surprisingly mild day so nobody really shivered. All due, Seth ap Tomos said, to global warming. The sound of those unaccompanied harmonies reverberated through the shadows in the church like ghostly sounds from the seventeenth century. The candles were meant as symbols of light in a pagan darkness. It was all haunting and memorable and everyone was deeply moved. We were being married to each other and to the place.

But the greatest surprise occurred during the wedding breakfast that Seth ap Tomos and his carpenters of song insisted on providing in that large room at Coed y Glyn. When I at least was beginning to relax, an unexpected guest presented himself in a mud spattered leather coat with goggles perched ridiculously on the peak of his cap. It was Barry Parrott who emerged from a low sports car covered in mud. It appeared he had got completely lost on the way. None of the road signs meant anything to him. He never felt more of a foreigner, he said. He had found the shop at last and had been redirected here. He had been in Australia for several months filming, and had only just heard the awful news about his dear friend and colleague, which he could see merely by looking around, was awful news no longer. I made something of a show of welcoming him and I could see Bethan was very pleased to see him. I explained to whoever was close enough to listen that this visitor had been present when the bride and bridegroom first met, could even claim to have been partly responsible for throwing them together and that it was wholly appropriate that he could join us as our guest. So it all went very well and everyone declared themselves to be pleased and happy.

Except perhaps, within less than a week, my wife and

partner Bethan. It seemed that Barry Parrott had driven, hot foot so to speak, all the way to the backwoods of Pentregwyn in order to persuade her to join him in executing a wonderful commission for a series of documentary films on the present state of racial and class relations in seven major English inner cities. She had rejected the invitation out of hand. It would have been disloyal to her vision for the shop and the regeneration of the village. It would have been disloyal to Curig and all the other friends who had supported them in their hour of trial. And worst of all it would have been disloyal to me. I understood her well enough to realise that within days she regretted her great refusal.

It did not take me long to rise to the occasion.

'If you want to do it,' I said, 'do it. I'll look after the shop. And I'll look after Curig.'

He was still happily engaged in editing what he had come to call Sulwen's Papers. Olwen Caradog's machinations to inspire the Presbytery to give him a call came to nothing and he didn't seem to mind at all. Bethan said my unselfishness made her love me to bits. I was the light of her life and always would be. All the money she earned on the film would be ploughed back into the shop. I told her I didn't need to love her any more than I did already, but while she was away I would learn to love her Pentregwyn and her people so that when our little Cynddylans came about they would imbibe the attachment with their mother's milk. My purpose was to give her the space and freedom that she yearns for so that in the end we could both submit of our own free will to the exploration that counted most: finding the source of awe like an invisible stream running through the parish. She liked that. We were in an agreement that was quite ecstatic.

And that was how our married life began.

Pwyll Pendefig Dyfed

Ac fe debygai ef y'i goddiweddai ar yr ail naid neu ar y drydedd. Er hynny nid oedd yn nes ati na chynt.

Pwyll Prince of Dyfed

He assumed that at the second bound or at the third he would overtake her. Yet he drew no closer to her than before.